Murder at the Mela

Leela Soma

Best Wishes

Leela.

x x,

RINGWOOD PUBLISHING
GLASGOW

First published in Great Britain in 2020
by
Ringwood Publishing, Glasgow.
www.ringwoodpublishing.com
mail@ringwoodpublishing.com

ISBN 978-1-901514-90-2

British Library Cataloguing-in-Publication Data
A catalogue record for this book is available from the
British Library

Printed and bound in the UK
by
Lonsdale Direct Solutions

Praise for Murder at the Mela

"Leela Soma and her fictional creation DI Patel have the inside track on the mysteries of Glasgow's Asian communities. A beautifully written, ground-breaking addition to Tartan Noir - with a twist!"
Norman Bissell, author of *Barnhill*

" ... DI Patel is a new star in the making! Skilfully blending murder with the realities of race, religion and affairs of the heart, this is a crackling good book."
Cauvery Madhavan, novelist

Dedication

For my parents

Prologue

July 7th, 2015

It was the tenth anniversary of the 7/7 London Bombings. All the TV channels were covering the same images again and again. The story of the survivors, the services to remember the 'ocean of pain', held at St. Paul's Cathedral were broadcast on a loop. The mourners observed a minute's silence, and petals fell from the dome as the Bishop of London said the Tube and bus attacks had united a city in 'agonised outcry.'

He remembered it all. The pain he felt was searing. He touched the scar on his face. He watched the programme in a drunken haze. Each moment brought back the agony of the physical and psychological pain he had endured. He wanted to get away from it all, but he had nowhere to go. The bedsit he lived in was disgusting. He hated his life. He wanted to end it all. One can still suffer for nearly a decade and never get the images of loss from one's mind. His new life in Glasgow, and the drinking, had failed to get the demons out of his head. Yet, it was the bottle that was his salvation. He drank more and fell into a stupor. The next few days passed, but he recollected little.

He had had too many near misses with the car. He had trouble parking often and had scraped the passenger side. He couldn't afford to fix the dents in it. It was still running and the few days he was sober enough to drive, he managed to get from A to B. The car suited him well, for these erratic ways of living on the edge. However, he could never be sober all the time or take charge of his life. His life had spiralled down to nothing, a bottomless pit that he could not rescue himself from. In some ways, death would be a blessing. At least it would get the awful images from his mind that made sleep evade him most nights. His hatred had become like a cloud that grew bigger and bigger and seemed now to engulf his very being. He'd plan and get avenged, or would he? Well, in his case he wouldn't. It would never be cold. Coping with every wakeful moment was a desperate struggle.

When he had a sober moment, he felt good, he thought he had achieved something, and then the dark side arose, the shivers, the images of that fateful night. He reached for the bottle to obliterate it all. Is this what he had imagined life would be with his relationships? Such self-loathing and hatred made his life hell. He almost wanted to go and tell someone of his agony, but some survival instinct in him made him stop himself.

Drink, booze, spirits, to blunt the edges of hatred, no feelings, no thoughts, just a zombie. Was this all he could cope with? The pain in his heart grew as he went over these same questions again and again.

Chapter 1

April 2015

A few weeks earlier, Patel walked into his office, opening a door to a promising future, his new job as DI Patel at Glasgow West End Station, or 'Partick' as most police referred to it. He hung up his coat and looked out of the window. His love of poetry sometimes surfaced. A few words of Goethe came to mind:

> *'Life's field will yield as we make it*
> *A harvest of thorns or flowers.'*

The excitement of getting the promotion had faded. The huge burden of the new job descended quickly to cast a pall over his first day. Both excitement and worry weighed on his mind.

The office looked exactly as it always had when DI Martin Crolla had been there before he was promoted to Detective Chief Inspector. Martin would be helpful to Patel as he would be his mentor easing him into the job. However, Patel felt that he had to prove himself to be competent. He was aware that having been fast-tracked on the High Potential route, that some of his colleagues were jealous of his promotion. He had heard some colleagues joking: 'the ink isn't dry on his warrant card from his last promotion and now he is getting promoted again.' But all his colleagues felt he was worthy of the promotion, as he had been excellent at his job.

DS Alan Brown seemed to be the exception. From

his school days, Patel had experienced racism, often being the only Asian in a class or at sports clubs, but he always took an optimistic view that it would die down as he and his peers at school grew up together. Those jibes had only made him more determined to be better at all the things he chose to do. He was the fastest cricket bowler at high school and the best at his studies. His one love was poetry, something he just enjoyed whether it was the Indian ones his grandmother sang to him when he was little, or the ones he read at school, it was an abiding passion. His colleague at work, Alan, proved to be the bane of his life. They had sparred right from the beginning. His overt racism, disguised as humour, really annoyed Patel.

'Here comes curry and chapatti,' when Patel walked into the canteen, often accompanied by Alan's raucous laughter. John Doyle, Alan's sole friend at work, would try and dissuade him from making such remarks.

'Mince and tatties, just shut up will you,' Patel had retorted, his face reddening, ashamed that he had to stoop to Alan's level to get back at him. His hands had been itching to punch his face.

'Now, now, just banter, Patel. Take it like man, for fuck's sake,' Alan chuckled as Patel walked away.

Patel's colleagues would often confront Alan: 'Stop it, Alan; we could report you for this. Racist jibes at Patel would only get you into trouble. Why don't you start working hard, eh? Get the grades Patel gets?'

'Och away, you wouldn't do that to me,' Alan would say and add, 'I work hard too.'

The day of the interview for promotion still played in Patel's mind sometimes. Alan had even tried to unnerve him at the interview as they both waited to be called in: 'Patel, nae chance. It's all mine,' was Alan's warning as he came out of the interview room, looking

2

flushed and smiling broadly.

Patel smiled to himself, Alan's bitterness reminded him of the old Ortega quote: 'Rancour is an outpouring of a feeling of inferiority.'

Alan took it badly when Patel got the job. As others swarmed around Patel to congratulate him, Patel saw him sulking in his corner. Alan walked out of the room, swearing and muttering as he left.

DS Joe McKay, Patel's close friend heard Alan's complaints as he walked into the office to congratulate Patel, and so he stopped him in his tracks.

'That jammy bastard getting the DI's job! Bet it was just because of his colour. Bloody token black! Diversity, fast track, I don't give a shit. They keep promoting them. Fuck them! What about people like me, eh?'

'Look, Alan, this is bang out of order, I'm going to tell DCI Crolla,' he said.

'No, you won't. I dare you to. Do you know what I am going through, eh? I need this promotion and the pay so much more than that geezer.'

'Stop your racist comments,' Joe insisted.

'You wouldn't dare. I'm still senior to you by a few years. Don't you forget that McKay.'

Joe gave up and shook his head in despair.

Later that day, surprisingly, Alan came over to Patel and had congratulated him, with eyes that poured out hatred. Patel decided to forget Alan's sneering look and get on with his work. He checked on his administrative duties for the day. He already had a pile of things to get through. His work as a DI was challenging. He missed the comfort of his old desk, strewn with paper and a work overload that he had enjoyed.

Now, in his new room, with the DI plaque on the door outside, where everything was shiny and neatly

3

kept, he could find anything he needed. There would be even more paperwork and communicating with his staff, which would be yet another chore, and he did not relish the endless meetings! He wanted to be back on the street, solving crimes. He had always been ambitious, holding a secret wish to be the first DI, even perhaps the first Asian to be Chief Superintendent. Or he would work all the way up the ladder to become a Chief Constable.

Another three months and I'm sure Alan will ask for and get a transfer and get it, thought Patel, as he settled into his chair to get on with his new job. He shifted the files on his desk and got on with the backlog that Martin had left behind.

'Settling in, Patel?' Martin came over with his cup of coffee and some files and sat on the other side of the desk.

'Yes, a bit nervous. No honeymoon period in our kind of job, is there?' said Patel.

'Patel, just carry on as before. Don't hesitate to ask me anything you need. I also noticed that you've applied to join the Major Investigating Team at Govan. Good to have ambition, and focus. Well, prove how good you are in here, Patel, and I'll write a very good reference for you. I know you've got great potential. Right, back to business here. I need that report on that heroin stash recovered from that car boot in Possil as soon as possible.' Martin got up to leave.

'Ha, nothing changes, and thanks. I am keen on joining the MIT.' Patel smiled.

'Nope, not much changes,' replied Martin. 'Here's some more for you,' he placed another stack of files on Patel's desk and walked out of the office, picking up his cup of coffee.

Patel worked solidly on. As the day drew to a close,

he remembered that he had brought a photo of Usma. Her dimpled smile made his heart skip a beat. He put the photo in a desk drawer.

Usma would have left for her shift on street patrol by now. He wanted so much to be with her tonight, at the end of the first day of his work as a DI but that was not to be.

His drive home was slow. He took his time to avoid going back to an empty house. He missed her.

Growing up as an Asian in Glasgow, Alan Brown's constant jibes and Martin's encouragement were representative of the two contrasting aspects of his life. He was made to feel both an insider and an outsider, often trading places within the same day.

Chapter 2

It was the end of a long working day. Patel's mobile piped, reminding him that he had to visit his parents. His new job kept him so busy that he needed an alert for the party so that he wouldn't forget. He grimaced at the phone, sighed, and then walked into his house. A quick shower followed by a change of clothes and Patel was back in his car in half an hour driving towards Bearsden.

He parked his Honda Civic and walked over to his parents' front door, noting all the huge Mercs and SUVs lined up on the street. The stone house in Bearsden had more cars parked on the long driveway. It was lit up as if it were *Diwali*, the Festival of Light, when *diyas,* the little clay lamps, were lit and kept all around the house. Outdoor lights were hung on the beautiful old tree near the porch.

Some of the houses also had big compound walls that made it even more private so people could see little from the road - not that many people did walk on the road. There were more cars during the morning rush hour, ferrying children to private schools in Glasgow or to the local primary, which was one of the best in the area. Houses were snapped up at high prices just to get the children into that primary school.

Going back, even for a visit, to his parents' house always brought that strange feeling of being a small child again. It was a mixture of love, embarrassment, and lack of understanding. Sometimes his work also kept him from visiting them. People closest to each other are often hurt or misunderstand. Communication seemed to be a really difficult thing to achieve in almost every family. His was no different.

He could hear some Indian music and conversation as he approached the open door. The porch had some pretty *diyas*, the flames casting lovely patterns on the walls. Through the glass door leading to the hall and front room, he could see a lot of people inside. He shrugged his shoulders and went in. The front room was heaving with friends and family. As he entered, he saw a huge banner saying 'CONGRATULATIONS DI PATEL' in red and gold with balloons of the same colours strung together trailing at both ends of the banner. On the huge dining table, in the open plan lounge diner, there were bottles of bubbly cooling in buckets and people were helping themselves to a glass each. His parents had gone over the top with the party, as per usual.

Patel's mother, Laxmi, came over and hugged him. She was wearing a maroon sari with a gold border; her heeled sandals gave her a few more inches than her five-foot frame.

'Come in, *beta.*' He smiled at her flushed face as she fussed over him and introduced him to all her friends. Her eyes were full of pride. His dad, Anand, raised a glass to him. He was a tall, distinguished-looking man, with almost white hair, wearing thick glasses. He had made an effort tonight, looking smart in a dark suit.

'I'll never get used to you doing this job, but congratulations,' he said. He came close to Patel and patted him on the shoulder.

Patel was grateful for his parents' support, even though they had been baffled when he chose his career with the police. Their close family friends were no help either. They bragged about their son or daughter taking up one of the professions that Asian families usually preferred, such as medicine, the law, accountancy and lately IT, as they saw a future in technology. His parents had constantly nagged him about his career choice. He smiled as he recalled the scenes he had had with them when he chose his career. His mum was not pleased at all. 'Why not a doctor?' she had said, 'look at your grades, all 'A's. The world's your oyster; you can be anything. You can choose your speciality, like dad you could become a consultant,' his mother had insisted. 'It is such a good profession, helping people.'

'Mum, the police also help people,' he had retorted.

In his final year at school, he was privy to his parents discussing in lowered voices, 'Our only boy, why is he going into this profession? Indians only respect doctors, lawyers or accountants, why has he chosen this strange career?'

He had felt worried that he had let them down, but he had persevered.

He recalled his grandmother's Bhagavad Gita quote that had helped him so many times during the hours of doubt in his childhood.

'Man is made by his belief, as he believes, so he is.'

Simple but true, she had said. Always believe in yourself. It had stood him in good stead all these years.

They came around to accepting his choice later as his progress at Tulliallan Police College was good and he earned accolades there as one of their best officers. They were proud of him and arrived to see him at the graduation when he had passed his course with flying colours. Now, this rapid promotion to a DI came as a welcome surprise to them.

A gang of older people, his parents' friends milled around him, slapping his back, shaking his hands, and congratulating him. From the far side of the room his sister, Anita, watched the people crowding around him. She was slim and tall, like his father and him, with her glasses perched on her nose, and was looking pretty in her sari tonight. She rescued him from the older people saying she needed a quick word with him. She winked as she offered him a glass of champagne that he refused.

'Go on, indulge today. Get sloshed.' She placed a champagne flute filled with bubbly, firmly in his hand. 'My dear brother, you're not on duty now. The new DI in Glasgow whose favourite dram is the smooth Glengoyne whisky! I know, I know, but hey, make an exception today. A glass of bubbly is better for a celebration. By the way, I'm very proud of you. Never said it before,' she hugged him.

A big lady in an orange sari, bedecked with jewels on her hands and neck came gushing over to him. It was Mrs. Prema Parikh, the 'Aunty' to all. She claimed all Indian families and their lives to be her own and her gossip helped the community become aware of all its news. Births, deaths, marriages, weddings, and jobs were grist to her mill. She had arrived in Glasgow long before the other Indians and was well respected, so her presence was desirable at the party even though she wasn't a relative. However, her memory for details of all families and spreading rumours in the community was often feared.

'Congratulations, *beta*. Next thing we need is to see you nicely settled down with an Indian wife"said Mrs. Parikh bringing a *ladoo*, the traditional sweet used in all celebrations, to stuff in Patel's mouth. Anita quickly took charge and steered her to the side.

'Aunty, how is your diabetes? I hope you've not had too many of these.'

Anita prised the sweet from her hand. Mrs. Parikh looked a bit stunned. Her guilt at consuming more than she should have made her cower a bit, especially as Anita was her GP. She was quiet as she walked over to the group of ladies talking about the latest Bollywood movie and how some of the scenes in it were shot in Glasgow.

'Look at this new kitchen, it's like a Bollywood set, *na*?' she exclaimed loudly as she touched the granite countertop. 'Is that a fridge for wine bottles?' she asked Anita as she saw a glass-fronted cabinet. 'And I love this central island.'

Another lady, Neela, joined her as Anita withdrew to look after other guests. Prema guided Neela towards the sliver platters with more Indian sweets.

'I must admit, Laxmi and Anand have such good taste in everything from food to doing up this huge house,' Prema continued talking to Neela. 'I think those goddess statues they have in the lounge are antiques from India,' she whispered.

Patel stood with the glass of champagne in his hand as he was approached by some of his friends.

'Hey, DI Patel, congratulations!'

Andrew Ramsey, his hair thinning on top, almost forming a semi-circle around his skull, like a halo, came forward and shook his hand. A slight paunch, his shirt taut against his beer belly, one of the buttons ready to pop open. He looks like his father, thought Patel as he smiled at him. Andrew was happy for him. They had been friends since they were at primary school.

His old friends from school days and university were there and a few of his colleagues from work. Martin, Joe, Kara, Brian and Kenny, who had been promoted to a DI in Stirling, were all there.

Anita raised a toast.

'Congratulations to my baby brother. The villains in Glasgow will be worried now,' she joked.

The sound of glass clinking and a loud, 'To Patel,' rang out.

'Now all we need is a few words from you, dear brother,' said Anita.

'Come on, no one wants to be bored,' laughed Patel.

'Go on, where is that speech you were writing all day?' teased Martin.

Patel cleared his throat. 'Right, I can't thank the family here, as no one wanted me to join the police force,' he chuckled and pointed the glass in his hand at his dad. 'As for my colleagues, the less said the better.'

The evening went well. He felt both humbled and happy.

As he was leaving, his mum hugged him and whispered '*Beta*, so proud of you, the first Asian Scot DI. Now all you need is a nice young wife, and we can look forward to grandchildren *na*?'

His mum had smiled happily, making her plans for his future. She had repeated what most of the older Indian ladies had wished for him. His mother knew of the heartaches he had gone through. Few of his relationships had worked out. Tanya, the last one, had complained of his long hours of work as a policeman. She wanted him to have a 'normal' nine to five job. The four years with her had been full of ups and downs. When he had to cut short their holiday in New York, a holiday that they had planned for many months, Tanya broke off the relationship.

As he drove home, more thoughts of Usma swirled in his mind. Her lovely clear brown eyes, that sweet smile and the curvaceous body that made his heart race just in the few months of knowing her. Both Usma and he had deliberately kept their relationship a secret.

They both knew that there would be strong opposition from both families. Their clandestine affair had been well hidden though they had wanted to live together. Neither family would approve. They both knew how it was going to play out. A Hindu marrying a Muslim! That would never be approved by his parents and Usma had dreaded broaching the subject to her parents.

He only wished Usma could have been there with him to enjoy the celebration.

Chapter 3

Nadia walked into the Kelvingrove Park from Malcolm's flat. She had no other thought but to find her gold necklace. Her grandma, Nazreen Bibi, had worn it with pride on her wedding day, jewellery that the whole family had saved up for with hard work over many years in Pakistan. The scars of hardship etched on Nazreen's face. She had undergone many stillbirths, then her only son was born, her pride and joy, and had given her a reason for living. Later, wizened with cancer, Nazreen had held the necklace in her wrinkled hands and softly beckoned Nadia and bequeathed it to her on her deathbed. It was like a clear photograph in Nadia's mind. She was only a child, but she remembered looking at the gold, heavy and distinctive in design, and the stamp of the jewellers in fascinating Urdu. The calligraphy was beautiful. Guilt filled her as she walked through the park. How could she lose something so precious?

The skeletal trees swayed; the pale moon glimpsed in between the branches like snatches of light in the darkness. It was like being on the set of a horror movie, the atmosphere electric with nothingness. Nadia's thoughts returned to the evening with Farah. *Bhangra* dancers with their bright orange and red clothes, donning purple turbans were drumming the *dholki* and dancing with a vigour that had all the people around tapping their feet and enjoying the beat. The Scottish pipers gave it local colour and made it special.

Nadia and her family were drawn to a group of Polish dancers in their lovely costumes in one of the tents and had admired the display. Over three thousand had thronged to Kelvingrove Park. The colourful spectacle drew in bigger crowds every year. Mansur, her wee son, had been excited, running around and demanding chips when all around people were eating some exotic new Indian dishes, like *bhel-poori*, *dosas*, and the ubiquitous samosas and biryanis. They had laughed at his choice of food. People had worn bright *salwar-kameezes* and even some of the Scottish people had some Indian tops and jewellery on. Jewellery! Nadia shuddered as she remembered why she was out in the dark now. She hummed a Bollywood tune to keep the fear of the dark away.

She walked fast, trying to shut out the fear and looked away from the swaying trees and bushes. Her eyes scanned the path and the grass searching for the jewellery, hoping that the bright gold would glint in the pale moonlight. She was retracing all the places she had been with Farah during the Mela earlier that evening. Nadia was engrossed in the task when she felt a ripple of fear grip her. Was that the sound of a branch splintering? Were those footsteps that she heard behind her? She turned around quickly, but she saw nothing but dark shadows. She walked on. A shiver ran down her spine knowing that the place was empty, not even a cleaner or park steward around. She glanced at her watch. It was late. Was she ever going to find the necklace?

Darkness.

The sounds of silence were more acute in the dark.

A rustle of a leaf, a tiny paper wrapper fleetingly picked up by the breeze seemed to make a noise.

She hugged herself. The warmth helped her. Her

eyes scanned every bit of the path and the grass around her.

She heard another crunching sound. Was that someone treading on some dry leaves? She could feel beads of sweat on her face. She pulled her coat tightly around her to protect herself from that chill of fear she felt. She could feel her heart palpitating, her pulse quickening, as she sensed a figure move beside her.

'Who's there?' she asked, her voice trembling.

Silence.

She waited for a few minutes, standing stock-still. Nothing. Complete silence. She shivered, feeling hot and cold at the same time.

Something glinted in the grass near a bush. She ran towards it, almost weeping as she grabbed a pathetic piece of foil. Then she heard a sound and turned around to see an outline of a face in the dark right beside her. The blade of a knife glinted.

'Please, please don't hurt me ...' words stumbled out, fear making her mouth go dry. Her voice was more of a croak, hardly making a sound. Before she could summon up the courage to look closely at the person, she felt cold steel touching her overheated skin. The knife plunged. Blood dripped onto her clothes. She sank to the ground and as her lifeblood flowed out, her eyes closed. The trees swayed in the breeze as the red liquid seeped into the grass. Soft footsteps faded in the distance.

Death

He had accomplished what he wanted. He had followed her into the park. He went as close to her as possible. She turned to look at him, exposing her soft throat, and he drew the sharp blade against her neck. Feeling her weight as she slumped against him gave him a shock, just for a moment. He quickly pushed her away, and stepped back, as a sudden gush of red splattered on the bush beside them. He watched as her body buckled down and fell on the ground. The blood gushed out of her neck forming a pool in the dark. He saw her body go into spasms. Then he waited till the breath left her. Job done! He didn't feel any guilt. What should he feel after killing someone? The anger did not subside, that void in his chest. It was still filled with hatred. He checked that his clothes were not blood-stained; he'd worn a plastic mac that had some blood stains on it. He took it off now to dispose of it later. He cleaned the knife with a leaf using his gloved hand and stashed it in his pocket. He removed both gloves, and then put them in the same pocket of the plastic mac. He glanced once more at the body. He felt like he was outside of his own body, high on a drug.

He slunk away into the darkness.

Chapter 4

The park lay in darkness. The streaks of light from the streetlamps made strange shapes on the path. Caroline Dunn walked on, swinging the dog's lead, keeping an eye out for Sheba, her golden retriever, who kept running off to the bushes along the way, to mark her territory. The detritus of the Mela was on the far side.

As she approached Sheba, a stale aroma of curry wafted over; paper bags and polystyrene boxes were strewn around with remnants of pakoras, samosas and red sauces seeping through; a discarded mess that was the annual sight. Sheba barked excitedly. Some empty stalls had still not been taken down, and the wooden shack-like structures stood mute in the early, misty morning. She loved her early morning walks with Sheba, but today Sheba kept barking from the same spot. Caroline ignored her, thinking of the evening she had at the Mela a couple of days ago. The colour, the music, it was a joyous festival that she enjoyed every year. Sheba continued barking staying stationary. Caroline walked over to the bush further up where the dog had its nose to the ground, tail wagging vigorously.

Caroline stood in shocked silence. A blood trail led to what looked like legs covered in jeans partially hidden behind the bush. She didn't want to touch it. The blood made her wary. Numb with fright, her body shivered. She was not sure what to do. After a few seconds spent stifling a scream, she took her mobile out, and with shaking fingers dialled 999.

'Ambulance, please ... someone is lying here, blood all over, maybe a body ...' Caroline explained slowly.

'You stay right there. The ambulance will be there, and I'll also transfer your call to the police. I'm sure they'll be there within minutes,' reassured the call centre operator.

*

Partick station swung into action as soon as it got the call from the operator. Detective Sergeant Brian Hunter called the police response officers on patrol nearby.

'Golf Sierra, Glasgow North West, Charlie 26 - attend a call at Kelvingrove Park. Female, injured.'

Two uniformed police officers, Ross Liddle and Lorraine Telfer, were soon there. They got out of their car quickly and rushed over to Caroline. Lorraine took her hand. It was cold. She looked white as a sheet.

Brian from Partick station arrived shortly afterwards. The paramedics from the ambulance had pronounced the victim dead.

Brian called DI Patel.

Patel picked up his mobile. The screen cast a blue glow on his tired face.

'This is DS Hunter. Just to let you know we've found a dead body in Kelvingrove Park, near the Mela Mefhil Stage, close to Parkgrove Terrace.'

'I'll be over right away,' said Patel. He pushed aside the warm duvet and got up quickly. The sun was just rising, casting a faint light as he rushed into the en-suite. His tall figure reflected in the shower screen, as he hurried to get ready. The seriousness of the early morning call made his mind whirl with a list of things to do immediately. Dressed in black trousers and a pale blue shirt, he raced down the stairs. In the hall, he grabbed a pen and scribbled a note for Usma just in case she came in after her work.

Body found. Call you later.

He left the note on the dining table and hurried out of the house.

Was this going to be his first murder case since he became a DI? he wondered.

He drove over to Kelvingrove Park, picking up Joe, his sidekick, on the way. Joe waited outside his flat, dressed, and ready, his mop of brown wavy hair smoothed back. His grey eyes lit up when he saw the car stop beside him.

'Joe, hop in, a nice early start, eh?' Patel tried to keep it light.

'Yes, sir,' said Joe. He felt excited as Patel accelerated the car.

Meanwhile at the park, Brian, as the Crime Scene Manager, began work and started the log. He also gave out some commands to the two officers.

'Get this crime scene cordoned off.'

Brian cast an eye over the site. 'Was anyone else around?'

'No, sir,' said Ross as he quickly put the yellow tape around the area and secured the entrances to the park.

Lorraine took Caroline's hand again. It was cold and the woman looked pale, the veins prominent in her neck. Lorraine moved her away from the proximity of the body and sat her on a bench. Sheba sat at her feet. Lorraine asked her name and waited for her to calm down and then took notes. She spoke in soft tones.

'Caroline, why were you up so early?'

'I always take Sheba out for a walk before I go to work.' Caroline's voice was low.

'Were you at the Mela?'

'No, not yesterday evening. I was visiting my mum.'

'Did you see anyone else during the walk?'

Caroline shook her head. Sheba looked up as Lorraine wrote down her notes.

'We need your address. We may need to contact you again.'

Lorraine saw that Caroline was trembling. Her eyes were filled with tears, the shock giving way slowly to reality at the thought of making her way home.

'Would you like to be taken home?' Lorraine asked her gently.

'Yes, yes ... please,' said Caroline.

Patel parked the car in the Kelvingrove Park; he and Joe pulled white suits over their clothes and walked over to the scene of the crime. Joe kept up a brisk pace beside him. The grass still had the early morning dew, the moisture sparkling in the morning sunshine. Patel's eyes were combing the park, taking in everything: the buildings around, the path they were walking along.

'Joe, I'll check the scene if you can talk to the uniforms and see what they have,' Patel said as Brian came over.

'Sir, Joe, all we have is a young Asian woman's body found by a dog walker.'

Joe immediately went over to the constables to get details.

The body sprawled behind the bush was covered with blood. The red formed a gory design on the young woman's clothes. Patel switched his torch off and surveyed the scene. His keen facility to read a scene of a crime and taking in all the details surfaced. The white crime tent was being set up, the park gates had been closed and all public access suspended. A police constable was setting up some floodlights. The force photographer was busy. He was taking photos of the body from every angle. The mist was lifting, but he needed lights to get clear photos. His team were working well.

Dr Jamieson, the police casualty surgeon, a sprightly sixty-year-old with hair greying at the temples, arrived. He opened his case and as he put his gloves on, he acknowledged Patel. He checked the body and declared her dead.

'So?' Patel queried. 'What can you tell me?'

Jamieson looked up at him. 'Carotid artery; a clean cut.'

Patel watched him as he turned the corpse over carefully, checking for wounds. He applied some pressure as he moved his hands all over the body and paused to gauge the temperature and to see if rigor mortis had set in.

Patel waited for the doctor to stand up. More photographs were taken.

'Doc, any idea of the time of death?' he asked him and moved aside to let the others cover the body with the sheet.

'At a guess, maybe around six to eight hours? We will get a more accurate time when the post-mortem is done in the lab.'

He closed his case and walked back to his car.

Some of the terraced houses lining the street to the park had lights on; the police activity had woken up some of the residents.

A black car arrived on the scene and an official-looking gentleman got out. It was the Procurator Fiscal who did not usually arrive at the scene of the crime, but Patel had called him. It was a suspicious death in the venue of the biggest multicultural festival in Glasgow.

'So, it was a drug death when I saw you, last time. That was some time ago, right, Patel? So, you had to wake up early? What a dreadful thing to happen after the Mela, eh?' Jim McKern shook his hand.

21

'Yes, just awful. Another request, Jim: you know Muslim funerals take place within twenty-four to forty-eight hours. We need to be sensitive about these cultural issues. I know under Scots Law the body belongs to the Crown. As the Fiscal you have the power to release it as soon as the post-mortem is completed,' Patel said.

'I'll bear that in mind. Young woman, I am told,' Jim shook his head. 'Right, give me all the details you know.'

Jim noted down all the details. As the Procurator Fiscal, he was the person in charge of investigating all sudden, suspicious deaths, prosecuting the criminals and directing the police.

As he was about to leave, he shook hands with Patel again and said, 'I just remembered now. Congratulations! I heard that you've become a DI.'

'Thanks, Jim.'

'Good luck, Patel.'

Patel was glad that the procedure to register a suspicious death was underway. He watched as the stretcher to take the body to the mortuary was set up and two men placed the body on it and lifted it to the waiting ambulance.

Chapter 5

Hanif Khan unfurled the prayer mat and looked up towards the family photo on the wall. His parents, his sisters and his older brother were all smiling happily at the photographer. The photo had been taken on his sixteenth birthday. How naïve he had been then. Wanting to belong, following the latest boybands and dressing like them; smoking, drinking with his school mates just to act cool. He shuddered at his foolishness, that silly teenage time when all he wanted was to be like the other boys at school. Like Hugh, the cool guy who always had all the girls. The style, the confidence he had and managing also to be in the good books of his teachers.

Hanif had always been good at schoolwork, near the top of the class, a right wee nerd as they called him. The teachers liked him because he handed in his work on time. He worked hard and he was polite and intelligent. Teachers hailed him as an example for others to emulate. He felt proud when he got good grades, but it made him squirm when the guys in the class made him feel like the oddball. 'Hanif the Hunch', they called him, because he was always hunched over a computer. The square-eyed geek. They laughed behind his back and called him HH. That nickname made him cringe now. The last year, the sixth year, he stayed mostly in the library or came home when he had free periods. His parents noticed him getting morose and withdrawn.

Some family friends commented on his behaviour change, but his parents were glad he was not one of the tear-away young teens. They had their hands full with their older son Rafiq. Their daughter Farhana had calmed down after a tiny rebellious phase when she was fourteen. Now that they had married her off early, she had become a model wife and mother in their eyes. Hanif was their baby; they were proud of his school work and were looking forward to the day when he went to university. He would be the first in the family to attend. This was surprising, considering he had a mother who could hardly read and write and a father who had only just gotten to grips with his paperwork! They were immensely proud of Hanif.

'He wants to get the highest grades in his Advanced Highers even though he has been accepted for studying medicine at Glasgow Uni,' said his mum to her friends, her pride evident in her face when the results came out in his fifth year at school.

They cleared a room for him to study now that Farhana was away and made sure he got whatever he wanted. That September they watched him enter Glasgow University and their hearts burst with pride. They invited a lot of friends over and gave a big meal to celebrate his results at school and starting university.

'A doctor in the family soon. My *beta* will cure me of any illness,' said his mum, beaming with happiness at her youngest.

Within a few months of starting university, Hanif started to put his beliefs into practice. His parents approved and were surprised at his interest in all things Islamic. He became a regular attendee at the mosque, prayed five times a day. He asked his mum to get him some *salwar-kameez*, the Islamic wear for men and started wearing them to the mosque.

'No one understands how much better I feel now,' Hanif thought. 'I belong, I am something, and I am in the centre of a group that validates my existence like never before,' he said to himself. His computer was open on the Facebook page of Glasgow University Muslim Students Association, GUMSA. The events planned for the new session were not very different from Fresher's week last year. He would try and meet the new students who come for a visit on open day and get them interested in GUMSA.

The mosque, the computer, his house, and the few meetings with his new friends in their flat, this was his new world. Hanif looked at the mirror as he got ready for the Morning Prayers. His beard was only a couple of inches long. It was growing very slowly. He was impatient. He wanted to grow it much longer, take pride in his identity. He wanted the world to know that he was a man of faith. Hanif adjusted the skull cap on his head, which matched his waistcoat and dragged his shawl closer to his chest.

Life had become harder as his beliefs were challenged by what he experienced at university. There was a feeling of elation and freedom in life at the university. Unlike at school people here were friendlier and were inclusive, invited him to all the social gatherings, and were respectful of his faith but also ready to debate with him. He felt confused about the path he had chosen. Should he let go and enjoy life? Eat, drink, have sexual partners like some others did? Hanif found himself filled with self-doubts and sometimes slipped up in his ritual observations, which made feel guilty.

He knelt down on the mat and said his prayer. Afterwards, he dressed for the day ahead. He checked on his schedule. There was plenty of time to attend his lecture and then to check on some of the Muslim students.

Chapter 6

At the park, Joe put on his latex gloves and examined the contents of the victim's plastic bag that one of the DC's had handed him. He checked the woman's bag and called the station to give the details he had. A Bank of Scotland ID card and her work tag were in the bag. He scribbled her name, 'Nadia Ahmad' and her address, 'Rhiannan Road, Cathcart' in his black book, which he would show to Patel later. There was no mobile phone, something that would have been of real use. Very few people left home without a mobile. He wondered if the murderer had thrown it away.

'Hey, Joe,' Kara gave him a wave and smiled as she walked over to him. Her blonde ponytail was just visible under her police cap, her pretty blue eyes winked at him and she elbowed him saying: 'Want some help?'

'Yup, we need all the help we can get. What's the smile for? Good night in the boozer, was it?' Joe said relaxing, glad to see his mate there.

'If you must know I was at the Mela last evening, dancing away to the *bhangra* band.' The smile on Kara's face disappeared. 'Shocking! I couldn't believe it when I heard about this.'

They went over to Patel. Joe told him the few details he had gathered from the bag and from Lorraine who had spoken to Caroline.

'Check if anyone in the houses across from here saw or heard anything,' Patel said to his colleagues.

Patel's thoughts were running through the minutiae

of the process. The brown folders with the voters' roll would be here soon, and door-to-door would start work immediately. They would need to check all the data against the National computer, HOLMES (Home Office Large Major Enquiry System). A murder in a park or a public place was always a big challenge.

Kara and Joe chatted about the case as Joe handed over the zip-lock bag to Kara, so she could take it back to the station and hand it to forensics.

'Joe, come along. We need to see her family right away,' Patel said and walked towards his car.

'Coming, Boss.'

*

A young woman was reporting to the camera. She wore a flowery summer dress under a white jacket. Patel recognised her from the TV. She seemed totally at ease in front of the camera, enunciating each word carefully. Joe and Patel listened to her as they walked towards the car.

"The body of a young Asian female found in the park. What a sad end to this year's successful Mela. Earlier last evening, we reported that there was a fracas between a young BNP gang and some Asian youths during the Mela, but it was quickly quelled by security. Was this related in any way? Very few details coming in,' she said. She finished by saying,

'And now back to the studio,' and then indicated to the cameraman that they should follow the police officers. They rushed over to meet them.

'Christ, how did they get here so early?' muttered Patel.

Patel walked faster to get away from them, and as they caught up, he said clearly,

'I have nothing to say. It's too early.' The policemen strode determinedly to the car.

Patel got into his car and put the seat belt on. He rolled the car out of the park and onto the main road. Both men were deep in thought as the car sped on.

'Joe, the Mela finished at eight p.m. We need to find out how long it took for the stallholders to leave the park and if any council cleaners cleared the park at night.'

'I'll get onto it, sir. Wonder how many people hung around after the music bands and stalls owners left. It was a Sunday night, so most would head home, especially as it was more of a family outing. What do you think, sir?'

'I was wondering if, the murder victim, Nadia, had stayed on after the Mela for some reason, Joe. Maybe talking to someone she knew?'

'That's possible.'

'She must have been killed there. Not easy to carry a body around to that place, so she must have been in the park. There were no marks to indicate that the body had been moved. Maybe the family will give us some answers, eh?'

The car progressed along Great Western Road.

'Not many murders take place in the West End of Glasgow and Asian murders are quite rare. This is going to be quite a challenge,' observed Patel.

'Yes, sir,' said Joe.

'Let me get more information from the SOCO team, sir,' said Joe, busy on the phone recording further details on the case.

Commuters on their way to work had filled both the lanes on Great Western Road. The purple blazers of Glasgow Academy were in sight as parents dropped kids off at Kelvinbridge. Patel swore under his breath. The cars in the parking bays were full. Parents got musical instruments, huge PE kits, and other paraphernalia out the cars and dragged out the kids to get them to school. But it was the summer holidays! Must be extra-curricular activities that these private schools indulge in, he thought to himself. He had to inch past Roots and Fruits and the exotic Persian restaurant, the Shisha bar and finally reaching the lights at Byres Road. Red light, of course! The iconic Oran Mor, the old church that had been converted to a pub and arts venue, stood proudly across from the Botanic Gardens. Glasgow University students crossed at the lights and he saw people rushing to work in the busy West End. He sighed. He knew the traffic would be busy right up to the traffic lights at Anniesland before he turned into the Clyde Tunnel. A slight drizzle fell yet the sky was brightening, a July morning that held a promise of a sunny summer day. As the car left the tunnel, he got a call. Joe noted with a tinge of envy that the car had a Bluetooth hands-free phone. He hoped that he would be a great policeman like Patel and get promoted quickly and be able to own a car like this.

It was Clare McCall, the consultant forensic pathologist.

'Hi, Patel, just called to say I'll be doing the post-mortem. Nasty piece of work.'

'Could you do the PT within twenty-four hours please, Clare. The victim is Muslim, and the family need the body as soon as possible for the funeral rites.'

'You'll have the report as soon as possible. Awful to see such a young woman on the table.'

'Thanks, Clare, you're ace.'

He was relieved. He got on well with Clare; she was a good friend and an efficient woman with a great track record.

Kara had called Joe with some more sketchy details. The door-to-door surveys had started. The area of the park where the body was found was screened off. Computer information on the victim and colleagues at work were being checked out and the victim's Bank ID card was a godsend. It would be easy to get to the bank and get a list of all the employees working in the branch in St. Vincent Street. Joe related all the information to Patel who was concentrating on the driving though thoughts surged through his mind.

For a minute Nadia's image flashed into his mind. Why was she in the park that night?

Had she been having an affair? Was that why she was out at that time of night? His thoughts moved on to Usma. He used to meet with her late at night when she had lied to her parents and stayed with him. How many times had he dropped her at a friend's house at an ungodly hour?

Joe kept Patel up to date with all the new information he received. The usual traffic jams up on Great Western Road had slowed down his visit to Nadia Ahmad's family. Breaking news of the loss of a family member was never easy. 'Life and death, joy and sorrow, gain and loss, these dualities cannot be avoided. Learn to accept what you cannot change.' The quote from the Ramayana that his grandma used to read to him came to his mind. He had watched his senior officers doing that difficult job and saw how some families reacted. The emotional outbursts were heart-rending at times. Some stayed stoically quiet, the shock making them numb. Now it was his task to carry out that same job with sensitivity.

A good half an hour later, they had crossed the River Clyde and were in the Southside. This is my first murder as DI. I must get it solved soon. I have a good team. I'm lucky! Patel thought to himself.

Chapter 7

Nadia's family is the priority. What dreadful news to break to them on such a fine morning, thought Patel, as he drove towards their house. Rhiannon Road was just off the main Cathcart Road. This was a residential area with a lot of red and blonde sandstone tenements, terraces, and villas. Some of the shops on the main street were opening as he drove past. A few early customers were heading into Tesco Express.

Patel drove into the driveway. The Ahmads had an old sandstone house, which was semi-detached. He noted that the garden looked unkempt. The weeds were smothering the flower beds and the brown patches of moss looked like a random design on the strip of lawn. Joe and Patel rang the bell. One of the steps in front of the door was battered. The windows and doors could have done with a lick of paint as the tired green shade looked drab in the sunlight.

The only part of his job that he found hard to come to terms with was talking to the next of kin, if it was a sudden death, especially a murder. The worst was when he had to tell parents of very young children the cause of a sudden death. Patel hoped that his first case as a DI would be solved quickly and help this man by giving him some closure as soon as he knew who murdered Nadia.

An old woman opened the door. She had her hair covered with a scarf and was wearing a brown flowered *salwar-kameez*. She tugged at her shawl and wrapped it around closer to her neck.

'*Salaam alaikum,*' she said softly.

'*As salaamu alaikum,*' Patel returned the greeting respectfully. He remembered reading up on the scholarly debate on what kind of greeting should be used for a kaffir, or non-Muslim. He quickly added, 'Can I see Salim Ahmad, please?'

She nodded and ushered him in.

'Salim,' she called out and a young man, medium height and dark hair came down the stairs, tucking his shirt into his trousers.

'I'm DI Patel and this DS Joe McKay.'

They showed him their warrant cards.

'What's up?' He looked worried.

'I need to talk to you. Can we sit down, please?' said Patel.

The young man led them into the living room.

'Please, sit down,' Salim said. He indicated a sofa in the living room. It was an old-fashioned room with an old settee. There were some toys scattered around and lots of photographs of the family on the wall. The green flock wallpaper was like the paper in old Indian restaurants, harking back to the 1970s. A scroll of the Koran with writing in gold was inscribed on a velvety wall hanging. The quote said: 'Allah defends those who are true,' in Urdu. It was one of the few quotes that Usma had taught him, as it was short and easy to remember. There was a small statue of the Kabah in a glass case on the mantelpiece and a Koran text on a table, covered with a green cloth with a gold border. Patel took in all the details, a familiar sight in some houses of Asian Muslims on the Southside.

'It's about your wife. I'm sorry,' he said to Salim.

'Nadia! What ... What's happened? An accident? Is she okay?'

'No, not an accident. She's dead.'

'What! She can't be … she was staying over at Farah's.'

Salim's face crumpled; tears glinted. He sat down heavily on the settee. Patel could see that the news of his wife's sudden death was unbearable. His face was drained of colour.

'I'm so sorry. It appears that she was murdered.'

Salim stared at him blankly. Tears rolled down his cheeks.

'My boy, oh my God, my boy Mansur,' He sobbed quietly.

'I need to ask you, sir. Were you here all night?'

Patel felt a deep sense of sympathy for the newly widowed young man. As the DI in charge of the investigation, it was a question he had to ask, but he almost felt like hugging Salim.

'What! What do you mean? What kind of question is that? Of course, I was here! I was with my boy all night. Nadia, I must see her. Now!'

Patel coughed. 'Can anyone confirm that you were here all night?'

'Of course! Ask my mum. I … I can't believe what you are saying. Where is she? What happened? Oh my God.'

'Ammi,' he called out.

I'm afraid I need more details. Who lives in this house apart from you, your wife and the child?' Could he have worded this question better? Patel thought to himself.

'Just my mum … Amreen Bibi.'

The mother came in from the kitchen.

'What is it?' she asked Salim.

'Ammi …' He went to her.

He explained to his mother in Punjabi that his wife

33

was dead.

For a moment, Amreen looked confused. Then she hugged her son and wailed.

'Tell him that I was here all night. Oh, my god! Nadia is dead.' Salim shook his head.

Amreen looked more confused; she turned her head from Patel to Joe then back to Salim.

'You were here last night? Oh but ...'

She looked at Salim; Patel noted that fear crept in her eyes.

Salim looked at her and said loudly, 'Remember I was here all night, Ammi?'

Amreen sat down heavily. She cried and wiped her tears with her *dupatta*, the scarf that almost hid her face now.

Patel decided this was not the time for more questions. He said to Salim in a quiet voice, 'We need you to come and identify the body. Please tell your mum that Family Liaison officers will be here this morning, to talk to her.'

Salim nodded.

A young boy of four or five came running down the stairs in his Disney cartoon pyjamas. Patel's eyes widened. His heart felt heavy as the young boy rushed over to his father.

'Daddy,' he cried. Salim lifted him up and kissed him.

'Why are you crying? Where is mummy? Why is *Dadima* crying?'

Questions tumbled out of the little one's lips.

Salim wiped his eyes.

'*Beta*, I need to go with this man. *Dadima* will look after you.'

The boy looked at Patel and then ran over to his grandma. Amreen held him tight.

Salim headed for the door.

'I must see her,' he kept mumbling, as tears coursed down his cheeks.

'Let's go, Mr. Ahmad.'

Patel took his car keys out.

Salim said a few more words to Amreen Bibi and joined them.

Patel and Joe followed him out the door. They both heard the young boy's muffled cries and gran's soothing words trying to calm him.

As Patel drove, he explained some more of what he knew. He told him where Nadia's body had been found. Salim seemed stunned. The city snaked past as they headed to the new mortuary.

'What was she doing at the Mela? We left well before closing time. She and Farah were going to enjoy a "girlie" night. I ... I can't understand.' Salim shook his head.

Salim sat in the back of the car, his head down. His hands were gripping tightly the front passenger seat that Joe sat in. Patel watched him in the rear-view mirror as he drove. Joe saw that his knuckles stood out white and pale.

'By the way, did she leave her mobile at home? Patel asked Salim. 'There was no mobile phone in her bag. We need to take her number. We can trace any calls she made.'

He looked in the rear-view mirror. Salim was sitting in the back seat, pale and shaking, saying nothing.

Patel felt sorry for the young man, but at this stage, everyone was a suspect. The closest members of the family had to be questioned and observed closely. He drove carefully towards the old Southern General Hospital, which was now completely replaced by the dazzling new Queen Elizabeth University Hospital, whose buildings stretched far up to the sky. A yellow helicopter was visible perched on the helipad. The way towards the hospital where the new mortuary was situated now was difficult to reach because there was lots of traffic around the Clyde Tunnel.

Patel glanced again at Salim who was sitting with a dazed look, not taking anything in at all. Patel thought of others he had had to drive to the old Glasgow City Mortuary, near the High Court of Judiciary, which was a small grey Victorian building. He thought of the old, grim viewing room compared to the high spec, shiny, new one they hoped to see soon. He had had the privilege of looking at the new facilities. The new mortuary section was huge in scope built to take in over two-hundred-plus bodies in case of any terrorist activity. How things have changed since 2001 and the Glasgow airport bombing, Patel thought to himself. There was a small group of people from the pro-life lobby standing outside, on the pavement opposite with a banner that read, 'Pray for an end to abortion.' The US-style pro-life campaigners had been protesting since the new hospital had opened. Patel thought of the tenacity of their deep-held beliefs and how they continued their silent vigils.

Patel drove into the huge car park in the hospital. They walked into the atrium of the new hospital that looked more like a big airport or a five-star hotel. There were food courts, café-style tables and the reception desk was in the corner. Not like the shabby old hospital. It had been transformed. Everything looked so different from what he had been used to. They had to walk through a long corridor to get to the mortuary.

They were met at the door of the mortuary by a young blond woman, dressed in blue scrubs with a badge that read Anatomical Pathology Technician. She led them to a waiting area. She came back shortly and took them to the viewing room. Patel was aware of a small TV monitor on the wall. The next of kin could identify murder or accident victims on the monitor, at a safe distance if they wished. There was a viewing window with some blinds, and they would be pulled back if the family wished to see the corpse in the flesh instead of the TV monitor. Patel asked Salim if he wanted to use the TV monitor, but he shook his head.

'I want to see her,' he whispered.

Patel nodded.

Joe stood outside with Salim as Patel went in.

Clare McCall was in the room. They spoke briefly.

They both came out and asked Salim to come into the viewing room. He walked in hesitantly as though his feet couldn't move. Inside, Salim looked over Clare's shoulder. His eyes were looking in the direction where a trolley stood. He was silent in shock and sheer disbelief.

A covered body lay on a steel gurney.

The tube-lit room still smelled of a strange mixture of sickly chemicals that was unique to mortuaries. It was something Patel had never got used to. He crinkled his nose and stepped aside as Salim waited for Clare to reveal the body. She removed the sheet that covered the young woman's face. Salim held on to the side of the trolley, shaking his head in disbelief.

He whispered, 'Oh no, this is ... yes ... my Nadia.' Tears rolled down his cheeks. He touched her face and bent down to kiss her. He withdrew sharply, the cold grey skin almost too much to bear. He took a step back and tripped on a small steel tube that lined the floor separating each gurney.

Clare and Patel both reached out their hands to support him. Salim stood for a few seconds, looked at the body again. More tears wracked his body. Then he gave a deep sigh, wiped his tears, and nodded quietly. His hands went up to his mouth as if he were holding back from being sick. Patel gently but quickly guided him out of the room and made him sit on a chair in the corridor and persuaded him to put his head between his legs.

Clare came out of the room and she got him some water from a cooler.

Patel looked at the pale and haggard Salim. Clare gave Salim a cup of water. After a short gulp from the tiny plastic tumbler, he got up in a daze. He shook his head, still not able to take it all in. Salim clasped his hands together and rubbed them, as tears ran down his face, shaking his head again as if to say, 'No, not my Nadia.' He tried to speak but words came out that sounded more like choking sobs.

She glanced at Patel and nodded to him. He ushered Salim away from the corridor saying a quick thank you and goodbye to Clare. The three of them, Joe, Salim, and Patel, walked out of the door, the sunny day making a mockery of such a tragic scene. Glasgow's usual grey clouds hiding the sun would have been a blessing this morning.

They got into Patel's car. They drove in silence for a while. The traffic was inching out of the big hospital and on to the dual carriage leading to the Clyde Tunnel and then onto the city centre.

'You get that bastard who did that to my Nadia,' Salim suddenly said aloud.

Patel said nothing.

A trickle of sweat gathered on Salim's forehead. He brushed it away with the sleeve of his jacket. 'I need to see my wee boy,' Salim sobbed.

'I'll get someone to take you home,' Patel said gently.

They arrived at the station. Joe got out of the car quickly and went ahead to find a DC to take Salim back to his son and mother.

The station was busy. Joe saw there were three men gathered round the reception area. A young DC had brought them in. He recognised two of them, Big Mo and Gazza. This was the infamous duo that was often brought to the station on breach of peace, often the worse for alcohol consumption and once before for possession of drugs. There was a new person with them. The DC was addressing him,

'Daniel Kelly, eh? Joining our infamous pair, are you? So, how many pints did you have?'

'My best pal Danny's guid company, so he is. We wis at yon pub ...' piped in Big Mo, his short T-shirt not quite managing to cover his belly. The man beside him, Gazza, was thin and scrawny looking. He had wild eyes, and his thinning brown hair lay flat on his small head.

Patel glanced at Daniel Kelly with interest. The tall, big man with sandy hair and a scarred face seemed quite inebriated. His reply to the DC was garbled. The DC was asking him to repeat himself while shushing Big Mo.

Drugs and alcohol were problems that kept police busy in all parts of Scotland. The annual reports of crimes related to the twin evils that beset the community were fresh in Patel's mind. He had been reading the reports for his station; the numbers peaked at the weekends. Regulars like Gazza and Big Mo were picked up often. So, Daniel might be another drunk to add to that list. He shook his head as he headed towards his office. The image of the young woman in the mortuary came back to him. It was hard not to think of death.

Joe went over to the canteen to get them both a strong cup of coffee. He brought the steaming cups to

Patel's office.

'Just what I needed. Thanks, Joe,' smiled Patel as he took the big cup of coffee from Joe's hand. 'So, what do you think of Salim?'

'Looked pretty upset to me, sir,' said Joe as he sipped his coffee.

'I am not saying that Salim did it, but guilt can make someone emotional if they're confronted with the victim of their crime. It's just a thought. I really feel sorry for Salim and his young son,' mumbled Patel.

Joe smiled.

'Boss, I called the office while you were in the viewing room at the mortuary. The murder investigating room is all set up and the team are ready and waiting,' said Joe.

'Good work. We have to be on our toes. This is a murder case, Joe; every person needs to be thoroughly investigated.'

Chapter 8

Patel watched as a young policeman helped Salim into a squad car. He heard footsteps behind him. He turned around as Joe entered the room. They walked over to the incident room briskly, trying not to think of the image of the young woman's body on the gurney. As Senior Investigating Officer, Patel had to get the murder investigation strategy correct.

When they reached the meeting room, the group of police officers he had always worked with were there, Brian, Kara, Colin, Ben, Alan, John and eight others. Patel made a mental note to ask Martin for more officers and resources for the huge work ahead. He was pleased to note that the whiteboard was up and ready, with a picture of Nadia, along with known details of the case and location of the murder. Patel gave a summary of the case.

'Sir,' Joe added, 'She worked at the Bank of Scotland in St. Vincent Street.'

'Good, Joe, now make sure you get all the info on the family and friends, and Nadia's work colleagues. Kara and Brian, get the Govan Police Gang Task Force; see if there is any connection with the gang squabble early on in the evening at the Mela.'

'Right away, sir,' said Kara.

'Alan and John, check the bank accounts of the entire family if possible. Ben and Colin, start interviewing the neighbours and friends of the victim. Joe, you and I will get over to Nadia's friend, Farah. She was supposed to be staying with her last night.

'Get cracking!' was DI Patel's parting shot to the team.

*

Later that night, DS Alan Brown parked the car outside his flat. Through the living room window, he could see his daughter, Tracey, comforting her baby, holding him in her arms and pacing up and down their tiny lounge. He was probably screaming his head off. Alan checked his watch. Eleven-thirty. He did not want to go in. He wished he had stayed longer at the pub. He sat in the car, closing his eyes, and resting on the car headrest. Finally, at midnight he went inside. As soon as the baby heard him, he started a whimper and then cried. Alan went to his bedroom and lay in bed, tossing and turning. No promotion and now this at home.

He couldn't sleep. His thoughts turned to his friend John's attempt to help him that evening. They often shared the usual after-work pint. John observed his partner downing more than a usual couple of drams and a beer chaser and had chatted about it with him.

'What's up, Alan?'

'Eh? Just enjoying my swally.' Alan grinned, gulping his whisky. 'Don't give me that look, all disapproving.'

'It's not like you, Alan. The last few weeks you've been like a bear with a sore head.' John locked eyes with him looking for a straight answer.

'The usual. Life is shite.' Alan took another gulp of his pint this time.

Alan looked away. John had been his friend since primary school, his companion in so many escapades as young teens. The careers advisor at school had sat with them and pointed out that they could make something of their lives if they joined the army or police force as they were intelligent but lacked discipline. It was John who had been keen, but he and the guidance teacher had had a hard time convincing Alan to join the police force. It was a career that had straightened Alan out. He moved up the ranks by taking the exams and training to become a detective, until his wife suddenly left him for the Asian shop keeper she worked for. As a single parent he struggled, went back on the drink, but Tracey, his daughter had given him the strength to go on. John helped him through each of the crises, a shoulder to cry on. Sometimes it was more than Alan could handle. And now Tracey was letting him down. 'Just like your mum, you whore!' he had screamed at her. But afterwards, regretting his words, he hugged her and promised to stand by her, because she meant the world to him. Just seeing her struggling with the baby, a painful reminder every day was hard on him.

'If I can help in any way ...' John offered.

'Naw, not sleeping much.'

'Drinking too much. That's never going to help, is it?'

'Naw, you wouldn't understand, man. Too much happened last year. It's all getting to me, I guess.'

'Try me. Tracey and her tantrums? Usual teenage carry-ons. Listen to me, I've seen it all. From thirteen to eighteen, we just have to keep nagging them and hope their pals don't lead them astray,' said John, looking at him. The concerned expression on his face caused Alan to relent.

'It's more than that,' he said, 'I've been a useless dad. I need another drink.'

'Hey, we all feel that. Come on, pull yourself together. You don't need more of that stuff.' John moved the glass away from Alan.

'She's ruined her life. That Paki bastard of a

43

boyfriend has just dumped her.'

'What! I thought you said they'll be getting together now that the baby is here?' John laid a hand on his shoulder.

'No, he just dumped her, now she has his bloody baby that never sleeps. Jesus, life just stinks.' Alan drained the glass then banged it on the table.

'But Tracey is young, she'll get over it.'

'She's just sixteen and ... oh just get me a drink,' Alan bellowed. A few punters looked towards them.

John went over to the bar and ordered another round. He walked back to their table with their drinks and sat down.

Alan downed the next drink and glared at John. 'Don't breathe a word to anyone. I don't want any pity.'

Alan was late for work the next day. John wrinkled his nose; the heavy drinking to forget his woes could be smelt on his breath as he sat beside him. All of the team members working on Nadia's murder had gathered in the briefing room for the usual morning meeting before the day's work. Patel was just starting the proceedings. Alan saw that Patel had noted his late arrival. Alan wondered if Patel would add this to the list of black marks on his record.

'Kara and Brian, you complete the door-to-door today. Rope in some more constables if you need them. Forensics and post-mortem reports, make sure they are at my desk right away.'

More instructions were given to each member of the team. Alan listened with scant attention, but his ears picked up the last instruction.

'Alan and John,' called out Patel, 'I'd like you to help out with the door-to-door. It is a big area to cover. HOLMES should have the details you need. Right! Chop chop, back to work now,' he concluded the briefing.

Alan scowled. He hated the door-to-door work, and his head was sore; the bright sunlight and hot weather bothered him. He rose slowly from his seat and said 'Shit' under his breath, but John laid a quick hand on his shirt sleeve and threw him a cautionary glance. Along with the others, he left the room. The morning work began.

Would an eyewitness emerge from the door-to-door enquiry? Patel thought as he got ready for the next visit.

Chapter 9

Farah heard the alarm and decided to ignore it. Outside, dawn blushed. The brush-strokes of a sun rising in the East enhanced the beauty of the white clouds in the sky. The magic of summer sunrise waving goodbye to a dark night broken by birdsong; a sweet rush of notes to start the new day usually awakened her.

Not today. She tucked herself under the duvet and opened her heavy eyes. The curtains were drawn back. The dark lining in the curtains ensured there was no blinding sun through the curtains to wake her up, but that was no use, she must have forgotten to draw them in last night.

She heard the shower. Craig, her young husband, was getting ready for work. A few minutes later, he came over with a towel around his slim body, sat on the bed and hugged her. She screamed at the water dripping off his hair and onto her face. Now those extra few minutes under the warm duvet were ruined. She was fully awake now. Craig was getting dressed in a smart suit. Farah was happy that he had chosen the blue silk tie that she had given him for his birthday. She got up and made her way to the kitchen with him. The kettle boiled and she made him some coffee, as he sorted his briefcase and checked his phone.

'You and Nadia had a good night then?'

'Yeah, it was a good night, but she left to see her pal later.'

'Hmm, did she?' he replied. His phone pinged with

a new message; he looked down to read it. He gulped some of the coffee from his mug.

'Right, I'm off,' he said and left the half-full coffee mug on the granite worktop. He gave her a peck on the cheek and rushed off to work.

Farah moved around as if on autopilot. She took the little pod of coffee from the Tassimo tin. There was a choice of various flavours of coffee, all stacked up neatly in the coffee pod rack. It had to be a strong one this morning. Not decaffeinated or latte, caramel, Oreo, or the other sugary ones she normally helped herself to. She chose the Kenco Colombian Roast, switched the machine on and listened to its whine, as she looked for some paracetamol.

The aroma from the Tassimo machine filled the bright room. The piping hot coffee was perfect. Farah curled her fingers around the big mug and sipped the heavenly beverage. She looked out of the big French windows. The garden was blooming, rhododendrons, azaleas, the red pieris' with their red-hot tipped leaves and the pale-lilac clematis winding around the fence with more blossoms than leaves. A contented sigh escaped her as she took another sip and glanced at the clock. She took two paracetamols and hoped that the headache and wooziness would leave her soon. The coffee helped, but she was still tired. What with being at the Mela almost all day, then Nadia coming over, followed by that phone call from Malcolm, she was still up well after midnight! She deserved the long lie in. Craig must have slept through it all. He was a heavy sleeper. Lucky him! He always left early on Monday morning as the traffic tended to be pretty heavy.

Should I just have a lazy lie down on the sofa? she thought as she walked into the lounge. She was proud of this room; all in white, with hand-picked works of art hanging on the walls and a collection of Caithness glassware and crystal in a big glass display cabinet. Craig and she had saved hard to buy this rather large modern villa just off Hyndland road, behind the tennis club.

She went over to her studio. It was full of easels, paints, and her projects from over the years, some finished, some not. She looked at the huge canvas she had recently been working on. It seemed to summon her forwards. She took a sip of her coffee and then put the mug down on her desk. She picked up her brush and started to work on it and soon was immersed in it. The headache was forgotten as she concentrated on the brush strokes. She stopped, stood up and looked at it from a distance. She was not happy with her work this morning. Too tired, better to come back to it later she decided.

Farah retraced her steps to the kitchen and on the way, in the lounge she glanced at their wedding photo in a pretty silver frame. How happy they looked! She, the radiant bride, and Craig, looking down at her dimpled smile was dashingly handsome in his kilt. How lucky she had been having this charmed life. Okay, so they had no children and that was a void that had made her so unhappy. It was Nadia who had helped her through that awful period when she was just a weeping mess, every month, and all through those years of infertility treatments. Farah had somehow come to terms with it. Childfree, she said now, instead of childless. Maybe simple semantics but it did make her feel better, not bitter any more.

Farah and Nadia, they had always been there for each other. Farah sighed again.

Poor Nadia, her friend from primary school, lost her father when she was only ten. She was always looking for love. They had such a good few years together as a foursome, Roger and Nadia, her and Craig, always going out together, picnics, and trips to the seaside, or clubbing and meals out at weekends. When Roger's drinking got the better of him it was not an easy time for Nadia. Then it was Farah's turn to be there for her when Nadia had gone through that awful divorce and trauma. At least in the last few years, Nadia had settled down with Salim. Her little boy Mansur filled her life with happiness. Another sigh as Farah rinsed the coffee mug, placed it in the dishwasher, and went up the stairs to get dressed. She was soon out of the shower and changed. She was going to rest today, read a book and take a stroll maybe in the afternoon.

I must call Nadia to see how she got on with that Malcolm and what time she reached home, thought Farah. It was strange that she had not texted her! Their WhatsApp chat was endless. Nadia would even chat to her on the way to work every morning! It was a wee bit of catch up on daily wittering, as they laughingly told each other. Nadia would have been busy getting Mansur ready for school, and all that early morning palaver. She must be tired like me, I'll call her later, maybe during her lunch hour, she said to herself. She grabbed the glossy magazine No.1, Scotland's gossip magazine that lay next to Hello and copies of Vogue and Asiana on the coffee table and settled down on the sofa. She fell asleep. It was nearly lunch time when she opened her eyes.

The doorbell rang.

It was a shock to see two men at the door.

'Farah Bolton? I'm DI Patel and this is DS McKay.'

They showed their warrant cards.

'We'd like to have a word with you about your friend, Nadia.'

'What? Why? Is she okay?'

She led them into the lounge.

So not short of a bob or two, thought Joe. He made a quick note in his black book.

'Nice place you have here, Mrs. Bolton,' said Patel gently as they all sat down.

'You said Nadia ...?' Farah's eyes were wide open, with a glint of worry in them.

'Was Nadia staying over here last night?' Patel asked her.

'Yes of course. Why? What's happened?'

'Did she spend the whole night here with you? When did she leave?'

'Look, what's this all about? Is she okay?'

'Well, it is bad news, I'm afraid. Nadia was found murdered this morning.'

'Oh my God! No, no ...' she cried.

'When did she leave your house, Mrs. Bolton?'

Farah was shaking, her face drained of colour.

'Do take your time and tell us all you know.' Patel's voice was gentle.

The tears rolled down her cheeks.

Joe walked towards the kitchen. The scent of freshly brewed coffee filled his nostrils. He took a glass from the draining board and filled it with water and took the glass to the lounge.

'Here,' he said, and handed her the glass.

Her hands were shaking. She took a sip, and then put the glass on a coaster on the coffee table.

'Oh my God. I can't believe it.' She paused. 'There was a carry-on last night. Nadia found that she had lost her grandma's gold chain that she always wore, and she was going back to the Mela to look for it.'

Patel's eyes widened. 'The Mela? Did she go there alone?'

'No, she did not. We tried calling some of the organisers but couldn't get anyone on the phone. She was upset. I told her that it was daft to go back late at night. That was when Malcolm called.'

Patel's eyebrow shot up in surprise. 'Malcolm?'

'Her colleague, Malcolm Watson. They work in the same branch.' Farah's sobs broke through again. 'Are you sure she's dead? She can't be ...' her voice trailed off.

'She left your house late at night to see this Malcolm?'

'Yes, she did. She was his best friend!' Farah protested. 'He was going through some personal stuff and he needed her. He doesn't live far from here, anyway.'

'Did she call you when she got there?'

'Yes, she did call me to say Malcolm was in a bad way, but I assumed he would go with her to look for the necklace. Look, this is way too hard for me. Poor Nadia, she was just helping a mate.' Farah started to cry.

She looked up as a sudden thought made her sit up.

'Salim and her wee boy. Oh my God, I must go and see them,' she mumbled through her tears.

'Do you have Malcolm's address?' Patel insisted.

'Near the Mandir, Park Grove Terrace, number twenty. I think it's a floor up. I'm not sure.'

'Anything else, Mrs. Bolton? You know that even the smallest detail would help us?'

'Oh, Nadia said as Malcolm's flat was on her way home and close to the Mela, she would go to look for the gold chain,' Farah added quickly. 'I was so sure he'd go with her,' she said.

They tried to get more details from her, but Farah wanted to hurry over to see Salim and Mansur.

'We may come back to you for more details and a

statement from you.'

Patel and McKay left.

Farah sat stunned for a moment. Nothing made sense. She picked at the cushion, hugged it close to her and cried. What had happened last night? Why had she let Nadia go to Malcolm's? She tried to work out the sequence of what happened, but the image of Nadia in her lovely pink *lehenga*, the pretty Pakistani evening wear, kept flashing back. It was confusing. Farah had drunk a lot of wine, but Nadia had said no, she was going to detoxify and be teetotal for a while. They discussed going to the park to look for the gold chain. Then Craig complained that he had to be at work in the morning and went off to bed. Malcolm rang. Nadia had changed into the jeans and top that she had brought for the next morning and rang for a taxi to get to Malcolm's, even though it was late.

'I'll call you. I'll be back soon. Malcolm is just being a drama queen, just sounds like he needs a shoulder to cry on, I'll go and see if I can find my necklace. Don't worry, he'll come with me,' she had said, leaving the overnight case and jumping into the taxi.

It had all happened quickly, the call from Malcolm and then Nadia rushing off.

I didn't even ask where they found Nadia! she thought now.

She ran up the stairs to get her bag and make her way to the Ahmads'. She called Craig before she left.

'Oh my God! Did that Malcolm...kill her? Jesus! I thought he was her best mate!' Craig was stunned.

'I don't have a clue.' Farah stifled her sobs.

'Are you okay? Shall I come over?'

'No, I am going over to see Salim. Call you later.' Farah hung up.

Farah drove over to the Ahmad's on the Southside,

as fast as she could. Last night was like a dream, surreal. Allison Street was busy, filled with people shopping. Boxes of mangoes, various exotic fruits and vegetables outside the shops, creating bright and colourful displays on a summer morning. Farah noticed the shops as she had to brake suddenly. A young man walked out of one of the shops in front of her car at the pedestrian crossing. I really should be concentrating on my driving, she thought, and then took a deep breath as she drove to Nadia's house.

Nadia's little boy, Mansur, rushed over to her as soon as Amreen Bibi opened the door. It was as if the little boy wanted reassurance from his mum's best friend. She hugged him tight, rained kisses on his sweet face and tried to stay calm for him. Her heart was beating fast. The familiar house without the chatter and presence of Nadia felt different. Amreen took her to the kitchen and put the kettle on. They settled down for a cup of tea after Mansur calmed down and stopped asking 'Where is my mum? Is she not with you?' Questions that made them both shed tears and search for answers to allay that anxiety in the young child's mind. How does one tell a six-year-old his mum is dead? Farah thought, as she hugged Mansur and distracted him with a game that was on her mobile phone.

Grief: that journey with no destination. Grief enveloped the house as only death can, an ambience that is felt by people all over the world but to each family unique and heart-wrenching. Farah felt the grief of the family deeply as she stayed with them for a while, comforting all of them with her soothing words.

Chapter 10

Patel remembered one of the first stations he worked in, as a young police constable. Maryhill Police station was a bleak 1970s building, four floors of brown brick with a windowless tower standing behind. It was on the main road, opposite an equally dismal block of flats. The blue and white sign was familiar to some of its inhabitants. The main road, an artery from the north to the city centre, was dominated by a huge twenty-four-hour Tesco and a line of takeaway curry shops, Jaconelli's fish bar, and a betting shop. A high rise set of flats faced the police station. The noise and the smell of fish & chips would stream in if the windows were kept open in the summertime. Patel would shut the window as he worked at his desk. He missed the old station with so much life around the place.

Patel checked all the information that the team had brought in from the various sources. Nadia's bank statements, interview reports on her work colleagues, and some of the interviews with the house to house calls from Kara and Brian.

He called Joe to his office. They went over their visit to Farah Bolton.

'We need to take a statement from her and her husband again. But we need to see this Malcolm Watson and hear what he has to say. I wonder if he was one of the few who didn't answer the doorbell when Kara and Brian were doing the house to house calls,' Patel said to Joe.

'Let's go and talk to him.'

The houses along Park Grove Terrace were old stone tenements. The blonde sandstone was still resplendent after a century of Glasgow's bad weather. In the West End of Glasgow, the old flats looked out on Kelvingrove Park, a green, luscious place in the heart of the city. The dark entrances had bare stairs that led up to the flats. Houses ran almost the entire road on both sides and were occupied by students, young couples, and first-time buyers. There were cars parked nose to tail on both sides of the road.

Joe noticed a layby beside the Hindu Mandir and parked in it. Patel glanced at the Hindu temple, which evoked memories of his parents bringing him and his sister over most Sundays when they were both children. As he walked beside Joe, he noticed the name emblazoned Hindu Mandir with a big OM written in Sanskrit.

Number Twenty was like all others in the row of tenements. Some of the flats were well maintained but Malcolm Watson's flat did not look very welcoming that morning. The sun drifted behind some grey clouds casting a dark shade on the houses. Flat 20A was up the stairs. The door was painted brown and the brass on the Yale lock and handle were covered with verdigris. It could do with a good clean and polish, thought Joe as he knocked on the door. It took a few rings on the doorbell and some banging loudly before it was answered.

The door opened a fraction.

They heard an angry man's voice, 'For God's sake, stop banging and ringing!'

The door opened fully. A tall, sleepy looking, dishevelled young man stood there in his crumpled jeans and a stained T-shirt.

Patel lifted their warrant cards, 'DI Patel and DS

McKay. We need to talk to you.'

'What about?' The man looked half-awake.

'Nadia Ahmed came over yesterday evening. We need to talk to you about her.'

'Look, I'm too knackered, come back later.' He was about to slam the door on them.

'No, this is important, Mr. Watson.' Patel said, taking a step inside.

The man let them in, looking puzzled.

They sat down. Joe and Patel looked over the room, it was in bad shape, and it reeked of alcohol. Bottles of lager, a mug of cold coffee, some magazines and yesterday's newspaper were all lying on a dining table. The couch was covered with some kind of fleece throw, scrunched up and not very clean. A TV remote lay on the floor. The lampshade near the couch was covered with dust and the brown shade of the walls made the flat look dismal. A small TV was screwed to the wall, the cable running along the skirting board and the plug point had an extension with various cables from a DVD player and an Xbox and other electronic devices. Beside the couch were two empty bottles of whisky and a glass with remnants of a drink. A scatter cushion designed with bright orange and brown flowers was lying on the floor. Their eyes scanned the room looking for any small clue that might help the investigation.

'The news is not good, Mr. Watson. Nadia is dead.'

'Nadia, dead?' He gave a dry laugh. 'Don't be ridiculous. She was fine last night.'

'This is serious. You may have been the last person to be with Nadia. When and with whom did she leave the flat last night?' Patel's voice was low and firm.

'I've been sleeping. I've got a hangover! What do you mean? Yes, she was here. God, I must have been so drunk that I fell asleep. She said something about her gold chain, but I was drowning in my own piss here. Fucking hell, what do you mean, she's dead?' He sounded dazed. 'Nadia dead ... dead? No, no that can't be. She was here ...' Sobs welled up and tears gathered in his eyes.

'What was such a crisis that you called her?' Patel continued.

'I ... I Jesus fucking Christ! I was devastated.'

Patel and McKay waited for details.

'I'd rather not say.'

'What? Mr. Watson, this is a murder enquiry. You need to help us with all you know!'

'My partner left me. We were getting married in three weeks.'

'I'm sorry to hear that, Mr. Watson.'

'Nadia was my best friend.' Malcolm almost spat out the words.

'Well, then you better explain.'

'No, no way. Just leave me, eh? Just go.'

'So, Nadia, what time did she come to your flat and what time did she leave?' Patel reiterated.

'I told you, I've no idea what time. I'm wasted, man! Can't you see that?' His eyes drooped and he held his head in both his in hands as if it were pounding.

'She was here around, say, eleven, so how long did she stay? Surely you must have heard her leave?' urged Patel.

'I've told you; I was well gone when she came. She tried to make me drink coffee; I just drank more from the bottle.' He indicated the bottle of whisky that lay nearby. 'I don't want to think. I can't.'

'Did anyone else come here, Mr. Watson? Can you remember anything at all, even the smallest thing that would help us?' Joe demanded.

'No, I'm so sorry. Jesus, Nadia, Nadia dead, Jesus

Christ, she was here ...'

He shook his head in disbelief.

'Well, after you sober up, we'll get you down to the station and you can give us a proper statement, perhaps even tomorrow as it is nearly four p.m. now, Mr. Watson.' Patel frowned. This was an unnecessary delay. One of the rules of investigations is that the person is sober when interviewed. This was obviously not so.

Patel got up. 'Drink some coffee. Get yourself together and we'll see you tomorrow or when you can think clearly. He put down a card with the address of the police station on the table, and they left.

In the car, Patel observed, 'Not much use, was it? Hope we can get something useful tomorrow when he's sober. I just can't believe he blacked out so soon after her arrival. Also, clamming up when we asked him about his fiancée. That sounds too suspicious. Not a very good alibi, is it?'

'No, sir, looks like he had made a night of it. Not a good alibi at all,' Joe concurred.

'By the way, check out his fiancée. If he were getting married, his colleagues would know. Wonder who she is.'

'Kara and Brian are talking to the bank employees, sir,' said Joe.

'Well, Malcolm was the last one to see Nadia alive. Once he's sobered up, we'll get a better picture of what happened.

Patel and Joe discussed what they had so far in the case as they drove back to the station.

*

Malcolm looked around the flat. Was Nadia dead? He could not get his thoughts together. What happened?

When did she go? He did remember her coming in and how he had cried with her and kept drinking. She had come as soon as he had called. She had never let him down. He was well gone by the time she had arrived. That first bottle of whisky was done, and he had worked his way through the next one.

'Malc, look at the state of you. Don't let anyone do this to you,' she had cried, hugging him.

She had prised the glass out of his hands. 'This bottle is not the answer. Anyway, you're not much of a drinker, are you? Where did you get the whisky?' she had chided him.

He was struggling to understand why he had been jilted by his fiancée so close to the wedding.

'My life is over. I ... can't live anymore ...'

'Look, your words are slurred, and I can hardly get what you're saying. Drink some coffee.'

She had bustled over to the kitchen and put the kettle on. While she was busy with the coffee mugs, he had slumped back on the settee and had drunk some more . The next thing he knew the policemen were banging on his door.

'Oh my God. Did she die because I called her over? Jesus, what have I done?' Malcolm cried again as he keeled over and fell asleep on the sofa.

Chapter 11

Ah ... his creaking old bones ... Ali Hassan got up and stretched himself out like a cat. Fat splodges of raindrops fell on the window, but the grey dawn would turn into a sunny day, he hoped. Radio Awaaz played an old Bollywood favourite. He hummed the tune.

The mirror in the bathroom showed a white-haired man, handsome once, with clear brown eyes that missed nothing. All those years in the shop, rising early and working long hours had left him still active at seventy. The big cash and carry work he now left to his sons. He wanted some rest after years of toil. He knew nearly everyone in the Asian community and that was his 'work', a benign father figure whom people respected and looked up to.

He dressed and went down for his breakfast. His wife Salma was at the dining table with their breakfast and the daily papers. She handed him a mug of steaming white coffee and he saw the parathas, the soft ghee-filled chapattis, which were his breakfast favourite on the plate in front of him. She went to the kitchen to make an omelette spiced with green chillies and onion, brought it in a few minutes and served him. She sat down beside him and then rubbed her knees. He gave her a quick smile and said, 'Knees playing up?'

She nodded and grimaced. She sipped her coffee, put it down and then tucked into her plate of parathas.

He picked up his mug, slurped his first sip of the hot coffee, and then started on the hot parathas and omelette.

'So, Nadia is running around with this *gora*, the white boy,' said Salma putting her mug down, '*Sharam nahi*. Shameless, flaunting it. And she is married! She has such a beautiful son.'

Ali was busy eating his breakfast.

Salma tutted as she sipped her mug of coffee.

'He's just a colleague,' Ali said calmly.

'That's no excuse. Having cups of coffee with him in Costa in Buchanan Galleries for all to see?' Salma threw a glance of anger at Ali. How could he treat it as though it didn't matter? This is what happens when girls are allowed too much freedom, going out to work and forgetting their own culture, she told herself as she sipped the hot coffee.

'Well, she does work in town,' said Ali and opened The Daily Record.

'Nothing good will come of this, *inshallah*,' said Salma as she tucked into a paratha. A frown caused wrinkles on her forehead.

'Look Salma, don't gossip, and say things that you know little about,' warned Ali and turned to his paper. He hated hearing gossip about Nadia for whom he had a special affection.

Salma moved to the kitchen. He heard the banging of the dishes as she put them in the sink. He loved her to bits, but this habit of gossiping about a girl they had looked after was too much for Ali. He shook his head. He had helped Nadia when her mother was suddenly widowed. Salma and he had taken them under their wing. Nadia did have a few distant relatives, but they were down South, in England. He considered her to be the daughter he never had, though they had grown apart when she turned into a teenager. He had shifted his help in the last few years to her mother who had the beginnings of dementia and had been in a sheltered home in the last few years. They visited Mrs. Hussain in the sheltered home once a month at least.

'I'm off to the office first, then going to have lunch with Raj Singh, so don't make any lunch for me,' he said as Salma came in to clear the table. She stacked up the tablemats and coasters in a neat pile. 'I want to find out all about the Mela and how the business did out there,' he added.

Salma sighed loudly.

Ali came up and touched her shoulder and said, 'Those parathas were delicious. Now you take a rest and look after that knee, and stop that gossiping, okay?' he said with a smile.

He put his light waterproof jacket on and picked up his car keys.

His business kept him busy, but he still liked to be involved in the Mela. The Asian community worked all year to stage a fantastic show, inviting bands from London and further afield and businesses vied for stalls to show their wares. He had been at the Mela for a short time with the grandchildren, over the last two days. Now, over lunch, he would hear what his friends thought of the Mela from a business perspective. Later he would ask his sons what they thought about it. Was it a success? Did the businesses make money? Now he had to drive over to the office and check all the takings from the cash and carry business and make sure the stocks had arrived and the manager was doing the work. It was always good to keep an eye on the day to day running of the business as it gave him a focus in life.

He looked forward to catching up with all the news on his round at lunch time. The rain had cleared, and the summer sun shone brightly, lifting his spirits. He set out in his silver BMW and sped along towards the cash and carry office. The CD player was on and he listened to his favourite music and drove on, unaware of the tragedy that had befallen the very girl that Salma had mentioned to him at breakfast. Oblivious to the murder, enjoying the feel of the sun warming up the day, Ali steered the car, happily singing along with that famous maestro of *qawalis* and Sufi music, Nusret Ali Khan. Hassan's tuneless voice tried to keep up with the fast-paced song and the high-pitched vocals of Nusret. He shook his head, saying, 'Wah! Wah!' and sang along as he sped up the car. He arrived at the office; spirits high with the music ringing in his ears. The sun's warmth made him smile. He worked solidly through the morning.

Close to lunchtime, he was on the road again, on to the Clyde Tunnel to get to the West End. Each year the businessmen met to have an informal audit of how the Mela had fared and came up with ideas for changes if they were needed. They met at the recently opened Akbar restaurant close to the Mitchell Library at Charing Cross. He would get lots of gossip about how the business world was in these days of austerity, and best of all, the food was always delicious. The chef made sure the food served for Ali's table was more in keeping with homemade style than the fare they served out for other clientele.

Raj Singh was a good friend, with his finger on the pulse of how the Mela was organised. Ali wondered what problems, if any, might need to be ironed out for next year. The Mela meant 'to meet' in Sanskrit. The Mela in its infancy had been a small affair, held in the old Kelvinhall Transport museum. It had grown beyond its tiny beginnings and in the last few years was held in the huge Kelvingrove Park to accommodate the thousands who patronised it.

He felt a shiver of excitement whenever he passed the new Transport Museum, which was a wonderful building on the banks of the River Clyde. It was designed by the world-renowned Zaha Hadid, its unique shape rose along the spruced-up Clyde walkway. As he drove along the Clydeside Expressway, the river shimmering silver in the summer sun and the beautiful buildings of the Hydro, the Armadillo, the new BBC and STV buildings all making the skyline different from the old cranes and shipbuilding heritage of old Glasgow, he smiled at how his thoughts had jumped from the origins of the Mela to the River Clyde regeneration works.

Twenty-five years ago, when the Mela started, he was much younger. He had so much energy then. He could work from early morning to well after midnight and feel he could do another few hours if needs be. He had retired from all the hustle and bustle of managing the shops and getting stalls ready for the Mela. Now he was the elder, whom others looked up to for expertise on this annual event that was important to new and established Asian businesses in Glasgow.

He felt his age now. Well, I have grown older and weaker but the Mela has grown from strength to strength, he thought. He had had some stalls of textiles and fancy goods at the first Mela, which was initiated in 1990 as part of the celebrations when Glasgow became the City of European Culture. Glasgow had been kind to him and his family. It was his home, well, his second home. His attachment to Pakistan had always been stronger. Lahore, the second-largest city in Pakistan was where his family had moved to after the partition of India during the British rule. Originally from Kashmir, his family had found more opportunities in the big city. Kashmir was a disputed territory between India and Pakistan since Independence. The two countries had gone to war twice over this piece of land and the border incursions were a daily occurrence. The fact that India ruled this Muslim majority state annoyed Ali. Despite his friendships with Indians in Glasgow, he wanted Kashmir to be taken over by Pakistan. This was something even staying over the twenty-five years in Glasgow could not change.

The black glass and the huge blood-red neon sign of Akbar's restaurant on the white façade made a striking picture at the edge of Sauchiehall Street. Ali parked and locked the car. He stretched his arms above him, grateful for the fact that there were always some unoccupied parking bays in the side street, Berkeley Street, very close to the restaurant. Since a parking fee had been imposed from eight to six, the bays tended to be free during the day.

He went inside the restaurant and saw that Raj Singh presided over a table with a few of the other businessmen. No one noticed Ali as he entered. None smiled at him. The usually jocular Raj looked sombre as he rose from his seat and came over to greet Ali. Seeing their gloomy faces, he assumed that maybe the Mela had some new problems.

'You must have heard the shocking news. We thought you might have gone straight to the Ahmads'.' Raj said.

'Shocking news? Why? What's happened?' Ali's brows rose in surprise.

'Nadia Ahmad was found dead in the Kelvingrove Park early this morning,' Raj explained.

'No, *inshallah*.'

He said nothing for a few minutes.

He understood why no one smiled. It was the death

65

of young Nadia. The shocking news of Nadia's murder must have reached them all, while he was listening to his favourite music all morning! They recounted what they had heard that morning on Radio Clyde and some had seen a brief flash on the news on Scottish TV. They had waited in a sombre mood to see if Ali would have more details, but it was a shock to him. He was devastated.

Ali and Raj decided this was not the time to discuss business. The group left the restaurant, not even fixing a later date. The news had left them all stunned. Ali decided to go over to the grieving family and see if they needed any help.

*

Later that night Ali Hassan stood on the porch of Patel's house. He rang the bell, hesitating and wondering if it was too soon to ask the new DI for details. Patel was a good friend of his. He would probably tell him nothing at such an early stage of the investigation. He waited with a worried look on his face, causing the wrinkles to furrow deeper into his skin.

Patel opened the door to Ali. He was pleased to see him. Patel had sought his help many times for police investigations involving Asian people, and for some insight into the Asian business community.

'Ali, how are you?' They shook hands. 'I was going to call you later. Come in and sit down.'

They walked into the living room. There were some files on the coffee table that Patel was working on and his jacket lay on the back of the settee. There was a cut crystal glass of vodka on the side table, half-full. Patel took the jacket off the settee and asked Ali to take a seat.

'I've been trying to get hold of you all afternoon.' Ali

took his light jacket off and handed it to Patel.

'Pretty busy day as you can imagine, Ali,' said Patel as he took the pile of files and placed it on the dining table.

'What's this I hear? Nadia murdered?'

'Did you know her?'

'Yes, I know the family, and there was some gossip about her. Salma was talking about her this morning.'

'What do you know of Nadia? Tell me please.'

'You've not told me anything yet! How did she die?'

'Found murdered early this morning. I can't tell you more, you know that. Anything useful you can tell me, Ali? Did she and her family come to your mosque? Do you know them well? Is there any gossip?'

'I know her, but in the last few years, we've hardly seen her. No, she was not one to come to the mosque. Salim, her husband did come sometimes, during *Eid*, with the little boy. I visited them today and told Salim to ask for any help he might need with the funeral. The gossip was that she was going around with a *gora*, a white man.'

'Do you know who this white man is, a colleague? Patel asked.

'No idea at all,' replied Ali.

'Can I get you a cup of tea or some juice?' Patel asked.

'Irn-Bru if you have any,' said Ali, smoothing his goatee with his hand.

Patel went to the kitchen. The fizz pop sound of a can opening echoed against the tiles in the kitchen.

Ali's mobile rang.

'Hello, Salma.'

Patel heard him talking. The snatches of conversation reached the kitchen. It was in Urdu.

Ali switched his mobile phone off.

Patel came back with 'the other national drink' a favourite with most Asians. 'Better than Coke or Pepsi any day,' Patel's mum had said 'and it tasted like the Vimto, that we had in India when I was little.' The orange bubbles popped in the tall glass. He put a small dish of nuts and crisps on the side table beside the glass. He waited for Ali, ready with his pen and a notebook.

'Salma will get more from her friend tomorrow, but we know that Nadia has had a hard life. Her dad died when she was young. She went through a terrible teenage time. She defied her mother all the time. She was married earlier to a *gora*, but it didn't last all that long.' Ali picked up the glass of Irn Bru and sipped it.

'That's interesting. Can you give me the man's name, the first husband, or where he works? You know the tiniest detail helps,' Patel said.

'No, I can't remember his name. That was a long time ago, her marriage to that *gora* did not last long. Ten years ago or maybe more so; my memory is quite hazy about her husband. But I'm sure I can get that for you. Salim's mother, who lives with them, was concerned about the young family, her son and Salim. She also mentioned that the body must be buried as soon as possible. You know our customs, right?' Ali looked at him.

'I have requested both; post-mortem to be done early and the body released soon. Though we will respect the needs and the wishes of the family you know that religion cannot override the judicial process. The body will probably be released as soon as we are satisfied that it is not needed for the investigation,' said Patel.

Ali frowned in anger.

'You're a Hindu, so you don't care. No one respects our religion anymore. There is so much Islamophobia. Everything we ask for is denied. And I've given my all to this country. Worked hard and paid my taxes, provided jobs for the locals.' His voice rose slightly. The vehemence of the statement surprised Patel. The rant seemed to come from somewhere deep within Ali.

'I'll do all I can to hasten the investigation. I want to get the murderer as much as you do Ali,' Patel stood up and put a hand on his shoulder.

Ali put his glass down. That old hatred between Hindus and Muslim had raised its ugly head for a few seconds. Ali had felt that underlying current of mistrust despite his friendship with Patel that went back a few years. Patel and he had had friendly banter about it when discussing politics in India and Pakistan, but things had changed perceptibly. Since 9/11, the London bombing, the Glasgow airport bomb and rising Islamophobia in the country, the divide between the Hindus and Muslims in Glasgow was getting wider.

Patel said, 'Look, Ali, it is important that we find the murderer as soon as possible. We don't want another victim, do we?'

Ali relaxed. That brief flash of disquiet was promptly quashed, and he said,

'I'm glad that you are in charge, Patel. If I come across anything useful I'll get in touch with you. I better let you get on with the work then. Get the murderer.

Chapter 12

The murder investigation progressed with pace. Late in the evening, drinking in the beauty of the twilight hour, Patel drove home. The skies changed from russet-shaded dusk to a darker hue. The house was in darkness as he parked the car and went in. Patel put the bulging paper files and his laptop on the settee.

'Usma,' he called out, hoping she had come over. Then remembered she was on the night shift. He phoned her.

'Hey, I hardly see you. I miss you, honey.'

'Well, Mr. Highheid'un how about getting me shifts so that I can be there when you get home? Need to go, short-staffed, summer flu,' she laughed and hung up.

'You know I can't help you there,' Patel sighed.

He opened the fridge and took out the ice tray. Then he took a glass from the cupboard to have a few good sips of his favourite Glengoyne whisky, the golden spirit, as he drained some into the glass and added some ice cubes. He had been a non-drinker until he joined the police force, his parents and family thought he retained his dislike of alcohol, but he had a taste for good whisky now. There was no restriction on his imbibing alcohol. It was something he had not taken to during his youth. He had wanted to be different from the hard-drinking friends who made it a habit of getting wasted, as they described it, at weekends. He had stayed away from that scene.

He put the mobile in his pocket. It had been a long

day. The drink had helped stave off that feeling of being dog tired. What was there to eat? He opened the fridge again. On the top shelf were the plastic boxes of his mum's cooking, various curries that she had prepared and packed meticulously. He gave a cursory glance at the boxes, picked one up and heated it in the microwave. Even when he was young, he remembered that her way of showing love was to feed him. She was a thoughtful mum who felt he needed sustenance. Usma's carb-free diet sometimes got on his nerves. The fridge was filled with meat and salads of all sorts, things he didn't care for. He prepared a quick-cook rice pack and ate his meal and watched the ten o'clock news. He switched the TV off after the headlines.

He grabbed the paperwork from the settee and moved them onto the coffee table. The folders fell to the floor. He left them there. He could feel his muscles aching. He stretched out his long legs and relaxed on the settee and closed his eyes for a few minutes. The ping of a text message on his mobile woke him up. An advert for an app! He was annoyed and deleted it. He sat up and glanced at the work he needed to get through. The files on support groups that he meant to read up on made an untidy pile on the floor. He picked the papers up and straightened them as he laid them on the coffee table. The reports of different groups in the British police such as women, gay, lesbian, transgender, disability, equality, Christian, Muslim, and the initiatives taken by each of the groups were something he had to familiarise himself with. He made a quick note on each paper to delegate it to the right person. His eyes rested on the last one, Staff Association for Minority Ethnic staff – SAME. Memories of his first meeting with Usma spooled over in his mind.

He had seen Usma, the young rookie policewoman,

at the SAME conference. She bumped into him in the lunch queue. They shared an instant attraction.

'Hey, watch all those deep-fried pakoras you're loading on your plate. They'll go straight to your hips.' Her voice was like honey dripping, a delicious sweetness. He cared little that she was teasing him. He was mesmerised by her lovely eyes, twin pools of caramel brown, in a cute face that gave him a cheeky grin.

He was tongue-tied for a moment, then, quick as a flash, he placed a few pakoras on her plate and said, 'Hey, you could do with some filling up,' he joked, a smile crinkled up his eyes.

She giggled, pleased at the compliment. She sat straight, her figure showing that she worked hard to keep herself fit. Few Asian girls that he knew seemed to care for their figures. Light skin and a pretty face were all they needed for his mum to say they were beautiful.

They ate lunch together.

'So, how did a cute lady like you join the Police?' he asked.

'Any career that would annoy my parents,' she said her eyes twinkling with laughter, blushing again at the word cute.

'That I can believe!' he smiled. 'Parents!' he said, shaking his head.

'And I knew I could meet handsome guys like you, in uniform,' she laughed a bit nervously. Her hands shook as she held on to the glass of water that tipped over and spilt on the table. He quickly put a paper napkin over it and cleaned the table and smiled.

'Was that the only reason?' he prompted, his heart racing with happiness.

She looked down. She was serious now, 'It was after the Glasgow airport terrorist incident. I was flying back from London; I even remember the date, 30th July 2000. I was horrified by what had happened in our city.'

'Terrorism, the new bane of our lives,' he commented. 'Our jobs are even more important, not just protecting the public at large but managing tensions in the community. Islamophobia and polarisation between communities that used to live in reasonable harmony before, things are all changing.'

'I agree, I think we Asian police have a huge role to play. I chose the Hate Crime and Racists Incidents and Positive Action working group to get more insight on the subject,' she replied.

'Well, we do see many reports about systemic racism in the police force. I experience it with a colleague of mine. This should be discussed at these working groups.'

She nodded. They spoke for a while on the conference working groups and moved onto music, her love of the outdoors and reading. Meeting her made the weekend conference magical. He made sure to enrol in the two same working groups as her, Hate Crime and Racists Incidents and Positive Action. Five years younger than him, just starting her career, but she was so ambitious, something he found endearing.

He drove back home after the conference. He worried about how his parents would react if they knew how he felt about her. Maybe it would come to nothing. It had been a fun weekend, but they had exchanged much more than just phone numbers. He mentally pinched himself at how close they had become in just a couple of days.

Patel texted Usma the very next day! They met again and within a few months, he knew she was the woman for him.

He tried to broach the subject with his parents on Anita's birthday. The family dinner was on a Sunday, nearly seven months after he had met with Usma. He waited for Anita and her family to leave. They sat in the lounge. His dad poured him a drink and said,

'So how is work going?' Patel knew that he never really understood his career.

'Fine, nothing special. But I have something important to tell you both. I've fallen in love. She's called Usma. She's beautiful, intelligent ...'

'Usma? Is she a Muslim?' Laxmi interrupted.

'Yes, Mum, she's ...'

Before Patel could finish his sentence, Laxmi got up from her seat, and anger glimmered in her eyes.

'No, no, not a Muslim. Don't bring such shame to your family.'

'Mum, you've not even met her; I can't believe I'm hearing this.'

Her anger now turned to tears.

'No, Alok, you know that is not on. Not a Muslim girl and you know why.' His mum shed more tears.

'Why? Mum, tell me why? I love her isn't that enough?' he had pleaded.

'Not just what the community will say, you'll be converted and think of the children you'd have ...' Laxmi shook her head.

'Children! For God's sake, I've not even mentioned marriage!' Alok banged his glass down and stood up. 'Dad, guess you have nothing to say.'

'Your mum is right.'

Patel had stormed out of the house.

He had to attend his grandmother's funeral later that year and the strained relationship with his parents had settled down to one of him being a polite and dutiful son whenever he was needed at the family home. Anita helped to smooth their meeting, making it bearable for her brother.

That was almost a year ago and now Usma and he were still not living together. The anger and hatred of both sets of parents about this was so strong that they did not want to go against the wishes of both their families. Neither of them wanted to marry without their family's blessing. Their wedding plans were going nowhere but at least they were together as often as possible, even if it was surreptitiously. Usma had moved in with friends nearby and often spent the nights with him.

He sighed as he took a sip of the dram and ice. He put the folders away. He picked up the remote with a sigh and switched the TV on. The twenty-four-hour news was on. The Chancellor's austerity measures were mentioned. Though the Police was a devolved power in Scotland, he knew that there would be more cuts to the police force.

'I have to keep an eye on my budget,' he told himself. Working on for a couple of hours, he turned in for the night, missing the warmth of Usma's body beside him.

*

Usma was back from work after a night shift. Out of the two of them, she had the longer drive, because she worked in the Southside of the city. The early morning drive without the traffic snarling up the roads was always relaxing. A sun-dappled morning again, summer was at its best. The flowers in the gardens bloomed with myriad colours, some casting their gentle fragrance that only Mother Nature endows. This was a time to relax and feel the warmth on one's face, a holiday ambience with children out playing. As she often had, she again sneaked into Patel's flat. Usma enjoyed snuggling up to him, still warm in bed, but she knew that probably he would be up and away for work. She was right. Disappointed, she undressed quickly and got into her pyjamas. She needed a few hours of sleep, but she wanted him to make love to her.

She stood by the window, opened it a fraction and breathed in the fresh air. She loved this time of year, the season of love and romance. She turned around as she heard Patel come out of the shower in the en-suite.

Usma watched his drawn face. He had hardly slept since this new murder case. Her heart skipped a beat as she saw him getting ready for work. She went over and hugged him tightly, kissed him hard on the mouth, then gently on his eyes. She held his face in her hands and looked at him, wishing she could kiss away that tension, that furrowed brow, that worry that was etched all over his face. She wanted him, right at that moment. Her body craved him, but he looked distracted, deep in thought. To get his attention she said, 'Hey, how is the case going? Any new leads?' she asked.

'No, just need to keep at it. Don't you worry your pretty little head,' he said and kissed her.

'I did ask some of my friends about Nadia but looks like she was close only to a few people. A full-time job and a mum, she must have had little time to socialise.'

'I'm sure we'll get the murderer,' said Patel, hugging her tighter.

'Do you need to leave so early?'

'You, temptress, you,' he whispered in her ear.

Later, she made coffee for both, but he shook his head.

'No time to drink it all,' he said, taking just a sip and putting the cup down. He gave her a weak smile, placed a peck on her cheek and left the house. She heard the front door shut and the car revving up. He had left early again, and she had hardly seen him since he had started

76

his new job. He left early and came home late and if she was on shifts, it was even worse. They were like two roommates, even though she had made a tremendous effort to be with him. She stayed away from her flat most of the time, to be with Alok. She was lucky that she had two good friends who always covered up for her if her mum called her late at night. She was about to go to the bathroom when she heard the papers drop through the letterbox. She ran down. The headlines in the tabloid were not about the murder, the case had been covered a few pages in.

'Young mum found dead in the West End.'

She wanted to discuss the murder of Nadia with him in detail, but they had little time together and it was hard to talk about work when he looked so tired and stressed. She felt the weight of Patel's work and the pressure on him from the media.

*

Patel drove fast. The roads were quiet. An Asian murdered, on his very first watch as a DI. He had never expected such a start to his new post. His promotion was what he had deserved. He had worked hard to get there. Now he felt the pressure. Martin was breathing down his neck, his words to him were playing like an audio spool in his mind.

'Patel, any leads yet?'

'No, Martin, we're working on it. It's only been a couple of days, I know you've mentioned 'the golden hour' before, but I'm working hard.'

Martin nodded. 'I don't need to tell you, but a murder in the West End gets people edgy. The media homes in on it. More than seven days then we will be heading for an enquiry team, Patel.'

'Yes, I know, Martin.'

'Don't want to be summoned by Detective Superintendent Arnott right, Patel?' his voice had an edge to it.

'No, sir.'

Patel had arrived at the station early and worked feverishly in the quiet of the morning, well before the morning bustle and endless demands on his time from others. He poured over all the evidence that they had collated. Clare McCall had sent the PT report. He called and thanked her.

'It was straight forward, a neat single cut to the neck, died of blood loss. Shame, a loss of such a young life.'

'Did she suffer?' Patel's words were out before he realised, his sympathy overflowing as he pictured the young woman losing her life in the dark.

'No, it would have been an immediate death.'

He reached for the phone to call Jim McKern, the Fiscal, to release the body for the funeral.

He had to find the murderer. Patel got back to the files on the desk. He went over Malcolm Watson's, Farah's and Salim's interviews again. Joe and some of the team had spoken to all the Mela stallholders and some of Nadia's colleagues. Was it some radicalised man, unconnected to Nadia committing an honour killing? That could become a really sensitive issue. Glasgow was perhaps a bit less conservative compared to the tight-knit communities down South in Wolverhampton or even London, but all it took was one person to feel his religion had been shamed by a young woman. He made a mental note to talk to Ali Hassan again.

Chapter 13

Salim opened the door a fraction and stared at Patel and Joe. He opened it widely and asked,

'Any news about releasing Nadia's body for the funeral?' His face was drawn, grief still etched on his face.

Patel and Joe felt sorry for the young man.

'Can we come in? We can give you an idea of what's happened since we last saw you,' said Patel.

Salim let them in and led them to the lounge. He stood near the fireplace as the police officers sat down on the settee.

'The post-mortem is completed. I've requested the body to be released. It shouldn't be too long now, Salim,' Patel reassured him.

Salim mouthed, 'Thanks'.

Patel thought the young widower looked so vulnerable. He must have been shaken about her funeral.

Salim looked up. 'Have you found a new lead?'

'Lots of people have been interviewed. There are officers conducting a door-to-door survey near the park to see if anyone saw anything at all. We have been questioning all the people who were in contact with Nadia,' Patel began, his voice quite gentle. 'Salim, I need to ask you again. Were you at home all night on the seventh of July?'

'Not again! How many times do you want me to tell you? I was home asleep with my boy. My mum was here. Nadia was staying over with Farah's,' Salim's voice rose with every word. 'Why don't you go and get the murderer instead of questioning me again and again?' His face was flushed, and his eyes were still red from tears.

'Mr. Ahmad, this visit is not only to question you. We need a bit more help,' DI Patel said, his voice firm but polite.

Patel and Joe saw Amreen Bibi hurrying into the kitchen, her bright orange *dupatta* swishing as she moved fast, covering her head with it. A strong aroma of curry hung about in the house. Perhaps they had just finished their evening meal, thought Patel.

'Well?' Salim was in no mood to wait for their questions. He looked tired, haggard even. He seemed to have aged over the last few hours. He sat down on a chair beside them, reluctantly. It was evident to the two policemen sitting across from him that the loss of his wife had affected him deeply.

'So, you were definitely at home all night on the seventh of July,' Patel began again.

'Okay, okay, I did slip out just for a pint with my friend. Look, please don't mention it in front of my mother,' Salim whispered.

Amreen came in and said a brief *'salaam alaikum'* to them and went back into the kitchen. She shot a glance at Salim, who did not meet her gaze.

Patel waited until she was out of earshot.

'So, when exactly did you leave the house and what time did you get back?'

'About half ten and I was back by half eleven, maybe even earlier.'

'So, which friend was this you were out with and where were you both?'

'You can check him out, just Imran who is a

neighbour; we go for the odd pint, just local. I told my mum I had to pick something up from his house.' Salim looked pale and worried.

'We will check that out for sure.' Patel nodded as Joe took out his black notebook and started taking notes.

'Now, Salim, we need to go over all of Nadia's friends, acquaintances. Can you think of anyone who would want to harm her?' Patel began.

'Harm her? Why? She was such a warm, loving person. Why would anyone wish her harm?' Salim looked aghast. He shook his head, looking down at the carpet. He seemed to forget they were with him, as he did not look up at them.

Patel coughed to get his attention. Joe tapped his fingers on his book.

Salim looked up, 'Look, there were some people who gossiped about her. I know that we are not 'conservative' Muslims, whatever that means. You know our community,' he said looking at Patel. 'Gossip is what makes the world go around for some of our people.'

'Mr. Ahmad, did she have anyone at work who may have had some grievance against her?' Patel continued.

'No, not all. She was well-liked.' Salim's eyes teared up. He looked at a family photo of the three of them, Nadia, Salim, and Mansur, on the wall, directly in front of him. It was taken at a studio; one of those offers that they had come across on Groupon. It was beautifully done. Nadia had Mansur on her lap and Salim stood beside her. She was in a turquoise-blue *salwar-kameez* with silver embroidery. He thought she looked stunningly pretty and all three looked so happy. Salim was drawn back by Patel's voice.

'Joe, do you have the photos of the colleagues I gave you?' asked Patel.

'In the car, sir, I'll get them,' Joe said.

Patel's eyes were cold as he looked at Joe, annoyed at him for leaving an important file when they were visiting the family. Patel was angry. Small slip-ups would have been easy to ignore before, but not in this case. He wanted everything to be just right. Joe could feel his eyes on his back as he walked out of the room.

Amreen Bibi came in with a tray full of freshly made pakoras, and some Irn Bru. 'Thank you. You really shouldn't have gone to the bother of making all this,' Patel called after her, but he helped himself to a pakora.

Amreen came in again with a plate of cut mango slices.

Joe arrived back with a file and took one photo out of several that were in the file.

'This was taken at last year's Christmas party at the bank where Nadia worked. Anyone have a grudge against her, Salim?' Patel's piercing eyes locked into his.

He shook his head. 'I know some of them, just acquaintances.'

'What about Malcolm Watson?'

Salim squirmed on the sofa. 'What about him? He was her close friend for years.'

'What do you think of her visiting Malcolm late at night?'

'What do you mean? Nadia knew him before I knew her. They are very old friends, for God's sake!'

Mansur came running in with a toy car in his hand and clambered onto Salim's knee. He demanded attention from his dad. The toy in his hand performed some actions when the keys were turned, and he wanted Salim to do it again and again. He kept urging his father to look at him and listen to him, not the police officers sitting in front of them. The wee boy had a tantrum when Salim refused to play with him anymore.

'Go to *Dadimma*,' he said firmly. 'I'm busy.' He hauled him off his knee.

'No, Daddy, Daddy,' Mansur screamed.

Salim tried to get him to behave. There was no sign of Amreen. Maybe it was her prayer time, or she was resting somewhere. Joe got himself a plate and took a handful of pakoras. It tasted really good. Patel glowered at him.

'Look, I need to take care of Mansur,' Salim made it clear that his priority was his son. He lifted the boy, who was clinging to his leg and held him close. There was not much point staying on.

The policeman left.

In the car, Patel said, 'Joe, always have essential information with you. You shouldn't have left that file in the car.' His voice was not loud but steely. Patel had always relied on Joe, and cared for him as a young officer, but this is was his first murder case and he wanted to ensure that everything ran smoothly. Patel's knuckles were white against the black steering wheel.

'No, boss,' Joe looked away at the houses and the trees whizzing past the window. 'Sorry. I was a bit distracted today, I was thinking of Lucy, it's two years since she passed away,' he added.

'Oh no! I am sorry Joe; I am too wrapped up in this investigation. That's insensitive of me. It must be a really tough day for you.'

'It is okay, sir,' Joe said softly.

They drove in silence for a while. Both were thinking of Lucy. Joe had been working with Patel for a while when he was with Lucy, a young officer full of happiness about his new job and young wife whom he dearly loved. He liked Patel's efficient, smooth way of working. He was a man of few words but got his work done. Patel had been sympathetic when Lucy had died. Patel had been there for him and made sure he helped by visiting her when she was in hospital and he had cheered her up with an iPod shuffle and a gift voucher. Lucy had downloaded her favourite songs onto her playlist. It was such a thoughtful gift. Patel had also organised a charity walk and raised a thousand pounds for breast cancer within weeks, which was touching.

Joe sighed.

Patel laid his hand on Joe's shoulder, a touch of sympathy.

Chapter 14

At the station, the team was busy working at their desks. Kara noticed Joe's taut manner as he passed her desk.

'Hey, what's with that face? It's fair trippin' you.' She laughed hoping some levity would raise a smile from her friend.

He ignored her.

'By the way, Brian and I visited the taxi firm and they confirmed that they had a fare from Hyndland Road to Park Grove Terrace, a Mrs. Ahmad. The taxi driver, Bob Kerr, did notice a blue car, a Ford Mondeo with an Irish number plate. He remembered only because it looked like his wife's car, the one she had crashed just a few weeks ago. He assumed it was one of the residents. He had to rush off for another fare.'

She offered him the report she had typed up on the interview with the taxi driver.

'Look I've even got it for you pronto, it's all in there.' She smiled at him.

'Thank you,' grunted Joe, not smiling back. 'I'm not in a good mood I'm afraid.' He turned and left to go to his desk.

'Got out of the bed on the wrong side this morning?' she called after him.

Joe hated that little slip up of leaving the folder in the car. He wanted to impress Patel with his efficiency and hard work.

*

On her street patrol, Usma was with DC Vikram Singh, a young guy, who had come up from Birmingham. She was learning so much more about Indian culture and family life from him. Patel tended to say little about his family, and she wanted to get to know more about Indian culture. In a way, it was good to have another Asian DC with her on the beat, and it was rare as the number of Asian Police was less than one percent in Police Scotland. Vikram was a tall stocky young man, strong and quick with his reactions to any challenges they confronted on the beat. She felt more confident with him beside her.

People behaved so differently as soon as the uniform was on. Usma felt a deep sense of duty and it gave her a sense of power to help the people, but they also faced some abuse as they patrolled the streets. Weekends and evening shifts were the worst.

Their colleagues assumed they were an item.

'Here they come, the Asian babes,' a sergeant had commented.

'Just working together, sir.' Vikram had replied politely as he was a senior officer.

'Aye, but you lot stick together, don't you,' he continued, muttering 'Bloody Pakis,' under his breath thinking they were out of earshot.

Usma let it ride and in some ways, it helped keep her real relationship with Patel quite discreet.

This was the kind of racism that Usma had discussed with Patel when they first met, and they had often talked about how to handle it. With this sergeant, as he was senior to her, there was little she could do about it. Like all young people who wanted to progress in their careers, she would have to think carefully before making any complaints about him. She had not mentioned it to Patel as yet as he had enough pressure with the murder case to solve.

From seven am until two, the day shift was bearable for Usma, as the hours usually passed quickly. Their patrol route was in the city centre today. Vikram and Usma had a clear idea of their route unless they were called away to some emergency. Argyle Street, Buchanan Street, George Square, and a round of the Merchant City, a good walk until lunchtime, then it got busier. It was the night shifts that were so much harder. She hardly saw Patel. Usma had been swithering about changing her job to one without shifts so she could be with Alok more. His promotion and the murder enquiry made her realise how little time they had together. Constantly being on guard and trying to meet in his flat when he was working long hours made it harder. Usma had a clear idea of how she wanted her career to progress. She had a plan which would allow her to make a mark in the Partnerships, Preventions and Community Wellbeing department. She had had enough of this police work that did not challenge her intellectually as much as she would like.

After her shift, she went home and made a clear decision. Usma downloaded an application form for Community Policing and filled it in immediately and put it in an envelope ready for posting next day. This would also help her pursue her interest in dealing with problems like racism in society at large and perhaps even allow her to confront racism at work, as she could come at it from a different angle. How could they help the public with initiatives when they have not put their own house in order?

She felt happier now, having made the decision. The only downside would be she would miss Vikram, a good friend. She would keep it to herself and wait until she got through the interview process and only tell Patel if she got the job. She took a long shower and cooked some simple pasta and waited for Patel to arrive, helping herself to a glass of red wine.

Chapter 15

The sheltered home at Govanhill was brown brick and pebbledash, a dreary building. Years of harsh weather on the front of the building had taken its toll. A plant in a huge faded ceramic blue pot beside the front door was dying; leaves dry and wilting.

Kara and Brian rang the bell. A young Asian girl in a nurse's uniform opened the door. They showed their warrant cards and asked to see Nadia's mother. The nurse introduced herself as Shabnam Anjum and welcomed them into the reception.

'Come on in, nice day eh?'

'Yes, it is,' agreed Kara, pleased to find that the pleasant young nurse was at ease with police officers.

'You're the DC Johnson, who rang about Nadia's death to inform her mother, aren't you?' she said as they walked along. 'So sad, but Mrs. Hussain as you know is not very well.' Shabnam smiled. 'I'll try and help you with Mrs. Hussain. We have told her about Nadia, terrible news, but sometimes she doesn't understand or process the news. Dementia is cruel, you know. We have a few Asian patients and they are not familiar with English so it helps that I can interpret for you. She only speaks Punjabi,' Shabnam said with a wide smile that lit up her face. She had a round face with long dark hair, with copper highlights cascading down her back.

'We don't get many visits from the city's finest,' she added smiling again at the two police officers. The cheery Asian nurse led them to Mrs. Hussain's room and explained that she was not the only patient who had the onset of dementia.

'She has her good days and not so good,' she said walking along the long corridor passing some patients peering out of their rooms. A couple were wandering aimlessly in their dressing gowns and stared at them.

Mrs. Hussain was sitting in an armchair facing the window. Her nightgown was fleecy winceyette, pink with green flowers. She had a cosy bed jacket on and warm slippers on her feet. Her grey hair was neatly brushed back and secured in a bun. Her room had a bed, a dressing table, and a small wardrobe, sparse, but neat and clean. There were no ornaments or pictures on the wall.

'*Auntyji*, here are two people who want to talk to you about Nadia,' said the nurse in fluent Punjabi.

Shabnam sat beside her and took her hand and squeezed it gently. She said to the worried-looking old lady, 'don't worry I can translate for you. Remember me? I'm Shabnam.'

Kara Johnson explained about Nadia's death. Mrs. Hussain looked out of the window. The news of the death of her daughter did not seem to register.

Did she not remember her own daughter? wondered Kara. She felt sympathetic towards this old woman who seemed to live in her own world.

The lady nodded, but still her eyes looked confused.

Kara and Brian asked all about Nadia from the time she was born. A glimpse of her early life would help to see if there was anyone in her life that would want to harm her.

It was a long morning. Each question was translated, sometimes repeated two or three times before Mrs. Hussain could give a short answer. Often the answers were vague or a mere yes or no that did not help at all.

Then all of a sudden Mrs. Hussein said.

'Nadia *beti*, Roger,' her eyes lit up. 'Roger *gori* but went to the mosque, good boy,' Shabnam translated.

'Tell us more about Roger and Nadia,' Kara encouraged her.

'Roger? *Na*, Rahim,' said Mrs. Hussain. Confusion reigned again.

Shabnam got a bit more from her. Then the memory faded, she shook her head mumbling something and clammed up.

'Looks like this Roger's Muslim name is Rahim,' explained Shabnam. 'Started mumbling about *sharab*, that means alcohol. Let's give her a break, eh?' said Shabnam. She got up and poured some lemonade in a glass and handed it to Mrs. Hussain. The lady drank it gratefully.

After a few minutes, Kara brought out a few photos of Nadia, Salim and Mansur, to try and evoke some memories, and this worked for a while, as Mrs. Hussain smiled at the photos and said, 'Nadia' aloud, then a glaze seemed to cover her eyes and she fell into silence. She nodded to anything that was asked or said.

'Well that's done, not much use but had to be done right enough,' said Kara to Brian as they walked over to the car.

Brian said 'Was Roger not her first husband? Roger, Rahim - that may be worth checking.'

'Yes of course. Shame to see what dementia does to older people,' Kara replied, her mind still on the old lady. 'At least we have interviewed her, a close member of the family and all that,' Kara said as she and Brian opened the car door.

Back at the station, she checked the file on Nadia to see if there was mention of the first husband's name.

There it was, Roger Anderson, but without details. Nothing.

Kara switched on the database to check Roger Anderson. He had no criminal record, so nothing showed up on the computer. More digging needed, she told herself.

That was another task, to get the details from the general registry of births, marriages and deaths from Martha Street or maybe get it online. She hoped that the date of the marriage would help give a timeline of Nadia's personal life. She hoped to trace Roger from his National Insurance number or other details.

Chapter 16

Ali Hassan and Salim had made a few calls already asking for Nadia's body to be released for the funeral. As the post-mortem had been done and the forensic evidence bagged and recorded, Patel acceded to their request.

As soon as the body was released, arrangements were made for the funeral. The golden orbs of the mosque shone in the July sunshine. The shape of the crescent moon on top and the green stained glass glittered like jewels in the bright light. The huge red brick building was imposing, an important landmark in Glasgow. The River Clyde beside it flowed serenely, shimmering in the sunshine. It was a stark contrast to a sombre day. Nadia's funeral was to be held that afternoon.

Police Scotland had a few people in plain-clothes to observe from a distance. Ali Hassan and the family were happy that it hadn't taken so long. The grieving process at any time is stressful enough, but for Salim, Mansur, and Nadia's family the process of waiting a few days after the death was weighing on their mind.

Patel had arrived to witness the funeral, as part of his work. He thought how different the rituals were to the Hindu cremation that he had witnessed at his grandmother's funeral. Both were grim affairs, of course. All the religious rituals at funerals made him pause for thought. These important rites of passage were sure to give comfort to the living, the relatives. Even the humanists and atheists had some method of saying goodbye to their dearly departed. Assuaging grief was a human need. He was not deeply religious despite growing up in a very conservative Hindu household. He looked on respectfully but he concentrated on the mourners. His observation of the mourners' behaviour was important for the murder investigation.

The Glasgow Mosque was filled with people. Nadia's relatives and friends arrived with the funeral cortege and the body was brought into the burial ground. Prayers were read out. Though women were normally not present at funerals, some had made sure to be there to say their goodbyes to Nadia. Farah and Craig were there. Most of her work colleagues from the Bank of Scotland also attended the funeral. Malcolm Watson, visibly distraught and crying, could be seen drying his eyes with a handkerchief. Craig Bolton was beside him, patting his shoulder occasionally to help him through this difficult time. There was another man that Patel had not seen beside Malcolm, must be a close friend of his, presumed Patel.

Ali Hassan stood by the graveside. The grave had been dug to face Qibla, in Mecca. Nadia's body was placed, lying on its side facing in the same direction. Her body had been washed by her mother in law and a simple white cotton kaftan covered it. Salim had placed the three fist-sized lots of soil, one under her head, one under her chin, and one under her shoulder. He poured three handfuls of soil after her body was lowered. The Imam read the last prayer in Arabic. 'We created you from it, and return you into it, and from it. We will raise you a second time.'

There were tears from Salim, and her mother, Mrs. Hussain, was in a wheelchair. Young Mansur was held tightly by Salim's brother who had come for the funeral from Birmingham.

Patel was not distracted by the rituals taking place but he wanted to watch any likely suspect close to the family who might be involved in Nadia's murder. In most cases of murder, it was often a close member of the family who had committed the murder. He concentrated on them. Patel had read up on the rituals. Patel watched the family and the extended family at the funeral.

He glanced over at the women's side to look for Kara. He saw a familiar face: Usma. There was an older woman beside her. Was that her mother? His curiosity got the better of him. He kept looking at her. Usma acted as though she had not noticed him. She was wearing a veil on her head and her mother looked formidable. Patel was seeing Usma in a very different light, wearing her traditional dress, looking modest, not talking much to the woman beside her and blending so well into her own faith and culture. Usma in these surroundings was totally different from the charming young policewoman who had mesmerised him when he had first met her. Conflicting feelings filled his mind. Aunty PP and his mother's face flickered before his eyes for reasons he could not understand.

Kara was mingling with the crowd in the women's section; Patel saw that the black scarf that she had worn had made it difficult for him to notice her right away. She was hoping to glean any new information on Nadia from her friends that might be relevant to the case. She wore a black scarf over her head as a mark of respect, and to be less conspicuous. The women were clearly in two groups, the older, conservatively dressed women stayed away from the young mixed group of Nadia's colleagues and Asian friends. Salim's mother was obvious as the wee boy, Mansur, ran between her and his dad. Mrs. Hussain, whom she had interviewed, was in a wheelchair beside them. She looked dazed and confused. Kara sat close to the young women and listened carefully as they spoke in broad Glaswegian accents.

'Aye, Nadia was a good mum, what a shame.'

'She was great at her work too, I'll miss her,' said one of her colleagues.

'You know she even found time to volunteer at Amina, the women's refuge, hope that had nothing to do with her murder. One can never be careful enough nowadays,' added another Asian girl in a dark blue *salwar-kameez*.

'Really? I didn't know that she was volunteering with Amina,' said her colleague.

She heard them talk more about Nadia's cheery personality and the evenings out that they had with her.

Patel did not want to spend too long at the funeral. He waited for the funeral rites to be over and spoke to Salim.

'Salim, my condolences, a beautiful ceremony,' he said and moved over to speak to Ali.

Ali was a grand figure of a man today. His grey hair gave some gravitas to this tall and well-built man. His moustache had tinges of grey, and the eyes behind dark-rimmed glasses followed the crowd keenly. Never one to miss a trick in any situation, he kept observing the crowd. Both Patel and Ali watched the mourners. Ali pointed out some of the members of Nadia's and Salim's family to Patel.

'I recognise a few here,' said Patel, looking at some young men whom he had confronted a few years ago when they belonged to a gang. 'Looking quite decent in their mourning suits, all grown up now. Probably married and settled down,' he commented to Ali.

Ali nodded in agreement.

'Come let us have some food. It is impolite not to eat. They have made such an effort to cater for all,' said Ali.

Ali led him to the room where people were milling around. Some were helping themselves to plates. The spread of food laid out for the mourners was impressive: a huge table laden with all kinds of snacks, lots of pakoras, samosas, kebabs, chicken tandoori, and even naans and a big pot of rice. Soft drinks in big two-litre bottles were placed on each of the tables and the servers plied the food to the mourners. Patel was surprised to see Big Mo and Gazza eating at the funeral, their plates filled with food.

Kara and Patel took a sip of Coca Cola each, a small amount of food and left soon after.

Patel and Ali arranged to meet up later. Patel said his goodbyes and left.

Kara pulled her scarf off her head as she got into the car.

'So, anything worth noting at your end?' Patel asked as he switched the engine on.

'Sir, Nadia was certainly popular, both with her own community and her colleagues, but from what I can gather she had a wild streak, defiance that annoyed the older members of her community, but most of the mourners praised her for being a good wife and mother. And I got a new lead. She volunteered at Amina, a women's refuge centre. I'll follow that up. That was all I could glean from there, boss.'

Patel nodded.

'Good. We need to check up on all new information, Kara,' he said, his eyes on the road. 'Strange to see Gazza and Big Mo at the funeral,' he added.

'Yes, I saw them when we went to get food,' she said.

They drove in silence, both thinking of the new experience of watching a Muslim funeral. Patel also kept thinking of Usma and the woman beside her. He had never seen her so morose and serious. There was something about how perfectly she fitted in with the women of her culture. He thought of his own grandmother's death last year and how the rituals had been completely different. This was the first time he was faced with the differences in their cultures. Birth, death, marriage; the significant events in one's life was filled with emotion. Patel felt a deep sense of unease. Would he be depriving Usma of her rich faith and culture? Would he lose his roots, which his parents had made such an effort to retain in the West? Nadia's funeral shook him up in more ways than one. Nadia! His personal life was not important. He needed to concentrate on the job in hand. His mind turned to planning the next step in the murder enquiry. An indignant sigh escaped his mouth.

On the Clydeside Expressway, the traffic moved smoothly, Kara glanced out of the window and saw changes brought by the gentrification of the banks of the river. The buildings lining either side of the Clyde and the greenery and walkway were a pleasant change from her memories of a turgid river meandering around the centre of the city, the banks often with overgrown weeds and litter sloping from the roads and building.

Wouldn't it be nice to be working in an office on the banks of the river? she thought to herself.

Once, she had been up at the BBC Café on the top floor of the building with a friend who worked in the television station. The views of the river on a summer evening had been spectacular. Kara delved into her own musings.

Her   thoughts   turned   back   to   the   murder

investigation. How would Mrs. Hussain, who had just buried her daughter, her only child, be able to cope? What would it be like to lose a daughter? That pain must be unbearable. She gave an involuntary shudder at the thought.

Chapter 17

She gasped as she stood against the door and picked up the newspaper. 'Brutal Murder in the West End' was splashed across the front of the newspaper. She read the paragraph below the big photograph of the murder scene. Her spirits dipped. But no, no one had a right to die that way. She felt disturbed when she saw the photograph. It showed the place where the body lay and it looked terrible. What a way to die? She read further. The victim had a young boy. She continued reading the article with a growing feeling of unease. A child now faced a future without his mother? How cruel fate could be?

Ten years and it was still raw. This story brought all those memories back again. She couldn't take it anymore. She threw the paper on the settee and got up to make a cup of tea.

The doorbell rang. She was still in her dressing gown. She knotted the cord of the dressing gown and opened the door warily. A man and a woman stood on the doorstep.

'I'm DS Johnson and this is DS Duffy. May we come in?' They showed their ID cards.

She was surprised. She did not open the door any wider.

'What is this all about?' she asked

'Can we come in, please? Marie Anderson, that's you right?' asked Kara.

'Yes. Do come in,' she said. 'I'm just up, what's this

about?' her face still streaked with colour from the tumult of emotions as she had read the newspaper. And now she was embarrassed for being still in her nightie. The blush heightened to a deeper shade of red.

'You were you married to a Roger Anderson in 2000?' Kara asked as they sat down on the settee. 'We need to talk to him. You are aware of Nadia Ahmad's murder,' Kara pointed out the newspaper that was on the settee.

'I don't know anything about him or where he is. I divorced him ages ago.' A deep sob broke out from her throat.

Kara waited a while then said gently, 'But do tell us what you can about Roger. Anyone connected with Nadia. It is crucial that they are contacted.'

More tears ran down the woman's face. Her distress was palpable.

'Do you have any idea where he is now?' Kara prompted gently.

'No. I lost touch with him over ten years ago. I think he went to Ireland, I'm not sure.'

'When was the last time you saw him?'

'I told you, maybe nine years ago. It was an awful divorce. I don't want to hear that man's name ever again. I've nothing more to say. Just go please.'

She stood up; her jaw set in a determined fashion.

Both the police officers rose, and Kara left her card.

'If you change your mind and remember anything you could tell us, please contact us,' she said politely as they left.

Marie shut the door firmly behind them.

Chapter 18

Joe had set the alarm early; Radio Clyde DJ, George Bowie's voice woke him up.

'Good morning, this is George and Susi on 102.5 Your Clyde One buzzing with news, music, start the day with Queen B's top hit.' Beyonce's *Halo* filled the room: loud, bright, and breezy like the sunny morning.

Joe lay there for a minute, the warmth of the duvet making him reluctant to get up. His favourite photo of Lucy was the one taken on their last holiday together in Ibiza, sitting on the bedside table. Her dark hair, windblown, framed a pretty face smiling into the camera for the selfie they had taken. Her petite body that had so enamoured him was hardly visible in this photograph, just the top of her pink bikini top, the string of the halter neck tied behind her neck. All the plans that they had made, the wedding in a couple of years when they had enough money, came flooding back.

The Commonwealth Games had certainly changed Dalmarnock, one of the poorest areas in Glasgow's East End. The athletes' villages were made into homes for the residents in the area when the old tenements were demolished. Joe's mum encouraged Joe and Lucy to buy one of the flats. The modern flat was perfect for a young couple. 'Tiny, can't swing a cat in it,' as his mother said to Joe, but it had all the mod cons. The flat came with carpets, a dishwasher and a fitted kitchen. The one-bedroom flat was all that they could afford. Lucy was still on a zero-hour contract as a shop assistant in a local shop. At least they had a foothold on the housing ladder, unlike some of his friends from school who were either unemployed or in rented accommodation. His police job did give him that edge, getting a mortgage at a low rate of interest. Joe was determined to work hard and secure a bright future for him and Lucy. They had been so happy here, at first. His happiness was snatched away as soon as Lucy developed breast cancer. He was devastated.

He wanted to feel her warm body against him, that floral smell, that sweet smile, the way she kissed him passionately on that holiday was still so easy to recall. The sea a bright blue, the sky cloudless, he could picture it all this morning, causing an ache in his heart. He pulled the duvet off and got out of bed. Then he changed his mind. He sat back down heavily on the bed; the rush to get ready and be at work early was momentarily thwarted. That strange feeling of waking up alone, not having Lucy's body beside him, hurt even now. He still had not got used to living on his own without her. Empty and lonely even after what was almost two years, thought Joe.

He dragged himself off the bed and stood under the shower. He got ready quickly and made it to the station before the rest of the staff filed in slowly. The cleaner had just finished. She gave him a cheery 'Good Morning' as she left.

Joe carried the cup of Costa coffee he had bought on the way to work over to his desk, sat down and switched on the computer, answered a few emails, then began the task of looking over all the files again. He shuddered at the photograph of Nadia. Murder of any kind was horrendous, but this young woman lying in that pool of blood was not a pretty sight. He grabbed the small number of brown files on the desk. A few house-to-house calls and statements had been taken by some officers and he read over them carefully. Then he made a note of all the facts that he could get from simply googling her name. She had public profiles on LinkedIn and Facebook. This might impress Patel. He wanted to make up for the faux-pas that he had made yesterday.

Patel walked in and strode into his office. Joe followed. He was sitting in front of his desk and the piles of papers were neatly stacked. Patel was methodical as always.

'Boss, LinkedIn gives her career profile from the time she joined the bank as a teller. It looks like she had done well and progressed in her career. She must have diplomas in banking too. Facebook updates I've only had a glance at, but at least she hasn't locked it in a completely private account.'

'Good work, Joe, but let's get the normal stuff done too.' Patel gave him an encouraging smile. 'Get the HOLMES on and check all her family and friends.'

Joe was eager to get more work done. He jumped to his feet and walked purposefully to his desk.

Alan Brown wandered into Patel's office. Joe heard him.

'Got your work cut out eh?' He gave a low whistle. 'I came over to give any help you might need Patel.' His voice was laced with just the right tinge of mockery.

Was he drunk? thought Joe, Such insolence. Surely, he knows that Patel can get him reprimanded. He may have been Patel's colleague, but he should not be so familiar now. The chancer. He could do without these barbs to his boss, but he noticed that Patel was dignified and kept a straight face.

'I'm doing fine, Alan. I'll use you when I need you.

I'm the DI,' Patel waved him away.

What a good way to handle Alan, thought Joe. He was glad that Patel was his DI. He was in sharp contrast to Brown, the cold, ambitious sergeant who made the life of any junior miserable. He cared little for Alan and his constant sniping behind Patel's back.

I'm going to do all I can to get this murder solved and prove myself to DI Patel, he told himself. He would make sure he followed up the phone calls from witnesses that came through as soon as the TV news was broadcast. And no doubt as soon it hit the telly they'd receive masses of crank calls. He picked up the pile of files on the desk to look through some of the statements of possible suspects once again; the husband, friends, and family. He thought of Nadia's body lying in the dark. First of all, what did he know about the deceased? She was around her early thirties, about eleven stone, with dark hair and dark eyes. He had never got used to seeing dead bodies, however many times he had to as part of his job. A corpse lying in the mortuary or in the laboratory for a post-mortem, its smell, made him feel sick.

Thoughts of his fiancée, Lucy, came to mind again. Since Lucy's death, any young woman's death, under any circumstances, was more difficult for him to face. His face reddened. He felt a jumble of emotions but forced himself back to the task. Be thorough, he growled to himself, as he read details of his notes.

Nadia was born in Glasgow to Pakistani immigrants who had settled in Pollokshields in the 1970s. She was an only child. Unusual he thought. Asian families tended to be larger. The father had died suddenly when she was in primary school and her mother had brought her up. Probably the stress of her dad's sudden death had made Nadia get into trouble at school. Though a bright and strong pupil, she went through a difficult phase and had been suspended a few times for defying her teachers. She got into fights after racist taunts from some of her classmates. Her school reported that she would carry on fighting until teachers separated the girls. The mother was withdrawn and apathetic according to school reports.

He laid out each of the other statements and started with the husband Salim's first.

Joe thought of Salim, his sorrowful eyes, the pained, haunted look imprinted on his face, the bristles, the five o'clock shadow that leant an unkempt look as he had exclaimed,

'No, no not my Nadia.'

He looked at his notes again.

He had seen him at the mortuary. His words had been more exclamations of shock.

Poor guy, Salim was a distraught man. Joe checked on the meagre details on him. A well-built man of around thirteen stone, maybe five-feet eight or nine inches tall. Well spoken. A university graduate. He had noticed the photos of Salim in his graduation robes on the walls of his home. His framed degree certificate was also in the lounge, a proud fact that was displayed for all to see. He seemed to be a loving family man, protective of his wife, son and his mother. The Asian practice of a couple living with the parents had been something he had witnessed before.

One of Joe's first assignments as a beat policeman was in the Southside of Glasgow. There were many shops run by Muslims and many Muslim households in Pollokshields. He remembered the *Eid* festival when the Strathclyde Police band played at the street party. The celebrations were supported by the dozen mosques in Glasgow and the sheer energy of the

Muslim population in the Pollokshields area.

Policing had been tough at times as fights broke out between racist gangs and the Asian population. He had been surprised to note that there were troubles also between Sikh and Muslim youths. Each community had gangs and he had to familiarise himself with the different cultures within the Asian population. It had been a steep learning curve for him, not to lump all Asians as a homogeneous group. Joe got back to his file on Salim. He and Nadia lived with his mother Amreen Bibi. Extended families were more common amongst the Asians. He had read in one of the diversity documents that more than fifteen per cent of Muslims in Scotland lived in extended families. Was it close family ties or was it expected of the sons? Joe wondered. At least Nadia's young boy had a grandmother in the house to look after him.

Interesting that Salim had married a divorced woman, he thought to himself. Kara was checking on the first husband. I must see where she has got to. I need to pay a visit to Imran, the neighbour, to check on Salim's alibi.

Later that day Joe decided to pass on some information on Alan's behaviour to Patel.

'Sir, here is the report on door-to-door interviews.' Joe stood beside his desk.

'Leave it on the desk.'

'Hmm ... just in passing, sir, I need to tell you something.'

'What's that then?' asked Patel, his eyes still on the computer screen in front of him.

'Alan, sir, he's looking a bit peaky. Maybe ill or something?'

'My heart bleeds for him. He's not lost his ability to have a jibe at me, has he, Joe?'

'This morning he lost it with a young PC who made a wee mistake.'

'That's Alan for you. I'll have a word with him. As long as he's pulling his weight in this investigation, I don't want to interfere.'

'I had a word with John, and I think Alan is going through some personal problems.'

'We all have them, Joe. As I said I'll look into it.'

Chapter 19

Patel drove over to the Southside. He had called and made an appointment to see Ali. He drove past the Clydesdale Cricket Club, which had opened in 1848 and was the oldest cricket club in Scotland. Cricket was one of his sporting passions that had been handed down from his father. He followed football too, but cricket was a game he had enjoyed as a young boy. He had participated and often watched test matches and the new IPL with his father and their family friends. In his mind, the sound of ball on the willow on a summer's day with a glass of beer in his hand was a wonderful way to relax.

The red sandstone house stood proud on Sherbrooke Avenue in Pollokshields, one of the imposing villas with mature gardens. Patel's car crunched along the gravel driveway and parked in the ample space in front of the garage. A mature tree cast a good shade. The porch door had rich Charles Rennie McIntosh stained glass features. He pressed the bell and waited. Ali Hassan opened the door and led him through a huge reception hall to a bay-windowed front lounge with a feature fireplace and from there into a smaller sitting room.

'Come in, Inspector Sahib, we'll be more comfortable here.'

Ali gestured for him to take a seat. Patel chose the end of a huge sofa. As he sat down he felt the luxurious fabric and comfort of the sumptuous sofa.

Salma was sitting in an armchair watching TV,

which was playing a Bollywood movie. She looked resplendent in a beautiful green and orange *salwar-kameez*. A red scarf with a paisley design was wound tightly around her head. That little mango design from India was so much part of Scotland, thought Patel, remembering that Paisley had been discussing making a bid for being considered as UK City of Culture in 2021.

'*Salaam alaikum,*' Patel said, smiling at Salma.

She rose from the sofa, greeted him with '*Wa alaykum asalaam',* and walked away into the kitchen. Ali switched off the huge, wall-mounted TV. Patel was familiar with the music that had been playing, an old favourite of his mum's.

Ali said, 'That was a sad funeral. Poor Salim and Mansur. I must thank you for releasing the body after a few days. I believe it was you who made that possible. Salim told me.'

Patel nodded politely. 'Ali, any more information that you can give me about Nadia? Did your wife find anything new, especially as she met a lot of the community at the funeral? Anything at all?'

Ali looked glum. 'Aye, there was a lot of talk about her running away with that married man when she was so young. That old gossip is revived again. But after divorcing that *gora*, she settled down with Salim.' Ali replied.

'My team seems to have drawn a blank. You said he left the country, the first husband I mean. Do you know anything about him?'

'No, I heard that he left for London, after the divorce. Not sure.' Ali shook his head. 'I don't think anyone has kept contact with him. Probably they only knew him as Nadia's husband and they were married for less than a couple of years, as far as I know.'

'Well, we will check on him. What about Salim and Nadia?' Patel watched Ali's face with interest. 'Was Nadia's marriage to Salim going through a rough patch?'

Ali checked his mobile as it pinged. He switched it off. 'Nothing important. Just a text for a new boiler from those infernal companies!' He smiled.

'I asked about Salim and Nadia,' insisted Patel.

'Salma says that Nadia was happy with Salim and had changed her wild ways. She loved her wee boy, Mansur.'

Salma walked in with some glasses of soft drinks and some savoury snacks on a tray. The light that fell on the tray made it look like polished silver. She urged Patel to take something to eat. She said something in Punjabi and Ali translated.

'She says why don't you stay for dinner?'

'No, thank you. That is very kind of you, but I have too much work to do. Has Mrs. Hassan heard anything new?' Patel smiled at her.

Ali spoke to her. She smiled back at Patel and said something to Ali who chuckled. Patel looked on expectantly.

'Tongues still wagged about Nadia's close relationships with her male colleagues, but she had never been one to toe the line. Now that she's dead they don't say much. Most people had lost interest in her and were on to the next big gossip. By the way, Salma thinks you look a bit like Hrithik Roshan, the Bollywood star.'

Salma looked embarrassed, tugged at her scarf, and sounded as if she was giving him a piece of her mind. He guffawed. She hurried back to the kitchen.

'Ali, I need to ask you. What do you think of Salim? Was he happy with the way Nadia behaved with her colleagues?'

Ali looked surprised. 'I know you guys always suspect the husband, but not in this case, surely?'

'We can't rule him out, you know. His mother gave him an alibi, but it turns out that he was out of the house for a short time.' Ali gave a glass of Irn Bru to Patel.

Patel took a sip of the drink. The sweet liquid with the strong flavour reminded him of his school days.

'Listen, Patel,' Ali said with a friendly pat on his shoulder. 'Salim took time to get used to her ways. but he doted on her.'

Salma coughed loudly. They both heard it.

'Excuse me,' Ali said and went to the kitchen.

Patel heard them talking. The name Nadia crept up in the conversation but he could not make out any of it. It sounded as if Ali disagreed with what Salma was saying. The snatches he heard sounded like Salma wanted less discussion of Nadia's relationships with men. Ali came back with a frown on his face and looking a bit flushed.

'What was that?' asked Patel.

'Nothing relevant, just new gossip. It's about Zena, a young woman who had gone for surrogacy in India to have her child. That was too shocking, so more tongues wagging. There were a lot of digs about whether it was her husband's child!'

Honour was deeply important to Asian culture. The concept of honour seemed to apply often only to women. Patel had worked on a few cases and one that had even led to murder when a woman was deemed to have lost her honour by marrying someone the family disapproved of. Was Nadia's behaviour embarrassing Salma and Ali, he wondered. Patel could not be sure if that was the truth. Did the couple know about Nadia and her 'honour' and were they reluctant to help him out with it? That was unusual, Ali was a reliable person. Patel decided to give Ali the benefit of the doubt.

'Well, if there is nothing more, I'll say goodbye. Do call me if you hear anything.' Patel stood up and they walked together to the door.

*

Usma would be waiting for him. Life had been so busy that it was a luxury to spend the evening with her. On the way home, he had bought her a bunch of roses and a bottle of Prosecco from the Marks and Spencer's attached to the petrol station. The drive to the suburb in the north of the city was pleasant, and the Clyde Tunnel was not busy. What a wonder to drive under the river, even if it was only a few yards. The marvel of engineering, thought Patel. The huge playing fields of Glasgow High School with its cricket pitches and the pavilion whizzed past him as he drove home.

He stepped onto the porch and slid the key into the front door. She stood there in the open plan lounge diner, putting her mobile down on the coffee table and looking stunning in a pale blue dress, her hair glossy in the light. He swept her up in his arms and kissed her. The flowers and bottle of wine were left on the coffee table as they ran up the stairs.

Later as they sat on the sofa, Usma raised her head from his shoulder and smiled.

'Hey, I miss you so much.' She kissed him gently.

He responded by hugging her like he'd never let the moment go.

'I know its early days yet, but I hope this case is solved soon and I can be with you every evening.'

'Any leads at all?' she asked and led him to the kitchen.

'I'll be chasing that Malcolm Watson, as he was the person who saw her last,' Patel said, his brow furrowing again as he thought of work.

'I hope you get the murderer soon,' she added, as she took the casserole out of the oven and he carried the salad bowl to the table. She had carefully laid the table and the candles were dripping and had melted a bit, but he smiled at her effort and commented on it. They ate with relish. The un-chilled wine was fine. They sipped it slowly.

When dinner was over, they stacked the dishes and switched on the dishwasher, moved to the lounge, and relaxed on the sofa. Usma placed her bare legs on him. His passion reignited and he stroked one of her legs, moving up towards her thigh. She turned and smiled at him, pushed him away, and then ran up the stairs. He followed her up to the bedroom. They crashed on the bed.

'Patel, I wanted to talk to you about something important,' said Usma as he fumbled with her dress. 'My job ...'

'Hmm ... not now,' he murmured as he kissed her.

Chapter 20

The 'summer heatwave on for a few hours' as they say in Scotland, was promising this morning. The sun streamed in and people were out in their skimpy summer clothes. The traffic was busy with three buses revving loudly waiting for the red light to change. The buses were full, mums with kids in prams, old and young travelling perhaps to the botanic gardens or parks nearby for a picnic.

At the station, Joe walked towards the young man sitting on a chair in the waiting room.

'Mr. Watson, good that you are on time. Let me take you over to the interview room,' said Joe and led the way along a corridor. He opened the door to a sparsely furnished room; the walls painted a dull grey. It had a table in the middle and four chairs two on either side. A video camera was focussed on the chair that Joe indicated to Watson.

'I'll be back with DI Patel in a minute,' he said.

Patel was on the phone in his office, Joe waited until he rang off.

'Boss, Malcolm Watson is ready for the interview, well sobered up today.'

Patel nodded, collected the file on Malcolm Watson and they walked over to Interview room three.

Malcolm was smartly dressed in a dark pair of jeans and a T-shirt with a linen jacket. He wasn't the dishevelled, bleary-eyed sleepy man in crumpled trousers and a T-shirt that they had seen when they had first set eyes on him. He stood up as the two approached the table. They took their respective seats after the formal greetings.

'Interview with Mr. Malcolm Watson, nine- thirty,' said DI Patel and they got started. 'You met with Nadia Ahmad. Tell us all what happened on that evening of July seventh when she arrived at your place.'

'Nadia was there before midnight and I was totally pissed, sorry, you know the state I was in ...' Malcolm looked sheepish at his admission. His eyes could not belie his state of mind. He looked uncomfortable and squirmed in his seat.

'Just tell us exactly what happened,' DI Patel's brown eyes bored into him.

'I told you, I was in a state and she tried to sober me up. I was traumatised.'

'So, you told us that your fiancée broke off your engagement that night, three weeks before your wedding. Give us some details. Who is she? Where does she live? Why did she break it off?'

Malcolm shook his head. He lowered his eyes to the floor and said nothing.

'Look, Mr. Watson, you were the last known person to see Nadia alive, this is serious.'

'No comment.' He looked away. There was silence in the room. 'My private life is private. Those facts can't be relevant,' Malcolm crossed his arms over his chest.

'Everything is relevant in a murder enquiry,' was a curt rejoinder from Patel.

'Were you in love with Nadia? Was that the reason that your fiancée broke off with you?' Patel's voice was harsh.

'No, No. How can you say that? We were just friends.' Malcolm's eyes were filling with tears.

'I'm waiting.' Patel's patience was wearing thin.

Malcolm looked respectable, a bank employee, obviously educated. He looked much better than when they had seen him the morning after the murder, half awake and drunk to the hilt, which made him look a wreck. What was he hiding?

Patel edged closer to him, his face inches from Malcolm and in a quiet voice said, 'Did you kill Nadia?'

'That's preposterous! I did not kill her. She was my friend. I think I need a lawyer.'

Patel's experience in murder cases told him that murders were often committed by people who knew the victim and that class, education, did not have any effect on that fact. He had seen cases where people committed heinous crimes either in moments of passion or hate or jealousy. Why was he reluctant to talk about his fiancée?

Patel tried once again. 'How long was Nadia at your place? When did she leave? Did she order a taxi to get home?'

'Look, I told you I can't remember a thing. I remember opening the door to her and very little after that,' he insisted.

'You said she made some coffee,'

Malcolm's face grew pale. 'She was so good to me,' his red-rimmed eyes filled up.

'She made some coffee then?' Patel continued.

'No. I said she said she would make it and went to the kitchen, but I was well gone by the time, probably before, the kettle had even boiled.' He placed his hands on the table, the fingers of the two hands entwined, the knuckles showed white as he clenched his fingers.

'Did your fiancée find out about Nadia, and that's why she broke off the engagement?'

'No, I've told you already. How many times? No, my fiancé didn't. There was nothing to find out.'

'Was Nadia threatening you about something? So, you tricked her into going to the park and finished her off.'

Malcolm sobbed.

'No! Look I did not kill Nadia. That's all I'm saying.'

Malcolm stayed silent after that.

There was little they could do. They could potentially keep him for questioning for twelve hours but they had no evidence, apart from the fact that he was the last one to see Nadia.

'Interview suspended five past ten.'

Joe switched off the video camera. 'Mr. Watson, you are free to go, but I doubt that this is over. Get yourself a lawyer and soon.'

Patel stood up, his tall frame domineering over the other two men in the room. A uniformed policeman opened the door and led Malcolm out.

'Joe, can you think why he's stalling?'

'Not really, sir,' Joe collected his notebook and file.

'See if you can get some info on his fiancée and make sure we schedule another interview with him as soon as he gets a lawyer.'

'Yes, sir,' Joe replied.

They picked up a coffee from the vending machine. Joe placed the file on his desk as Patel walked over to his office. On his desk was a report on the arrest of Bill Mason, a fraudster who had scammed some pensioners in Maryhill, taking money upfront from vulnerable old people. He glanced at it quickly and sipped his coffee.

Patel ruminated over the interview with Malcolm Watson. The young man was emotional about Nadia's death, obviously a very close friend, but why had he clammed up when he questioned him about his fiancée. Were Nadia and he more than friends? If so, why had he been planning on marrying someone else?

That afternoon, Patel and Joe had swung by Imran's house to check on Salim's alibi. It was only a couple of streets away from Salim's. Imran was a white man who had converted to Islam. Patel wondered if Imran found it easier to blend in the crowd of drinkers in the pub. Salim would have found it harder, be more conspicuous and worried in case any of his Muslim friends had seen him drinking alcohol. Patel understood the pressures of conforming to a different culture and the difficulties of those who were torn between the two.

Imran was courteous and confirmed that he and Salim had indeed had a pint that last evening of the Mela. The pub TV screens had been broadcasting the images of 7/7 attacks on the tenth anniversary and they had talked about it. So, Salim's alibi seemed quite solid. Just to make sure they went to the pub that Imran mentioned and the bartender seemed to know Imran and Salim, who were regulars at the bar. He confirmed that he had seen them both.

Chapter 21

'Good of you to call us, Salim,' said Patel as Joe and he walked into Salim's house for the third time.

The house was quiet. Farah had taken Amreen and Mansur away for the day, Salim explained.

They sat on the sofas and Salim said, 'I remembered: Hanif, Nadia's cousin I had forgotten all about him! He was hassling Nadia.'

'Hanif? Patel asked Salim 'Was that the young man I saw at the funeral, Ali said he was Nadia's cousin? What about him?'

'Yes, I do want to tell you about him.'

Even in his grief, his mind was clear as he related exactly what happened when he had brought Hanif home, a few months ago. He described the scene vividly.

'I had attended the mosque with young Mansur. Nadia had stayed at home that day. There were many household tasks that she had said she had wanted to catch up with. Some of the cupboards needed a good going over. Mansur's clothes and toys were taking over too many rooms. She had wanted to clear them out and make a pile for the charity shops and keep ones that were still useful. Hanif stood at the door with me, and little Mansur had raced in to hug Nadia. I invited Hanif in. Mansur was clinging to Nadia and chattering away about his visit to the mosque. He wanted a soft drink and was getting a bit annoying and Nadia had to see to him first. As soon as she got me in the kitchen, she whispered to me, "Why did you bring that idiot to our house?" I explained, "He's offered to play that new Xbox game with Mansur. Thought the wee man would like that. Surely no harm in that, so let's get the new game out," I told her and then I went to the bedroom and came back with the green bag, with the game still in its box. I found that Nadia had stayed in the kitchen making some tea. Hanif was leafing through the Koran that was in the room. After a good few attempts at the new game, we settled down to a cup of tea and some snacks as Mansur played with his toys. I asked as he sipped his tea. "So, how are your parents? How's your course going? Okay?" Hanif gave me monosyllabic answers back. I was surprised, he had been chatting amicably with me in the mosque and on the way home. He had a nice way with Mansur. My little boy liked all the attention he was giving him. Nadia sat quite still though, drinking her tea and watching Mansur playing with his iPad. I noticed that Hanif just stared at Nadia. It seemed as if he was taking in her sleeveless, low-cut top and tight jeans. Then he looked away. He did not meet her eyes. He tapped his toes. He looked unhappy. Even when he spoke up, I could see a kind of veiled anger. To distract him I asked,

'Any young lady keeping you away from your studies?'

There was an immediate change in Hanif's face. Tense and angry, he just blurted out,

'Not all Muslim women are flirts like your wife. You need to control her. Look at the way she's dressed even today ...' His eyes blazed.

I got up and I was about to strike him.

'Hanif, stop it. Don't you dare talk about my wife in that way, cousin or no cousin?' I remember shouting. I had pointed to the door and screamed, 'Get out, get

121

out.' With a few more choice swear words I sent him on his way. When he had gone, I sat down and wondered what had gotten into him. I had thought he was a bright young lad.

It was then that Nadia told me that the boy had accosted her and behaved rudely to her and Malcolm. I asked her then, 'Do you think he's getting radicalised, Nadia? Should I call his parents and warn them?' I was concerned that my wife was being hassled, and also that this bright young man was turning weird. 'Let's not rush to conclusions. Maybe it is just a silly phase,' Nadia said.

'Look, if he bothers you again, you text me immediately. Can't let this go on,' I said. A few months ago Nadia had mentioned that he had seen her in town with her friend Malcolm and was chiding her for being with a man. She laughed it off. I didn't take it seriously enough either.'

Salim finished recounting the incidents and looked up at Patel and Joe. He looked spent; the memories of Nadia and the horror of her murder ingrained in his mind. Patel could see what an effort it was for the young husband to tell them all he knew about Nadia's cousin Hanif.

'With all this talk of radicalisation of some young men, I am worried now. You understand that surely?' Salim said to Patel. He looked tense and embarrassed at the same time.

'I'll interview Hanif. It may be nothing. Thanks for letting us know about him,' Patel replied.

As they drove back to the office, Joe called the Counter Terrorism and Organised Crime office and Patel spoke to the chief there alerting them about Hanif. Patel would have the Prevent data on his desk as soon as possible.

'Was that young man crazy enough to murder if Nadia's behaviour went against his fundamental beliefs?' Patel wondered as he and Joe reached the office.

Chapter 22

The neighbours had phoned the police. Usma and Vikram knocked on the door. They could hear loud noises, children whimpering and a couple arguing. The weekend problem, or 'the domestic' as they called it at the station.

'What do youse want?' the man bellowed at them.

Usma and Vikram waved the warrant cards and entered the room; there was no hallway.

'Get him away from me,' a woman with a bruised arm and a bleeding hand shouted at them. Usma went over to check her injuries. A small child clung to the woman's feet.

'Aye, it's her agin, daeing me heid in, naggin, that's her middle name, I'll fucking kill her.' His whisky breath was like a wave assaulting them as he raised his arm towards the woman beside him.

'Stop it, now!' Vikram shouted and took hold of the man's arm and lowered it. 'I am arresting you for assault,' he clamped the handcuffs on him. They heard a police car screeching to a stop in front of the house. The officers from the car came in, read his rights to him, and led him away.

Usma noticed the clothes from the laundry basket were falling out. They were damp and twisted as if they had only just been removed from the washing machine. There room was untidy, filled with toys and newspapers. The TV blared. It was chaos. Usma sat with the victim and her young children. Her heart was heavy as she noted the empty bottles lying all around the table in the side of the room. The children looked malnourished and scared. They clung to their mother. Usma put a plaster on the woman's hand to stop the bleeding and talked to her. This was the third time Usma had seen her suffering at her alcoholic partner's hands. They had some tea and the mum and children relaxed. The man's alcoholism had affected all of them. The youngest child brought a tiny kitten from the kitchen. Usma followed her to the corner where three little kittens lay snuggling close to the mother cat. The cat and kittens looked underfed and uncared for. The child played with the kitten and Usma called the SSPCA to rehome the pet.

'Could you keep one of the kittens for me, please?' said Usma, surprised at her own sudden need for a pet.

'We'd be happy to. You need to come to our Milton branch and fill in forms,' said the lady on the phone.

'I'll be there to collect it on my day off,' she said and rang off.

Usma checked on the family a week later while on her street patrol. She reassured Betty that she would help her get a safe place to stay. It took a few weeks, but a safe refuge was found for the family. The man was given an interdict against having any contact with the family. The court proceedings would take a while.

Usma spent part of her day off visiting the SSPCA to check on the kittens. There was only one left. The tiny kitten meowed as she picked it up and cuddled it. She couldn't resist that wee ball of fur. Usma didn't hesitate. That last remaining kitten was hers in a matter of minutes. They had kept the last one for her at her request. Owners had been found in a few days for the basket of neglected kittens and the cat. That was the magic of Twitter and social media. The SSPCA officer was pleased that the young police woman had kept her promise and taken the tiniest of the lot, a weakling that needed a lot of care.

'This one is mine. I'm taking him home.' The shiny black kitten seemed to take to Usma, as she held him tenderly. It made him close his eyes and relax his whole body in her hands. She stopped on the way home and bought a litter tray, a bed, a feeding dish, and a grooming brush from the pet shop on Great Western Road Retail Park.

She decided to tell Patel both pieces of news when she was in his flat. She could wait no longer. Usma made dinner, played with the little kitten, and waited for Patel. She had made her decision; it would be a better quality of life for both of them.

Patel arrived home around nine that evening as he tended to do these days as the murder investigation became more intense. She was glad it was a casserole in the slow cooker, so dinner was not ruined. He heard the soft mewling of a kitten as he opened the door. Usma was holding a tiny black creature. Its green eyes opened wide to see the tall man.

'What is this? Taking care of it for someone?' he asked, placing the pile of work files on the table.

'Meet Coco, the new member of our family.' Usma explained how she got Coco. She handed him to Patel who took him reluctantly. Usma thought he looked worried about how they were going to take care of a pet, given their busy lives.

She poured him a glass of wine. 'Alok, I've got some more news. I've applied for a job as a Community Police officer, nine to five and I can be home for Coco.'

'What? When did you apply? You never told me.'

'I tried to, but you're either away or too busy with work. Do I have your full attention now, DI Patel?' she asked and patted him on the shoulder.

'I am all yours,' he laughed.

'Alok, no, this is serious. You know I joined the Police Force for a reason. I want to help our Asian people. I want more young Asians to get into the police force. There are so many problems within the community, and I want to help. With my knowledge of Urdu, Punjabi, and a smattering of Hindi, I can help so many. And a bonus! It is a nine-to-five job. I want to be home when you get home, I want to be there for you and Coco. The last few years have been difficult for me. The shifts left us such little time together.'

His tired face took it all in. Her eyes were shining, happy at her new life-changing decision. She was not even able to discuss something so important to her like her career with him, thought Patel, feeling protective towards her. He felt a surge of love for her.

She was talking rapidly now. 'The career path is good. I want to become an Equality and Diversity Advisor, eventually. I can take some university courses for that. I am so excited.'

Coco licked her face. She kissed him and cuddled him tighter.

Patel raised his glass. 'To your new job that I'm sure you'll get and our new life! I am so happy for you.'

'Hope the wait for the job is not too long. I'd like to spend more time with you,' she said. The dimples deepened on her cheeks as she smiled.

He kissed her and she patted him on his stomach and giggled, saying, 'Oh, and I've joined a gym. Maybe I can persuade you to accompany me sometimes?'

'More stuff to read,' said Patel eyeing a couple of reports lying on the side table. 'You go on up.'

Patel crawled into bed after working on the files for a few more hours. The wee kitten was lying in his basket on the floor beside Usma. He watched his partner sleeping, his love for her stronger still. She was making a lot of effort to be with him. They were living together whenever they could now. The kitten moved in the basket and made a tiny sound. Was Usma getting broody? he wondered. Was this her way of saying she wanted more than this odd way of just living 'together apart', as they referred to it, without their parents knowing anything? Did she want the wedding they had discussed before? He wanted it so much, but Usma had always said she wanted both families to bless their union. It was like a war, both families not willing to change their minds. Living together in this fashion was a compromise and she had kept hoping that their families would come around eventually.

He moved up closer to her and stroked her hair and kissed her lightly on the shoulder. She responded to him. Spooning in and cuddling her, he closed his eyes. His mind wandered from the comforting love of Usma to the pressures of his new job. Getting to sleep was getting harder with Nadia's murder always on his mind. He was not able to switch off. The responsibility was his, and he wanted the case to be solved soon.

Nadia's body lying on the mortuary table, Salim bending down to kiss her, reappeared in his mind. He had a sleepless night. Images of Malcolm Watson, Salim Ahmad, Farah Bolton, Ali Hassan, Hanif, and the gangs who had been clashing at the Mela, all spooled in his mind.

Chapter 23

Hanif's name did not show up on the Prevent data. Patel decided to ask Ali if he could meet the young man and have an informal talk with him. He was Nadia's cousin and it was part of the investigation to talk to all the people who knew her. Ali had agreed.

Patel had checked the madrassa online, as Ali and he were heading to meet Hanif there. He wanted to know more before going into the new place. There were a lot of details on the website, even photographs of the madrassa. The photos online showed a green door that had two big windows on either side, with vertical blinds on the inside. The madrassa looked like an ordinary house with two stories above the office-like interior, he presumed it had classrooms upstairs. That was the only difference. From outside it resembled the rest of the Street. A small undistinguished house which had been converted into a madrassa on Clydemure Street, in Pollokshields. It was an old blonde stone building. A plaque in Urdu and English above the front door stated that it was a kind of Sunday school for Muslims. They offered classes on The Koran and on Muslim Prayer. The madrassa was open to both men and women. Prayer times were updated every week.

'The classes are well established,' said Ali to Patel.

It looked like quite a small, intimate place compared to the huge great mosque in the Gorbals beside the River Clyde, a mosque that had become a landmark. The golden domes and the rich green colour against the extensive red brick building made an eye-catching sight for tourists. This madrassa served the local people, it seemed less formal than a huge mosque and it had a homely feel to it.

Patel and Ali Hassan stood outside the madrassa. This was way outside Patel's comfort zone, never having been to a madrassa before. He wondered if Usma had ever visited a venue like this. How little he knew of her culture. He must learn more, he thought to himself.

Ali rang the bell and a young man, Hanif, opened the door and let them both in.

Ali gestured towards Patel and said, 'Hanif, this is my friend DI Patel. He wants to have a word with you.'

'Why? I thought you said that you wanted a chat with me. Who is he?'

'Let's go through to the library, and then I'll explain,' said Ali and walked ahead.

They walked over to the library and sat down on the chairs. There were many volumes of books on the bookshelf that filled a wall in the room. Arabic calligraphy had its own beauty, and the predominantly green and gold bindings of the books and the numerous quotations that were framed and displayed on the walls lent a spiritual ambience to the room.

Patel said, 'Hanif, I am investigating the murder of Nadia. I believe you are related to Nadia Ahmad, right?'

Hanif squirmed in his seat. He stared at Ali accusingly and turned back to Patel. His face had a determined look, the jaw set firm.

'Yes, she was my cousin. So?'

'I heard that you were harassing her.'

'No, never! I just didn't want her behaving like a *gori*. That's not harassment.'

'When was the last time you spoke to Nadia?'

'Months ago.'

'How about the night of July seventh? Where were you?'

'Look, I know what you are getting at. I never killed her. I hated what she did, but she was my cousin, you know.'

'You've not answered my question.'

Patel looked at him, waiting for a reply.

'I was at the Mela just for a while, and then spent the night at home, doing some studying. Ask my mum.'

'Did you see Nadia at the Mela? Did you speak to her?'

'No, I just went there with a couple of friends, had something to eat and came right back. We must have left around seven.'

'Who were these friends?'

'Aziz and Haroun. You can ask them if you want.'

Patel asked for their mobile phone numbers and noted them.

'So, you were at home all night, from seven until the next morning. I thought you lived in a flat?'

'Yes, I do live in a flat but stay overnight with my mum sometimes. I told you, I was home that day after the Mela. Ask my mum.'

'Perhaps we should visit your house and see your mum. How about right now?' Patel kept up the pressure.

'Look,' interrupted Ali Hassan, 'I need to go to a meeting. You can take him to his house.'

'I'm not sure if my mum is at home now,' Hanif protested as Patel led him to his car.

Hanif sat in the passenger seat. The silence was deafening. Patel noticed him drumming his fingers on his thigh, as he asked him for directions to his house. The house was not far from the madrassa, they were there in five minutes.

Hanif led him into the house. He called for his mum

who arrived from a back room. She quickly put her veil over her head when she saw Patel in the room.

Patel asked in Hindi, if her son was at home on July seventh after the Mela.

She said nothing and looked down.

'My mum knows only Urdu. She doesn't understand what you're asking her,' said Hanif, a cheeky smile spread across his face.

'Well, you need to bring her to the station where I'll get the Urdu interpreter and get a statement from her,' said DI Patel, frustrated at his own lack of Urdu.

Hanif accompanied him to the door. His sigh was audible to Patel.

Patel drove back to the station fast. Hanif was a suspect and he had to get him down to the station for further questioning. Yet Prevent did not have him on the list. 'Would a young man kill his cousin because he disapproved of her behaviour? Many young men were getting ideas from online sites and Hanif was probably one of them,' Patel thought. Some of the persuasive online grooming that young women and men went through were not always harmful but led a few into more dangerous ideology. Patel was a good judge of character. 'Hanif was an intelligent young man who was immature, but not dangerous,' he told himself. He hoped he was right.

Chapter 24

Patel and Usma were doing some grocery shopping. Aunty PP! A simple supermarket outing was ruined by being waylaid by the community gossip-monger. Patel was trying to get away from her. She had talked from the moment he laid eyes on her. He smiled inwardly as he recalled the childish nickname they had given her. Prema Parikh had become 'Aunty Pissoff Parikh'. She never stopped talking. Usually, she got straight to the point of the most intimate details. When he was at school, exams were the main talking point.

'So, did you come first in class, *Beta*?' Or the sheer embarrassment of teen years, 'you are growing too tall *na*, why so many pimples?'

He edged away from her, but she almost pinned him against the wall of the supermarket.

'*Beta*,' she said. 'Why do I never see you nowadays? Forgotten all your old aunties? Big Inspector now!' She smiled; a bit of pride enhanced that gossipy big mouth.

'I'm in a rush, Aunty, just paying for this and leaving.' He gave her a charming smile as he indicated the shopping basket

Her beady eyes examined the basket.

'Just wine and microwave meals, no, no that won't do at all,' she continued. 'I was telling your mum just yesterday, time to find you the perfect bride.'

Patel saw Usma heading towards him with a baguette in her hand. He was quick, mumbled a bye to Aunty PP, and moved away. He brushed Usma's shoulders and rolled his eyes, towards Aunty PP. Usma understood. She walked over to the checkout but stood behind Patel. Aunty PP watched as Usma put a baguette in his shopping basket.

Aunty PP shook her head, but her eyes followed Patel standing at the cash till.

Who is that? A colleague? Aunty PP wondered. I must find out, she thought tutting. Wish this shop were not so big, I could have caught up with him, she muttered to herself and pushed the huge trolley around, her mind distracted now from the BOGOF offers that she wanted to purchase. Instead she decided to make up a list of young suitable women for Patel.

Patel and Usma rushed over to their car.

Usma slid in beside him in the car.

'Lucky escape,' he said and pressed her hand quickly. 'Better get out of here before the witch sees us.' He revved the engine and accelerated out of the car park.

'Hey, we can't keep doing this,' Usma said, her dimpled smile made his heart beat faster. He loved her too much; he never wanted to lose her. He nodded and drove home. Patel and Usma were lost in their thoughts as the car breezed through the summer evening.

Glasgow was at its best. An orangey sky sprinkled with little stars that were just visible, like jewels shimmering in the sky.

Aunty PP finished her shopping, but her mind was still on Patel and the woman that she had seen with him. She took out her mobile and called Laxmi.

Chapter 25

DI Patel turned away from the window and sat in his chair. He had been working since early morning. He looked at his watch; the strategy meeting would be soon. The murder investigating team needed clear direction and he made notes on tasks that each member of the team would undertake.

He checked he had everything ready for the briefing. The room was full. A murder investigation involved a large number of people that the public never saw. These were police who did mundane tedious jobs, sifting through endless tapes of security cameras, interviewing witnesses who were not very keen to cooperate, or thought it was a waste of their precious time. The digital world made the task even more onerous. Social media had to be viewed, registered as important or discarded. And the twenty-four-hour media wanted constant news and sometimes wrote their own skewed angle to sell more copies. The tiny details of people involved were seized on by the media and looked at for any morsel that could be conflated to present sensational headlines.

Patel's team gathered around the whiteboard. He addressed the group.

'So, Nadia Ahmad was with a friend, Farah Bolton, but left her around ten thirty or eleven to comfort a friend, Malcolm Watson, whose fiancée had dumped him three weeks before their wedding. He was the last person to see her alive. Two interviews with him and her friend Farah have not brought us any closer to the murderer yet. Has anyone got anything new?'

'Boss, we got nothing about the gold necklace. We managed to get a photo of Nadia wearing it from her friend, Farah. It was in the photos on her mobile that they had taken at the Mela. We printed it and took it to Gogna jewellers on Great Western Road to ask if they could give us some details about it. It was her grandmother's, so it was rather old fashioned according to the jeweller we spoke to, but they did say it was valuable. It is probably twenty-two carat gold and would have had a value of around two hundred pounds at least.' Brian stated the information gathered by him and Kara.

'That sounds quite valuable,' said Alan Brown, then lowering his voice, almost a whisper to his friend John sitting beside him, 'those Pakis wear bright gold that hurts the eye, right,' he said with a smirk. John shushed him, his eyes showing his displeasure at these uncalled-for comments.

'Could she have been murdered for the necklace? Maybe she had found it in the park and a stranger stabbed her and took off with it?' Kara stated.

'Did you follow that up?' asked Patel.

'The organisers and cleaners of the Mela found nothing. We asked the crime scene officers if they found any such item. So far, no jewellery has been handed in at the local police stations either. So, it is definitely missing,' Brian added.

'The jewellery could have even found its way down South, I know that gangs operate all over the UK, specialising in Asian gold theft. More burglaries happen during their festivals of Diwali and Eid. Not sure that this single item would have been targeted by gangs. Let's try and concentrate on facts here. No murder weapon found yet. Could you have another word with that taxi driver, Brian?' Patel added, 'Let's focus on finding suspects.'

'Yes, sir.' Brian made a note in his book.

'Any information on Nadia's colleagues who may have had grievances against her?'

'No, sir. She seems to have been very popular with her colleagues. In fact, she was the life and soul of office parties and very helpful to juniors, from what we were told, sir,' replied Kara.

Patel looked at the whiteboard.

'And what about her first husband?' Patel looked expectantly at the officers in front of him.

'We checked the wedding register. The first husband was Mr. Roger Anderson. We are trying to find more information about him. We interviewed his first wife, but she has not been in touch with him for many years. We also checked at Martha Street Registry office for the date of their marriage. He's not on the Police Database for any offences, sir,' said Kara.

'Kara, ask for information on Roger either from her close friend Farah, or Malcolm. They might know more about him.' Patel instructed. The meeting was over.

Kara immediately set about calling Farah Bolton to make an appointment to see her.

*

Bright and early next morning Kara and Brian were interviewing Farah at her beautiful home. She was still in a state of shock and distress and was willing to help in any way possible.

'So, did you know Nadia's first husband Roger, Mrs. Bolton?' Kara asked her as Farah brought them tea in china mugs and some millionaire's shortbread on a tray and placed it on the glass coffee table.

Farah sat sipping her tea and replied.

'Yes, we've been friends for ages. In fact, for a short time after she married Roger, we were a foursome often going for meals, the cinema, the odd gig and to each other's houses. When Roger's drinking got too much these outings just fizzled out, but I was close to Nadia always.'

'Do you know if Roger was still in touch with Nadia?'

'No, not at all. She made sure she had nothing to do with him. Poor Nadia. She even felt guilty and was unhappy that she had broken up his marriage.'

'So, Mr. Anderson was married before?' Kara asked.

'Yes.' Farah's eyebrows knitted sharply. She knew that the police investigated all contacts of the victim in a murder case.

'Do you know where he lives now, or where he works?'

'No, sorry, it was such a long time ago. There was some rumour that he had left Glasgow, but I was making sure that Nadia was okay rather than thinking of him. He was an alcoholic, wish we had known that before Nadia got into such a disastrous marriage with him.' Farah sighed.

'Can you tell me anything about his first wife?'

'Again, very little. I vaguely remember her name was Mary or Marie.'

'If you were close friends, do you have any photos of the four of you together?' Brian asked. Kara gave him a grateful look. That had not occurred to her.

'No, Nadia and I got rid of all mementos of Roger and her life with him. She didn't want any reminders of that traumatic last few months with him, or that divorce.' Farah brushed a tear from her eye.

'You don't think Roger had anything to do with her murder?' she asked.

'We can't rule out anyone. In a murder case, we need to check the people that Nadia has been in close contact with. Was he working when they were together?'

'No, he was lazy, never did much at all. Sorry, I wish I could help you more.' Farah looked despondent.

'Thanks for all that you've told us, Mrs. Bolton.' Kara and Brian got up to leave.

'Please find out who killed my friend Nadia,' pleaded Farah, tears running down her cheeks.

'I will,' promised Kara and left the house.

'Wonder if Nadia was just the second wife or if there were more in that Casanova's life?' stated Brian as they drove back to the station.

Chapter 26

Kara and Joe popped into his office and handed Patel a cup of coffee at the midmorning break, and briefed him on what they were doing that day.

'Boss, we've had that 'Young Shields' gang member, Mahmood in. He was cautioned with some of the others near the Kelvingrove Park earlier, chasing the 'Young Partick Fleetos.' A bit far for them to have come over to the West End.'

Joe hesitated as Patel sipped his coffee and ran his eyes over the mail they had brought in. There was more on the changes that were taking place at Police Scotland, reports on committees that he served on. He dismissed the officers and opened the mail and had started to read when he heard Joe coughing.

'Er... We are a bit short-staffed, boss, who'll interview Sanjay?' Joe asked.

'I guess it would have to be Alan and John.' Patel sighed and picked up the phone.

Trawling through the CCTV, getting the door-to-door work, answering the innumerable phone calls kept the staff busy. Patel had to watch the budget too in these austere times. He had to use all the resources at hand. He reluctantly summoned Alan and his partner John to interview the young guy brought in that morning.

Patel knew that Alan would relish this task. Patel was under pressure. Alan would want to get some kudos himself, prove to the highest in command that he was much more competent and would have made a better DI. But Patel had to rely on him today.

A few minutes later, Alan and John checked that the interview rooms were free.

'Right, get that Sanjay into Interview Room two then,' Alan said to John.

'Watch your language with the young man,' said John cautious as always.

'Don't you worry, I'll talk his lingo,' said Alan, a frown spread across his serious face.

The boy sitting facing him was one of the members of a well-known teen gang, the Young Shields, a swagger in his walk, and the 'I don't give a shit attitude' on his cheeky face. He sat upright in his chair, with arms folded against his chest and that casual expression of 'like you can do anything to me.' Alan was riled up by this performance. His fingers were itching to slap that idiotic face.

He switched the recording on after giving the boy the usual warning spiel. The boy looked nonchalantly at Alan. Nothing seemed to faze him, or at least his eyes gave nothing away. John switched on the video camera. Sanjay looked at the camera and gave a wry smirk.

'Name?'

'Sanjay,' the boy said and after a pause added, 'So what was I lifted for?'

'Date of birth?'

'Tenth of December nineteen ninety-seven.'

'Right, let's get started proper eh, Sanjoy.'

'It's Sanjay.'

'Whatever! Now, don't you get cocky with me!'

John turned round to catch Alan's eye, but he was staring at the boy.

Alan's bloodshot eyes were on the boy. The coffees

he had drunk had not relieved the headache from last night's drinking session. This boy's attitude grated on his nerves.

'Where were you on the evening of seventh of July?'

'Cannae remember.'

Alan glowered, 'I want an answer,' he growled.

'Probably in my room playing the Xbox. Not into *panga*, man.'

'What? Speak properly! And get that grin off your face!'

'Not in any scraps for ages. Ask my ma'!'

'So, when you were brought in on Sunday, July the seventh after that 'scrap' as you call it, Sonjay, and we let you go with a serious warning, you sat at home, did you?'

'It's Sanjay.'

'Did you?'

'Aye.'

'No, you were seen with a few of your mates 'scrapping' again with the Young Partick Fleeto guys. My men shooed you off on night of July the seventh at the Mela. Why were you in the West End anyway?'

'Naw. It wisnae me, nothing to dae wi' me.'

'See those security cameras. They pick up quite a lot.' Alan pointed to the camera.

Silence.

Another defiant look from the boy as Alan sneered at him, prodding him for an answer. The boy looked at the walls, ignoring Alan. He started to swing on the chair which made a strange noise as the metal scraped against the table legs, and the thin carpet on the floor looked like it would fray.

'You lot trying to get your own back for that Nadia's murder? Did you see it happen?'

Sanjay looked away, stared at the strip light above

him.

'Or was it drugs or some sort of revenge attack? I need an answer, now!' Alan thumped the table for good measure.

'No comment.'

Sanjay stared right back at Alan, challenging him.

Alan was infuriated. He wanted to shake an answer out of him. He wouldn't put it past this toerag, doing something violent to avenge a young Muslim woman's death.

Alan noted that his abrasive questioning made the young man even more indignant and he just clammed up.

'Try harder.' Alan smiled through gritted teeth.

Silence.

'This is a bloody waste of time. Get him out of my sight. The interview is over. Ten thirty-six a.m.,' said Alan reluctantly. He got up from his chair and switched the video off.

Sanjay got up and John led him out.

'Bloody Pakis. They know the bloody drill before they are out of primary school. Fuck!' Alan banged the door of the interview room and muttered as he made his way to the toilet.

July's heat had got to him. He sweated profusely and hated the warm weather. Summer was murder to him. He splashed cold water on his face. The mirror reflected a scowling ginger face, mottled red, with freckles of brown in angry splotches on his neck and forehead. It didn't help that he couldn't sleep through the baby's crying. He opened the door and swore under his breath seeing Patel walking towards him.

'Well, cracked that teen? Anything useful, Alan?' Patel with eyebrows raised waited for an answer.

'Just a bloody numpty, just cheek, no nothing useful.

Need to lock these loonies up." Alan's breath came out in heavy spurts.

'Losing your touch, Alan?' The teasing voice changed to stern, 'A report ASAP. Need to keep tabs on the gangs.'

A bright red colour spread up Alan Brown's face.

'I need a bloody day off after that shite of an interview with that low life, too many bloody gangs.' Alan's banging headache caused him to screw up his face.

'Drugs and territorial skirmishes too. Did you ask what that boy and the gang were doing so far from their own wee schemes?' Patel continued asking Alan.

Patel said he hoped that the clashes between the various gangs weren't going to escalate, thanks to the murder of an Asian woman.

Alan couldn't stop himself exclaiming, 'It was the Mela; the whole of bloody Glasgow was there. I need to go. Patel, you'll get your report,' wanting to get away for a hair of the dog or at least a coffee.

'Right, Alan,' Patel moved towards the toilet, opened the door, and went in.

Alan let out a sigh and headed towards the coffee machine. He'd write up that report and get the hell out of the office.

Meanwhile, John led Sanjay out of the room to the reception. The young lad gave a cheeky smirk to the desk sergeant and whistled as he walked out, with his hands in the pocket of his jeans.

'Pathetic, thinks he's a big man,' said John to the desk sergeant and walked back to his office.

*

Out of sight from the police station, Sanjay switched his smartphone on and pressed a number. His pal from

144

the gang picked up.

'Not lifted then?'

'Hey bro, no way, man!'

He gave a loud guffaw, put the mobile away, pulled his hoodie over his head and swaggered off into the grey morning and back to his petty gangland life.

Chapter 27

Patel's mobile pinged. He had a text from Anita:

Mum and dad want to have a proper chat with you. Dinner, my place, Friday 7 pm. Be there. Anita xx

The text from Anita made him squirm in his seat.

He knew that this was his parents trying to convince him that Usma was not the right partner for him. Should he just text back saying that he's too busy? Guilt raised its ugly head every time he had to meet his parents. He loved them and did not want to hurt them. Patel had been putting off seeing them. He had not seen them since the party. He had avoided them in case they persuaded him to part with Usma. And yet, his parents had always kept in touch either through calls or through his sister, Anita. As soon as he got the new job, they had given him that huge party to celebrate his promotion on becoming a DI. With mixed emotions, he typed a quick reply. The image of Aunty PP cornering him at the supermarket loomed large in his mind. Wonder if that old bat had been saying things to mum, he thought. Better see mum for a short time, he decided.

He texted back: *OK. See you all Friday.*

Patel had more than enough to cope with. A murder to solve and the lack of leads made him feel frustrated. He was still dealing with the fact that a young mother had been killed. Why is evil always present in the world? From what he had read of notes on Nadia she seemed a harmless young woman who had managed to make something of her life. Who wanted her dead? His years as a policeman had taught him that love and hate, good and evil lived side by side. There was a dark side to some people who either through passion or anger committed the ultimate crime of taking another person's life. Had Nadia annoyed or angered someone at the Mela that evening? Did she have any secrets in her life that even her husband or friends knew nothing of? He thought it amazing that when one delves into the life of a deceased person how many of the connections throw up some weird facts. He had to find the murderer. He recalled the old quote from the Yajur Veda, that his mum used to repeat often:

'Truth cannot be suppressed and always is the ultimate victor.'

He felt comforted that most cases of murder and other crimes were solved. One only had to work hard to find the clues.

He read the notes on Nadia again. Did she have any other hobbies? he wondered. All he could see in the reports of Nadia's murder was that she was interested in her work, her home and volunteering at the women's refuge. Considering she had a young child too, all that seemed enough to cope with.

Chapter 28

Malcolm had excused himself early from work and arrived home. He poured himself a whisky, switched the TV on and slid onto the settee. His eyes followed the scene on the TV but registered nothing. He nursed the drink in his hand, thoughts of the murder of Nadia and his interview with Patel preying on his mind. He went over the scene that night that Nadia came over to see him. He wished he had not been so drunk and had a blackout.

His mobile pinged. He switched it on, annoyed to see an advert pop up. He was about to switch it off when his fingers strayed over the photo gallery icon. He sat for while scrolling through his photos of Nadia. Tears ran down his cheeks as he thought of the years of friendship that they had. An ad for a Groupon voucher five pound for a ten-pound Costa card beamed on the screen. He switched the phone off. Nadia and he often slipped out of work to have a coffee at Costa. His mind spooled over to that time when he met Nadia's cousin, Hanif, in there. Was it in 2014, he thought? He remembered every detail.

Malcolm thought it was a joke the first time he saw the young man glowering at him when he was introduced to him. Hanif was impolite, not even offering a hello. He totally ignored him, speaking only to Nadia.

Nadia had explained and laughed it off. 'Young blood. He's some distant cousin called Hanif. He thinks he's grown up and he's strutting about laying down the law. He has learnt some nonsense about how we Muslim women are supposed to behave, or he thinks he knows. A silly young boy!'

Nadia dismissed him with a wave of her hands.

'You are one headstrong lady,' Malcolm commented, as he sipped his coffee. They were having their lunch out.

'I'm sure he's confused about his own identity. Young folk go through that phase. Except I never did! I knew what I wanted from the time I was ten,' she giggled.

'That young man's behaviour is very strange. You say he is intelligent, a medical student at Glasgow University?'

'Yes, the whole family is very proud of him. He is very intelligent, so I don't understand this sudden change in him.' Nadia brows furrowed for a minute then she gave her bright smile, 'Hey, let's get back to the desks and chain ourselves there until five.'

The second meeting with Hanif was when Malcolm was with all the staff members of his and Nadia's branch for Gina's fortieth birthday lunch. Gina was a theatre buff, so they decided to go to the Oran Mor in the West End, that beautiful old church that had been converted to a bar and restaurant, to watch A Play, A Pie and A Pint. Nadia was helping Gina to remove her big fortieth birthday badge from her jacket as the pin was sticking up awkwardly. Malcolm noticed Hanif hurrying towards the two ladies as they were nearing the top end of Byres Road. His maroon hat was low over his face which was filled out with a prominent beard. He wore pyjamas and a long tunic, which was unusual attire for a young student. Nadia did not notice Hanif until he came right up and touched her arm briefly. She said, 'Oh hello, Hanif. Out for lunch from the Uni?'

With a friendly smile, Malcolm joined them and said hello to him.

Hanif ignored him and said in an urgent tone to Nadia, 'You can't go in there.'

Nadia looked perplexed. 'What?'

Why would a young man talk to her like that? wondered Malcolm.

'Want to join us? It's a good play today,' he said, trying to be friendly to Hanif.

'I'm not letting you go in there,' hissed Hanif, his face close to Nadia. The anger in his voice surprised all of them.

Gina looked bemused.

Nadia shrugged. 'You what? How dare you!' She challenged him with a look of rage, 'Piss off! Beat it! Scarper!'

Hanif was taken aback and turned on his heels and muttered something under his breath and walked away.

'What was that all about?' asked Gina.

'Just an ignorant wee teen, forget it, let's enjoy your birthday,' said Nadia and they filed into the Oran Mor.

She had ranted and raved to Malcolm in the taxi ride home after the party.

'Why should I explain my behaviour to this young guy? How dare he question me? I'm going to call the police if it happens again, what a nasty piece of work. This has happened one too many times recently. Do you think he's stalking me, Malcolm?' she asked him. 'I'm certainly going to tell Salim,' she concluded.

At work the next day, Malcolm asked Nadia if she told Salim about Hanif's appearance at the theatre.

'No, no, when I got home, there was a carry-on. Little Mansur had fallen off of a slide and we had to rush him to A&E. I forgot all about it,' she replied.

That was not the only time. He appeared in Costa once again.

'Nadia. Aren't you ashamed?' Hanif stood beside her chair.

He had crept up on them. Her back was to him and she had not seen him coming over to them. He frowned at Malcolm who managed a faint smile.

This time Nadia had looked uncomfortable. She got out of her seat, took him aside and said clearly to him that she would be reporting to the police that he was harassing her. Hanif walked away, glancing at Malcolm who was staring at them, his face bathed in the sunshine. His bemused expression was question enough.

'That same bampot cousin?' he asked Nadia.

She nodded, 'I've warned him all right. I don't think he'll bother me anymore.' She smiled at Malcolm but he saw her sighing heavily.

The loud music of the commercial break on the TV broke Malcolm's thoughts. Malcolm was rudely awakened from his memories of the good times he had shared with Nadia and also that strange behaviour of her young cousin. He was distraught and sat with his head in his hands. Nadia, such a dear friend, he wished he could see her again.

Should he call DI Patel and tell him about Hanif? Malcolm wondered. The police seemed to think he was a prime suspect; he was the last to see her alive according to what they had said. No, he better not contact the police, he told himself. He had not seen or heard about Hanif from Nadia after those incidents. That was quite some time ago. He remembered that he needed to get a lawyer organised before the police came to interview him again. He had never been in trouble with the law before. Malcolm couldn't believe how his life had changed for the worse, recently. He felt tired and depressed. He had lost his best friend. His life was just awful, and his fiancé had ditched him at the last moment. If he could end it all, it might give him some peace of mind at least. He drained the last of the whisky in the glass, switched the TV off with the remote and lay down on the settee.

It must be Hanif who killed Nadia, was his last thought as he fell asleep.

Chapter 29

Spring 2004

Another sunny morning as he, an alcohol-ravaged man looked out of the window of the spare room. He saw a reflection in the glass. He took up a lot of space, with his huge frame in that tiny room. He was stocky, with a scarred face and dark brown eyes, the left eye drooping. His hair was dirty brown, thinning on top. He was not a pretty picture and he was conscious of it. The golden sunshine did little to make him feel any better. He had to sober up, see if he could make his way to the 'buroo', and get some money. He needed the giro.

He moved away from the window to get ready. As he shaved, he looked in the mirror at his drawn face, with dark rings around the eyes. He hated himself. The bile rose in his throat, from drinking too much, his mind regurgitated the same old scenes.

He had wheedled his way back to his wife. How many times had he been thrown out of his home? Women! Nothing he did pleased them.

He put on a pair of black jeans that had seen better days, a T-shirt that was once a dark shade of green, with a faded logo, almost indistinct now. He slowly made his way to the Jobcentre Plus. It was crowded. Men and women filled the plastic chairs. A couple of women stood outside smoking, one with a pushchair carrying a screaming toddler. The hour at the Jobcentre Plus made him more impatient for a drink. He collected his giro and cashed it straight away. Like being on autopilot, his legs took him to the nearest hostelry.

The darkness inside was reassuring, out of the sunlight and heat. He looked around, his eyes adjusting to the light streaming through the window. A few early birds were seated on the bar stools. The worn-out carpet a dark grey, now black, with patterns that made him feel dizzy. They were not conducive to his resting eyes. He ordered a pint and a whisky chaser, just what he needed.

He crushed the cigarette butt into the ashtray, thumped the glass of whisky down. People on the bar stools flicked a glance at him.

He tapped the glass on the counter, 'Another dram.'

'Not a please or thank you, the drunken bastard,' the barman muttered to himself.

He stared hard at him. 'What did you say?' he asked.

'Nuthin, here's whit you ordered and less of all that thumping and noise eh?' The barman grimaced at him, his thin lips mouthing the words, 'behave.'

He tapped the dram glass in front of him and glared at him.

The liquid gold flowed down from the glass; the warmth of its taste on his throat felt comforting. He closed his eyes briefly. Guilt and whisky, lust and guilt, the perfect companions. Had he read that somewhere? He downed the dram in one. A few more drams and he heaved himself off the barstool. He had to fill the rest of the day. He wandered over to the Gallery of Modern Art, with its iconic Duke of Wellington statue and a traffic cone on his head in front of the building. This always appealed to him. That flagrant disregard for authority was what he approved of.

Life was messy enough without people higher up telling him to get a job, stop drinking, apply for jobs, that morning the staff at the job seekers had bent his ear long enough. He also liked the fact that he could sit downstairs and have a cup of coffee to sober up in a quiet place after the hustle and bustle at the heart of the city. He cared little for the modern gallery exhibits upstairs that boasted artists like Andy Warhol, David Hockney, the names of these artists he had heard on TV or seen on newspapers were highlighted on the leaflets lying around.

Later he left the cosy interior of the library and walked outside. He filled his grumbling belly with a couple of sausage rolls from Greggs at the corner of George Square as he headed home. It was a long walk but the pubs along the way helped him quench his thirst for alcohol. The hours and the money melted away. He felt the change jangling in his trouser pocket as he moved from one bar to another, promising this would be his last. The smell of beer enticed him in. A mellowed haze of nothingness and dusk descended as he staggered home. Guilt gnawed his heart but drink helped him cope with shutting it away into a deep corner. His wife would be exhausted after the little one's bath and bedtime routine.

Somewhere deep in his subconscious mind, he knew he could rely on her. She had been his childhood sweetheart, his partner and mother of his child.

At the door, after the few fumbling attempts had failed, he reached down to pick up his clattering keys. She opened the door, and without a word, she turned on her heels and went up the stairs.

'Let me in ... lemme ...' he tried to get the slurred words and string them together. He raised his head and heard her banging the bedroom door.

She never banged on the door. She always thought of the wee boy, sleeping next door. She must be really angry, his befuddled mind registered, but his legs were taking him towards the drinks cabinet. He wanted to blot out her angry eyes. He staggered towards the cabinet; found there was no alcoholic drink in there. He felt a wave of anger rising. Frustrated, he went over to the back door and searched under the smelly old unwashed clothes, he had left them lying there for a week. She had not touched them. That had been a good place to hide that almost empty wee half bottle of whisky. It was still there. He took a swig and felt better. He slid down the wall beside the clothes and took a few more slugs until there was none left and he lay there almost unconscious. Later he woke, climbed the stairs and slept in the spare room.

*

Why had he come back? Why had she let him in, even if it was only on her terms? Very occasionally she had let him stay over.

She wished she hadn't.

How many times had she wanted to run away from everything? Away with her boy, find a new life. Anywhere, away from that drunken lump of a man who was still snoring in the spare room today? She had wanted a better life. Why was she so gullible? Why did she let him in, knowing her life was so much better without him? She muffled a sob and walked over to the settee, sat shocked and dazed, taking stock of her life.

She thought of that excruciating time when heavily pregnant she had begged him to stay with her. It was always the bottle, but that young slut had made the struggle to keep him even harder. Well, she could think of her in no other way. The years of bringing up the child on her own and then out of the blue, he came back wanting to get back with her and their son. Was it her loneliness that had made her accept him? Did she genuinely believe he had changed?

He loved the boy. She could see that. Her son liked having him around even if it was only a few days at a time.

The man lay in bed, sprawled on his tummy. The duvet had slipped off. She picked it up and laid it on the bed and covered him lightly. She could hear his breathing, almost a snore. Had she let him in? She couldn't remember. Coming late from the pub had become a regular habit for him.

She must have slept like a log next door. Those sleeping tablets were helping her sleep better. She closed the door. Let him have a lie-in she told herself, then walked down the stairs and into the kitchen and made a brew.

There was little change in his behaviour. He came knocking on her door every time he needed to find somewhere to stay for a while. She never understood her behaviour. She dreaded the way he assumed she would allow him in.

The phone rang. It was Cath, her friend.

'Not again, why do you let that waste of space in your life back in again?' Cath remonstrated when she told her that he was up in the spare room, snoring.

'He needs me.' Her voice was low.

'For God's sake, has he given you money for anything so far?' Cath demanded.

'No, not a penny. Just parks himself here when he needs me.'

'Does he bring anything for his son at least?'

'Never has a penny to rub together.' She tried to justify it, but her mind was frazzled.

'Well, you don't need me to tell you. How long has this been going on? Get rid of him. Do it now.' She rang off.

Cath's no-nonsense advice made her sit up. How many times had she thought about ending their relationship for good? Why had she hung on to him? She had forgiven him so many times because the thought of depriving Scott of a father negated her own feelings that he would never change.

She rinsed the mug in the sink and heard him get up and go to the bathroom. She had had enough.

This was the last time she told herself. She was going to throw him out.

He called out.

'Hey, how about a strong brew?' His voice grated on her. No more fetching and carrying for him.

She found her strength at last. She got up, packed his few belongings in a black bin bag and placed it at the front door.

'What's all the noise?' he rubbed his sleep-filled eyes, as he came out of the bedroom.

'Out, get out of my life,' she said very quietly and pointed to the bin bag.

'What do you mean? Where will I go?' His eyes widened.

'I've had enough, just leave.'

He stood there, just looking at her, laughing, thinking it was a joke.

'Get out!' she shouted.

He had never seen her like that. He picked up the bag and left.

A promise of rain tinged the low clouds with strips of a grey sky peeping out. The naked trees denuded of leaves stood like sentries inside a garden across the street. He walked to the main road and at the first bus stop; he placed the bin bag on the narrow seat in the bus shelter and sat beside it. He had no idea where to go.

The first bus arrived, and a couple of passengers got out. He sat still on the seat, numb, feeling lost. He had no idea of what he was going to do next.

Chapter 30

'Hello, hello, Laxmi?' Prema Parikh's excited voice screeched over the phone.

'Yes, it is me. How are y ...?'

Before she could finish the sentence, Parikh's voice cut through, 'I've been trying to call you all day. Your son, Alok, I saw him at the supermarket. I think I must warn you.'

'Oh, warn me? What about Prema?'

'Too many young women are after him.'

'What do you mean?'

'I'm sure I saw this pretty Muslim woman near him at the market, putting some bread in his basket. I mean how bold is that? One has to be careful.'

'Must be someone he's working with ...'

'Well, I'm not sure, she looked like she was after him, and you know these young women here, how forward they are.'

'So how is your husband? Is his BP under control and your diabetes?' Laxmi tried to change the topic.

'I rang you up for another important reason. It is my seventieth birthday next Sunday so I'm inviting you all for a family dinner, just our two families, but make sure Anita and Alok are there.'

'I'm not sure if Alok is free,' Laxmi hesitated 'I'll need to ask him.'

'Tell him I'll be hurt if he can't even come for my important birthday. Surely he can spare a couple of hours on a Sunday. I'll call him anyway. He has not changed his mobile number, has he?'

'No, but I'll let him know.'

'You tell him too. He must come.'

'Why is that?' asked Laxmi.

Parikh's voice went up a couple of octaves. 'You know my cousin Renuka, her pretty daughter Tina is here from India. She is just right for Alok.'

Now I get it, the reason for her phone call thought Laxmi. She was interested. She was desperate for Patel to make a good choice for his bride.

'I'll insist that he comes along then.'

They chatted for a while more on the latest news on NDTV the TV channel that they both watched and then hung up.

Laxmi sat in the easy chair in the conservatory. The sun's warmth made her feel comfortable enough to have a wee nap. She closed her eyes, but the words of Prema were troubling her. Prema must have seen Alok with Usma. She had tried so hard to keep their relationship from the community. If Prema got a whiff of it, it will be all over the tight-knit community. She wanted to protect him in some way, and she wanted Alok to see why she thought that Usma wasn't unsuitable for him.

*

The doorbell rang. Anita was standing on the doorstep holding a bag of shopping from KRK, the Asian shop on Woodlands Road.

'Hi Mum, I was passing the shop after a house call, so got you some packets of *Bhel* and some Indian vegetables. These okras and *mooli* were fresh today,' she handed her the bag.

'Come in, good to see you. I'll make you a nice cup of masala tea.'

'Perfect, let me put the kettle on and you can put the

161

shopping away,' said Anita as they entered the kitchen.

I am blessed, thought Laxmi, such a sweet daughter, concerned, loving and such a help to her and Anand.

They sat sipping their tea and Laxmi said to her,

'We've all been invited to Parikh's house next Sunday, her seventieth birthday. Will you get me a nice card and a gift, Anita?'

'Is Aunty Prema seventy? I should know that, being her GP. I've just been so busy that it slipped my mind. Of course, I'll do that, Mum.' Anita smiled. 'Mum's chai, the best in the world,' she said, having another sip from her cup.

'Prema has seen Alok with Usma. I'm so worried; you know how the gossip will be like wildfire all over the community. And knowing Prema, she will add more masala to everything she says. Before we know it she'll have Alok married to her.'

'That big gob of Aunty PP. She never gives it a rest, does she?' Anita shook her head.

'There is more. The real reason she rang was to tell me that her cousin Renuka and her daughter Tina are here from India for her birthday. She wants Alok to meet this girl. I've seen her photographs before. She's very pretty. I think it might be good to introduce Alok to her.'

'Mum, you need to stop this.'

'So, you want him to continue ruining his life? Remember what happened to that Shreya and Omar? They are divorced, already. Their marriage didn't even last five years. She even converted to Islam. Now she's left high and dry. No one will marry her and the two little ones, flitting between their mum and dad. What kind of life is that? I don't want that for my son.'

'I don't know what to say. Not every mixed marriage ends in divorce, Mum.'

'Can you tell me how many 'mixed couples' as you say, are in Glasgow? And how many are successful?' challenged her mum, a bit of anger flashing in her eyes.

'Mum, let's not argue. We've not even met this Usma.'

'No, and I don't want to meet her. She has lured my son because he is a bright man with good earning potential. The sooner they split up the better.' Laxmi had tears in her eyes.

'Mum, why are you so upset?'

'Anita, you know little about the atrocities committed by the Muslims. I am not talking about Mughal invasion or old history, not even the Partition. Look what happened in Ayodhya, as recently as 1992, that schism between the two communities will never be reconciled. And Kashmir, the two religions can never live in peace.'

'Mum, what happens in India should not affect our lives here.' Anita tried to calm her down.

'How can you say that? My roots are still in Gujarat, just like you feel Bearsden is home, I can never forget my origins, the place where I grew up.'

'Why don't you think of Patel and his happiness? Is that not important?'

'You know how much your dad and I live literally for both of you. We scrimped and saved to send you both to Glasgow High. We sacrificed a lot to make sure that you had good lives and careers. We didn't stand in his way when he went for this unusual career, did we? We are glad he did very well and has been promoted. Is it too much to expect that Alok respects our wishes in this one important aspect of his life?' Laxmi wiped the tears that fell on her cheeks.

'Mum, please don't be so upset.' Anita gave her a tissue from the box on the table beside her.

'Now with Islamic fundamentalism rising all over the world, I don't want our grandchildren to face problems in their lives.'

'Mum! What grandchildren? That is a long time away. You don't even know if they'll have any children. Christ, they're not even married yet.'

Anita heard a sob from her mum.

'Mum, please don't cry. I think we need to talk to Alok about this and how strongly you feel about Usma.'

'It's no use I've tried to, he just storms out of the house.'

'I'll talk to Alok,' Anita said reluctantly. 'Mum, I'll convince him to come to Aunty Prema's birthday. May not be a good idea to tell him about meeting a prospective bride.'

Laxmi face brightened. There was some hope. Anita loved her brother. They had always been close. She might convince him of his impossible choice. She could explain to him the difficulties of a couple living together when the families are of totally different faiths.

They sat in the warm conservatory, talking some more. When Anita left, Laxmi went to the kitchen to cook the evening meal. As she kneaded the dough for the chapattis her mind was still troubled.

She remembered quoting Swami Vivekananda, the Indian guru, to Anita when she was a young girl.

"All differences in this world are of degree and not of a kind because oneness is the secret of everything."

These sages write wonderful guides to live a good life, but some of their sayings are harder to live by. Would she find the strength to see past the difference in Usma's faith, she wondered knowing well in her heart that would be an impossible task. She did love her only son. Maybe that love would want his happiness more than her own, she concluded.

Chapter 31

Big Mo lived in one of the flats in Drumchapel. It was a grim estate, one of the 'Big Four' housing estates along with Easterhouse, Castlemilk and greater Pollok, the post-war social housing schemes. Sink estates as they were referred to in the media. Academic studies abounded with 'The Glasgow Effect' listing the problems of poor housing, unemployment, drugs, and crime all contributing to the lowest longevity in people born in these areas. Drumchapel in the north of Glasgow was edged by prosperous Bearsden and Milngavie, leafy suburbs, the commuter land to the city with sandstone houses prices comparable to the capital city. It was shocking to find the juxtaposition of poverty and wealth just a few miles out of Glasgow.

He had lain in the bare, damp house for a whole day, oblivious to the world outside. The alcohol had seen to that. It was an effort to get up and get dressed. He splashed cold water on his face to wake him up a bit more. He twitched his nose, at the stale smell of booze and vomit. The torn mattress in the bedroom, the sofa that had seen better days, patches of it worn out where he had sat most of the time, looked threadbare. The lack of a carpet on the floor made the place cold. He hated the flat. Life had been something that he could barely cope with. His parents were heavy drinkers, he had little chance of escaping the generational, 'living aff the buroo, man,' lifestyle and his stepdad had leathered him for any tiny faults.

Big Mo's tummy rumbled. He headed to the kitchen. He filled the kettle, switched it on and opened the cupboard. One tin of tuna in brine and a bottle of malt vinegar stood forlornly on the dirty dust-covered shelf. There was one teabag left in the crumpled blue pack of Typhoo, the label showing fifty percent extra on a pack of forty teabags. He placed the teabag in the mug and poured in the boiled water. He drank it hot, without milk.

He had been sanctioned again. Benefits were stopped as he had not turned up at his appointments. This was the three-month sanction for failure to find a job. He was sure he'd get three days of emergency supplies at least to tide him over. He'd need to head to the food bank and take that long walk to Allardyce Road, near the big Sainsbury's.

The rain came on as he walked over to the food bank. A young mother with a pushchair and a toddler struggled to get the door open. Big Mo helped her.

'Thanks, lots of people here today,' she noted as she got inside. The noise in the small room came from the bustle of boxes getting lifted, a woman at the desk asking a young man questions as she filled in a form and a baby crying in a pram. Big Mo edged in and saw a couple packing food into boxes in the back room. He waited in the passageway. A young man carrying a filled bag approached him.

'Shona here?' Big Mo asked him.

'Wait here, I'll give her a shout,' said the man hurrying away with the bag.

Mo found a chair in the front room, his fat thighs and buttocks spilled over the hard shape of the plastic seat, his long legs uncomfortably folded under the seat. He put his head in his hands. A blinding headache, a sharp stab of pain across his forehead made him close his eyes for a minute. His tummy rumbled. He could eat a horse. He was starving. When was the last time he had eaten? Was it that packet of chips in the lane while having a blether with gallus Gazza, a couple of days ago? What were they arguing about? It was that football goal and both had had too much to drink and argued stupidly. Mo had thrown the packet of chips at his face and ran down the lane. Gazza had chased him, swearing. Mo closed his eyes again for a minute.

'Back again, Mo?' said a chirpy voice. Shona, stood beside him touching him lightly on his shoulder. He looked up at the brunette, in a dark blue apron over her colourful dress. Her kind face and smile made him feel better.

'I am desperate,' he said, 'sanctioned off again.' He handed her the old crumpled voucher that he had not used for a while.

'Mo, you need to take care of yourself.' He knew that she had a soft spot for him, the way she always found time to talk with him.

Shona filled out the form and asked him to sign it. She went to the backroom and told a young man to pack a box full of his three-day emergency supply of food and necessities.

She brought him a cup of tea and a hot cheese toastie, sat beside him and chatted. Mo listened to her talking about the effects of alcohol intake. Every time Shona spoke to him, he wished he could change his life radically. It never lasted more than a few minutes. He took his box of food, thanked her, and left the food bank. He walked along, glancing at the old Argos, the boxing club at the community centre. He wondered if any kids used the clubs there. These were activities that he took part in when he was very young. Just walking now was a strain, heaving his weight around did not help his knees that gave him a lot of pain. He sighed.

The last few days were clouded in his mind. That little trip into town had given him a few bob to enjoy. The lassie had just withdrawn money from the ATM and he had watched as she chatted on her phone with the handbag zip still open. It took only a few seconds. That wallet he had pickpocketed had a large sum of money in it. He counted it; the lassie had withdrawn three hundred quid.

The pub sign tempted him. He just went in for a good drink when he had bumped into Jake.

'Hey, Big Mo, hauf an a hauf, eh?' He slid on the barstool beside him. Jake's blue eyes didn't leave Mo's face.

'Aye, treatin myself,' Big Mo grinned as he downed the shot. The amber liquid felt warm as it slipped down his gullet.

'So how about celebrating big time eh?' Jake lowered his voice. 'I got the right gear.' He patted his jacket pocket.

In the toilet, Big Mo had parted with a fifty-pound note. He could never resist a bit of Jake's good stuff.

He had wandered away from the pub and bought a pair of trainers and a tee shirt. He was on his way home when he met gallus Gazza near the Drum.

Gazza was his pal from their school days. They were a constant bother for the teachers: truanting, cheeky or getting into fights. But school was irrelevant to them. Their lives outside, with their little gangs and fights, were much more interesting. Gazza had some football skills but earned his nickname after the famous incident that got him suspended permanently from school. Big Mo remembered clearly how they had all crowded around that morning, reading The Daily Record with the page flashing the headlines of Paul Gascoigne, the

English footballer being admitted to the Priory after drinking thirty-two shots of whisky.

They had a dare and the very next afternoon their gang of four got a couple of big bottles of Buckfast wine and some plastic cups. They egged each other on; counting the number of times they downed the cup. Gazza won by taking as many as thirty-two, perhaps it was more. They lost count as they had to rush back to school. Gazza was sick all over the maths classroom.

'Fucking hell, man,' he had said loudly as the teacher tried to help him, compounding his problems.

'Aye, he's oor Gazza,' shouted Mo when the teacher was screaming at the boy to go straight to the head teacher. Mo had to join him and the two were suspended, but Gazza left permanently as his anti-social behaviour had been just too disruptive that year. Vomiting all over the head teacher's study didn't help him either. He was expelled from the school.

The name stuck. The local authorities found Gazza another school to attend but he never turned up. Instead, he hung around with Big Mo and the gang. Their friendship was steadfast and even if they fell out with each other they always got back together. Drinking, the odd bet and living in the same estate kept their friendship going. Lately, however, Big Mo was fed up with the number of times he had bailed Gazza out. He owed him a lot of money, a couple of hundred at least.

'Oi, awright big man?' Gazza came over to Big Mo. 'Ah see they trainers look new. Come into money eh?'

'Naw just treated myself like,' said Big Mo, his face belying what he had just said. 'You still owe me money. When am I getting it back?'

'Chill, Mo, look you'll get it, man, you know me.'

'Aye, I know you awright. Look I need the money.

Yous need to pay me back. I'm skint.' Big Mo warned him, 'Can't do this again and again.'

'Nae bother. You know I'll pay you back. We're mates right?'

Gazza patted him on the shoulder.

'I mean it, I'm skint,' Big Mo emphasised.

'Aye so am I, but I'll get the money fur you, nae bother.'

They walked along to Big Mo's flat after paying a visit to the 'offy'. The drink loosened Big Mo's tongue. He showed him the drugs that Jake gave him. Before long they were having a wee session of drugs and drink. Big Mo thought that the feeling of getting high was indescribable. It was so easy to forget all his worries and elevate himself to the top of the world.

Big Mo relaxed and fell asleep on the sofa.

The next morning in the cool of the day, Big Mo realised that Gazza had taken all of the drugs and his wallet was empty too.

That thieving bastard, I'm going to kill him, he swore to himself.

*

Kara watched Alan arriving late again to the office. His eyes looked like he had not slept at all with dark rings around them. He had been looking unkempt these past few months. Surely he is not depressed because Patel was promoted, she thought. At the morning break, she sounded out Brian about this.

'Yep, I noticed too, but I've been keeping well away from him, you know that tongue of his, like a whiplash if he is not feeling okay,' replied Brian.

'Maybe he's ill?' Kara was thinking aloud. 'Should I just ask him?'

'Rather you than me mate,' said Brain a smile

gracing his lips.

Later that day Kara saw Alan at the water cooler.

'Growing a beard, keeping up with the new fashion craze, Alan?' Kara gave him her charming but cheeky smile.

'Oh, just piss off will ya,' said Alan.

'Charming, no need to bite, just being friendly.'

He watched the plastic cup getting filled.

'You okay?'

'Jesus Christ, what's with you?' he took the cup and walked away.

Kara rolled her eyes and left it at that.

Chapter 32

Patel looked at the 'To Do' list on his phone. He sighed as he noted that a large part of the morning would be devoted to an important meeting about a new recruitment drive for ethnic minorities. He opened the file on the meeting and the photocopy of the news headline on Shekh Bayoh was on the first page that he had added to the report. Shekh Bayoh had died after being arrested and restrained by police in Kirkcaldy in May. It was that dreadful death that urged Police Scotland to make more efforts to engage with ethnic minority and under-represented people in the community.

Patel realised the importance of this recruitment drive. He had already seen a tiny increase in the force. He was mentoring a young officer, Ram Singh, who wanted to become a detective. He was willing to do more to encourage women and ethnic minorities to join the Police Force. This was a useful exercise and yet at this moment with an unsolved murder, Patel wanted to be out with his team, devoting his time to more important tasks at hand. But working for communal harmony was too important a duty, he felt he could not ignore it. Martin had said that he could delegate this work to others in the Division but Patel decided against it.

He was glad he had come early to the station to check on what instructions he wanted to give at the morning briefing. Martin would handle the briefings.

He hurried away to the meeting

*

Patel sat at the top table, along with Chief Inspector Judi Miller, Mr. Ali, the representative of the Scottish Police Muslim Association and Mr. Anwar the director of the Coalition for Racial Equality and Rights. The meeting was held to discuss the new BAME recruitment drive by Police Scotland. The force wanted to address the under-representation of BAME people in the police, where they formed only one percent of the officers in Scotland though the census showed they formed four percent of the population. The drive was also to encourage more women who formed only twenty-nine percent of the Force to apply for jobs there.

Patel listened as Miller introduced all of them to the media representatives present and started with a new change in the policy. For the first time in more than two decades, a driving licence would no longer be a requirement for joining the force, recognising the fact that many who may want to join the force do not own one. This was widely welcomed by the community and civil rights groups. But there were some concerns. The Pakistani Welfare Trust brought up the issue of the increase in stop and search tactics that disproportionately impacted on those of Pakistani origin living in Scotland. It's not only the Metropolitan police in London that overuse it, their spokesman pointed out.

More issues were discussed. When immigrants who had been working as policemen in their country of origin applied to join Police Scotland their qualifications were to be taken into account and assessed.

Patel gave a short presentation of how much progress there was in his own division in trying to recruit new members from the ethnic minorities and women to the force. He had done some research and noted that a simple change of dress code would make a difference. The Sikhs in the force were allowed to wear a turban. He quoted that over eighty thousand turban-wearing Sikh soldiers had died in the world wars for Britain. Sikhs were even allowed to ride motorbikes without wearing crash helmets as it was mandatory for men following the Sikh religion to wear the turban. He argued for hijabs for Muslim women to encourage more of them to join. This was well received. He added that he understood that any change had to go through a process of wide discussion before it is implemented. Patel also came up with more training to tackle racism not just with young recruits but with serving officers whose years of service sometimes made them unaware of their deeply entrenched attitudes whether it was on racism, sexism, or LGBT issues. He explained how it was incumbent upon each officer to not only be aware but raise the issue if they witnessed such attitudes amongst their colleagues. He set out an action plan on how to deal with such incidents at each station.

The meeting ended with a valid point raised by the director of the CRER. That this meeting should not end up as mere PR exercise and that the problem was not only recruitment but also retention. Decisions were made to engage more with ethnic communities through the mosque and other services used by the ethnic minorities.

These were useful meetings and Patel wanted to spend time putting some of these initiatives into action in his own Division. To tackle Alan's racist behaviour would be a good start. He had also been given a CV of a young woman officer, a Linda Chan who had passed her exams and wanted to be trained as a detective. He volunteered to arrange a work shadowing programme for her at Partick.

That evening Usma and Patel shared some ideas on how to tackle racism. Usma came up with an idea of making a short illustrated booklet for school visits. That would encourage all ethnicities and genders to join Police Scotland.

Chapter 33

The two police patrol officers were doing their evening shift. Sitting in the car, beside the gates of Kelvingrove Park and chatting quietly about their lives. Nothing much happens in the middle of the week, just the usual drunks, the odd dog walker or people walking home after a night shift. Constable Ben Strachan yawned loudly. His face was suffused with boredom. He opened the door and let the cold August air in.

'I need a piss, man,' he said to Constable Colin Pacitti.

They locked the car and walked over to the toilets. Trees flailed around in the strong wind, and the cool air stung their eyes after sitting in the warm car for such a long time. Condoms were strewn across the entrance to the men's toilet. A pungent smell of weed and urine hung about in the air. Some of the trees had started to shed their leaves. Their shoes crunched the dead leaves, making a strange noise in the still of the night.

'I see that the druggies have had a busy evening,' Ben joked to his pal.

Colin waited outside. He did not want to go into the toilets. He walked around the back of the toilets and wandered down a few yards away from the smell. As he walked away from the toilets, he shivered at the cold that seeped through his uniform. In the darkness, he could make out a man lying prone, on his side. Something was not right. Colin took out his torch and neared the man, to help him to his feet. As soon as he was close enough, he knew that there was something wrong. He checked the pulse, by placing his hand under the hollow of his neck. He could not discern anything. He recoiled, turned, and looked around for his friend. Was it really a lifeless body that lay there? As a young constable he had not seen many dead bodies. He was relieved to hear Ben calling out for him.

Colin spoke on his police radio and asked for an ambulance. At that moment Ben came striding over from the toilet, saw the man on the ground and asked,

'Another drunk?'

Colin filled him in, 'No, not legless after a drink. I think we have a body here.' Ben called the local police station. The dark crimson patterns near the body were highlighted as the torch lit up the scene of the crime.

Ben and Colin put the blue and white tape around the scene and secured the area quickly. They waited five minutes observing and noting anything that would be of use. Then Ben decided to look around the place to search for any signs of movement or people close by. Colin stayed beside the body. Before Ben could search the place properly, the silence of the night was shattered by the arrival of the crime officers. A couple of cars arrived and a Scene of Crime manager took over.

Patel and McKay arrived later with grim faces. The force photographer clicked away as Patel drew near. Dr Jamieson, the forensic pathologist, had just finished his initial examination and declared him dead.

'Male, stabbed several times in the chest. Died of bleeding. Must have been lying dead for a few hours at least. Post-mortem for more.' Jamieson wiped his hands on a tissue and took off his surgical mask. He looked haggard and tired, woken up at dawn, the hardest time for him to get up and be alert for such work.

Patel's brows furrowed. Colin heard him tell Joe, 'Fuck, a second murder already.'

*

Patel picked up the newspaper. The tabloids were also brought to his desk as the murders were highlighted as human interest stories. He read the newspaper, slowly sipping his morning coffee.

Second Murder in Kelvingrove Park!

The body of a young white male in his twenties, stabbed to death was found in the Kelvingrove Park early this morning. Is it related to the last murder? Only a few weeks ago a young Asian woman was stabbed to death in the park. The police are no further forward with that investigation. Now this young man has died. There are rumours that an Asian gang and some white youths clashed before the Mela, but this was brushed aside by the police. They claimed that it was quelled within minutes and that there was no trouble later at the Mela. Could this be a revenge attack? Was it a racist killing?

Patel sipped his coffee slowly. Two murders in the West End, the tabloid newspapers and the media were having a field day, he thought to himself, as he turned the pages to read up more on page eleven. The story of the murder was splashed out, with pictures of Nadia's murder appearing too. The paper seemed to have no qualms in linking the two or speculating about things.

There was also the ugly background to the racist gang warfare in Glasgow. His coffee had gone cold. He put the mug down. He wanted to turn away from the page, yet he was drawn to it. Some old cases were referred to in the article, facts that all of Glasgow remembered were in front of him in black and white.

178

He absorbed the words. The Southside of the city had seen an eruption of racist gang warfare after a young schoolboy was stabbed to death by a gang of Pakistani men. The dreadful details were dredged up once more. Why were they bringing it all back? Anything to sell newspapers, thought Patel, and then he saw his name mentioned in the papers.

The new DI Patel in charge is Asian. Has that triggered more racist's gang warfare? questioned the newspaper. He had no wish to read anymore. He closed the newspaper and took the mug of cold coffee, emptied the coffee in the sink. The mug hit the side and the handle broke off.

His mobile pinged. It was a text from Martin: *See me first thing.*

The piece of china lay there on the stainless-steel sink almost mocking him.

Nerves? There was enough stress in his life.

At the station, he walked over to second murder's incident room. It was a hive of activity, all related to the murder of the white male. He checked on the notes on the white board, gave a few instructions to the team and went back to his room and read all the reports that Joe had collated for him.

Two murders within a space of a few months had happened on his watch. Nadia and a white male? He had to find the killers of both and had to do it soon.

Chapter 34

The post-mortem report on Paul Graham showed that he had died of multiple wounds to his upper torso. The man himself was a lean drug-addict with poor health. His chronological age was thirty, but his body had seen so much abuse that he had aged biologically by another ten years.

Patel made sure that the team received the basic information in the report.

Paul Graham, aged thirty, unemployed and living at 35, Dewar Street, Drumchapel. He was not married but had a couple of children from two different women. He was known to police for petty crime and had once been imprisoned for possession of Class A drugs.

Patel was familiar with Kelvingrove Park being used by drug users and some male prostitutes. Graham was far away from his usual haunt of Drummy as they all referred to that estate just outside Glasgow. Was he meeting someone?

Kara, Brian, and Joe walked into DI Patel's office.

'Sir, we've done the door-to-door for Paul Graham, aka Gazza. Not much from any of the neighbours.'

'Those folk clam up as soon as you say you're with the Police, Boss' added Brian.

'He was usually seen around with that Big Mo,' Kara added.

'Did you check on the new trainers and Rangers top that he had on?'

'Sir, Gazza had been in Sports Direct in Sauchiehall

Street and bought the items just that morning. Cash purchases said the salesgirl, sir' said Brian.

'We need to bring Big Mo in for questioning.'

'Any others, like a wife or partner, close family that may have some information on Paul Graham?' asked Patel.

'We checked, sir. He had two partners and has kids by them. But he's not been living with either mother of his kids, just visits them occasionally.'

'Joe, pick up one of his partners and arrange for her to formally identify the body. And bring Big Mo in.'

The team hurried away.

A new board sat beside the one dedicated to Nadia, as both murders happened in the park. A photo of Gazza's body was put on the new board, along with a photo from his last conviction for possession of drugs. That was a few years ago. A younger, fitter looking Gazza looked incongruous beside a photo of the old emaciated looking corpse. The name of his partners had been added by Kara, a fact that Patel noted. She was hard working, and he was pleased to have her, McKay, and Duffy on his team. All young and working hard to assure themselves of a promising future in the force. Yes, he was lucky to have this good team around him. They were not shirkers like Alan who spent more time criticising others. Or like the older John waiting for retirement and who did as little as possible.

So apart from both murders taking place in the park, both by knife, late at night, were there any connections? Patel wondered. A young Asian mother and an unemployed man who had some drug problems. Unlikely to be a connection but could this be a revenge murder by some Asian thugs.

The media would have a field day if that was the case. Patel shook his head and set about meticulously organising the similarities and differences in the cases by re-reading the reports and jotting down essential information. As SIO for both cases, he needed to make sure both murders were given the same importance.

*

Patel called a team meeting. Nadia's murder was a priority case, and they were no further forward. Patel's knitted brow and stern look did not relax when he entered the room. He walked over to his place in front of the room. John and Alan were talking. Alan was making some lewd remark about some woman on his phone. Patel shushed the chatty pair and called the meeting to order. All thirty faces looked up.

'We need to find Nadia's murderer. Let's go over the whole case step by step. Joe, you can help me.'

'Yes, sir,' Joe said.

'We have ruled out Salim, her husband, and Malcolm, her friend, the last one to see her alive. I want each and every one of you to trawl through all the notes, CCTV tapes, interviews and reports and see if there is anything that we have missed.' Patel glanced over to as he heard a short, muffled laugh. It was from Alan.

Alan continued looking at the phone. Patel saw him nudge John beside him, pointing the phone at him. John looked away.

Patel strode over to him and took the phone out of his hand.

'Alan! Stop it right now.'

'Or what?' Alan stood up and smirked.

The tension in the room was palpable.

'Sit down. I'll talk to you later,' said Patel, his voice quiet but firm. It took all his effort not to push him back down on his chair.

Alan stood defiant; his face close to Patel's. He grabbed the phone from Patel's hand.

The nerve on Patel's temple twitched.

'I'm ordering you. I'll see you in my room, right now, Alan. Joe, you take over,' said Patel and stormed out of the room.

Alan stood still for a moment, and then headed towards the door.

'Fuckin hell! I'll get him for this.' he muttered and slammed the door as he went out.

A ripple of murmurs went around the room.

*

Patel stood looking out of the window in his office. He took a few moments to calm down.

Alan breezed in still with that defiant look in his face and stood with his arms akimbo.

'Don't you dare behave like that, ever,' said Patel. 'I'm the SIO, this is my investigation and when I give orders you follow it to the letter. I'm prepared to take it all the way for your dismissal.'

'You treat me like shit,' Alan replied. 'You're losing it, Patel. None of this university fast track promotion makes you better than me.' Alan's face turned a dark red, anger evident in his eyes.

'Right, if that's the way you want it; this will be your dismissal. Yeah, that's why you are still a DS. Get real, Alan, behave. If you don't toe the line, I'll just have to treat this as insubordination. I'll let Martin know later today.'

'Like I care,' retorted Alan, the sweat was pouring down his face and he dabbed at it with a tissue.

'You want to lose your job, Alan?' Patel's voice was steely.

There was a pause, the two men glared at each other.

'These are murder investigations; I need everyone to take it seriously and get them solved as soon as possible. I'll not stand for any more insolence. Martin and the whole team have witnessed your behaviour in that room. You can make it easy for yourself.' Patel laid it on thick. His expression brooked no argument.

Alan looked up at Patel, mouth drooping, shoulders slouching, his arms falling to his side.

'I've been working my backside off for this case, too. I do the work and others get credit. You'll get the bloody kudos at the end.'

Alan's voice was lower. 'It's not easy at home,' Alan's shoulders slumped, and he tried to suppress a sob.

Patel looked at Alan properly for the first time this morning. What Joe and others had been commenting about was right, Alan looked tired, his eyes were ringed with dark circles, looked like he needed a shave, the stubble flecked with grey made him look older than his forty years.

'Why don't you sit down, Alan? I have noticed that you're looking more tired and arriving late in the mornings. Is everything all right at home?'

Alan sat down; his legs were shaking.

'No, I am genuinely worried about you. That kid of yours, is she doing okay?'

'Why? Why do you ask me that now?' His aggressive tone took Patel aback.

'What's up?' Patel's voice was gentle.

Alan shrugged but looked down and mumbled.

'I've not been sleeping well. That baby of hers keeps me up. Never bloody stops crying.'

'Tracey has a baby? I thought she was just a teenager?' Patel was genuinely puzzled.

'That useless boyfriend got her pregnant and dumped her, didn't he? Okay gloat, if you want, Patel,

184

she's a mum at sixteen. Oh, just leave me alone.' Alan's eyes blazed with anger for a minute and then tears glistened at the corners. He looked down and held his head with both hands, Patel saw his shoulders heave, and Alan wiped his tears quickly with the back of his shirt sleeve.

Patel kept quiet for a minute.

'Alan,' he said softly, 'I didn't know about your problem why didn't you tell me? I know we are short-staffed, but you should get time off if you need it. I'll have a word with Martin.'

'No, don't bother. I'll sort it.' Alan dabbed at his eyes with a tissue.

'There you go again. This won't look good if you get a black mark on your CV. Promotion prospects will fly out the window. Think yourself lucky that I may give you a chance again.'

There was silence again.

'Patel, I'm sorry. It's just too much you know ...' Alan stood up.

'I understand, Alan. Just come to me if you need anything.' Patel said rising from his chair. 'And look, don't ever talk to me like that in front of my team again, Alan.'

'You're not going to give that written notice are you, Patel? I need this job.' his voice was pleading.

Patel did not reply.

Alan walked out quietly from the office. Martin was walking past and stopped him in his tracks.

'Step into my office, Alan,' he ordered.

Martin's office looked very tidy. This DCI was more organised than the present Super. The desk was clear, no sign of the various pieces of papers and stationery that used to be scattered about in Arnott's days.

'Alan, your behaviour is unacceptable. I have been

watching you. Since Patel's promotion to DI, he has only had hassle from you. I know at work we do not always get along with everyone, but this is not on. Do you know Patel could have charged you with racist behaviour on numerous occasions? He has been conducting himself well. I can't say the same about you. That display today was beyond reproach. I'm going to have a word with Patel just now. I want you to know that I'm certainly not happy at all with you.'

Martin did not mince his words.

Alan had no quick repartee this time. He stood there quietly; his pride battered. He apologised and explained the stresses he was going through.

'Sir, I promise I'll change my behaviour from today. This job is too important to me; I can't afford to lose it. I'm just finding life hard to cope with at the moment,' he pleaded.

Martin looked at him and said. 'You'll hear from me later today, Alan. You may go now.'

A dejected Alan walked out slowly. He worried about the applications he had sent away for DI posts and which senior officer he could use for a referee. Was that his career over with? he wondered.

At the canteen at lunchtime, Alan felt all eyes on him. The clatter of cutlery sounded louder than the usual banter that he normally heard. He picked up his tray filled it with his food and sat beside John who had accompanied him. Joe and the other team members looked towards him from their tables. Alan's appetite disappeared rather quickly. He left the canteen and went out for a walk.

Chapter 35

July 20th

Brian and Kara made their way to Alsatian Avenue, in Drumchapel. A ferocious-looking pit bull was tethered and chained to a tree stump, not unusual for that area. Kara noted the peeling paint on the door and the broken front step revealing the brickwork under the concrete.

'Got the wrong breed, not an Alsatian,' Brian joked, pointing to the dog.

They opened the communal door that was left unlocked, walked over to number 1A and knocked on the ground floor flat door.

A baby crying and the mother shouting at another child could be heard from a slightly open window, with a net curtain that was grey.

A short woman with bleached blonde hair tied in a ponytail opened the door. She held a snivelling baby in her arms. The baby coughed as she looked at the pair on her doorstep.

'What do youse want?'

Kara showed her warrant card,

'Janette McCafferty? I'm DS Johnson and this is my colleague DS Duffy here to see you about Paul Graham, Gazza'

'Nothing to do with me.' Janette was about to shut the door on them.

'He's dead.' Brian said in a low voice.

'What?' Her face turned pale. The baby howled. She

187

patted it and Kara saw a wee boy of about three come from inside and cling on to her leg.

'We need to talk to you,' said Kara.

'Come in,' she said reluctantly.

The house was a mess, kid's toys lying about, there was an old grey settee with a blanket and some kids clothes piled high on it. Plastic kid's plates with dried food on them were strewn about. Holly Willoughby and Phillip Schofield on This Morning were talking about Celebrity Big Brother and the latest eviction of one of the inmates.

Janette gave the wee boy a biscuit and she put a dummy that was lying on the pile of clothes into the baby's mouth.

'Look,' she said, 'I've not seen Gazza for a few months now. We've split up. I want nothing to do with him.'

'I understand,' said Kara. 'We just need you to come and identify his body. We can take you right away and there will be Family Liaison Officers, to look after the kids. Won't take long, I can promise you that.'

Janette looked distraught, but she nodded, took the kids, pulled on her tracksuit, and changed her slippers into a pair of trainers and went to the kitchen to get a bottle for the baby. As the young woman was busy, Kara and Brian looked around the room. Brian picked up a child's teddy bear that was behind the settee, may have lain there for some time, dusty to touch. The head fall off and inside was a stash of drugs. Brian took the teddy and put it carefully in a plastic bag and took it to the car while Janette got ready.

Soon they set out to the Queen Elizabeth hospital mortuary. She identified the body as her ex-partner Paul Graham, the father of one of her children.

Chapter 36

Hanif was confused. Some of the students behaved like Nadia, who had been murdered. His forehead creased into a frown as he thought of her. How many times had he seen her dressed inappropriately and laughing and sitting close to that same male colleague? A wife, and mother already divorced once and she had still behaved like the goris. He thought of the evening playing an Xbox game with the boy. His heart heaved a sigh. He felt deep sympathy for Mansur and Salim. Nadia was his cousin after all. Had he been too harsh with her? He started having doubts about his own ideas.

That talk with Patel had unsettled him. Why was Uncle Ali Hassan with him? Why do our own people let us down? Should Uncle Ali not be teaching our women how to behave and be modest or was it Hanif that was not moving with the times. He had had these thoughts recently. Was he getting brainwashed as some said? Seeds of doubts started spreading in his mind, but he brushed them aside, though he felt more confused now since Nadia's murder.

The Open Day activities organised by GUMSA were good. The Arabian Tea nights for girls and boys included their own ten pin bowling night. Some were joining in with the other lot, the kaffirs, the non-Muslims, drinking and high jinks. It made him angry. He wished he could make them see sense.

Just walking all along Byres Road, watching some of the antics of the girls near the Hillhead Subway, made him cringe. On University Avenue near the Union, he saw some walking out late, the new intake so obvious with their young expectant faces, holding the condoms given in their packs and laughing. Why are such intelligent young people leaning towards an alien culture? Why doesn't the madrassa, the mosque, even their parents instil more good values, he thought to himself. He felt confused again. Was he the one who was wrong? Should he let go of these old conservative ideas and enjoy life like the others? He felt a headache coming on.

He went home, shut himself in his bedroom, took some paracetamol, and lay down on his bed. Later, he spent more time studying and got through some work which he had neglected.

Chapter 37

An early morning run on her days off was always a routine that Usma enjoyed. She checked her sweatbands on her wrist, inserted the iPod earbuds in her ears, and set off. The Milngavie reservoir just a few miles from home was her favourite place for a jog. It was so refreshing to run on flat ground, away from busy streets and the scenery was spectacular at any time of the year.

The run around the reservoir gave her views of Glasgow city. On a clear day, one could see way into the distance. The planes taking off and landing also gave a pleasing sight of the white plume of flight contrails in the blue skies above. A riot of colour with rhododendrons in the summer and the sylvan woods with reds, gold and green in autumn, took her breath away. Usma stood looking at the hills to her left, the shades of green and brown against the blue sky like a landscape painting, something to savour. The scenery around the Campsie Fells this morning lifted her spirits. The autumn season was so short in Glasgow and was something she and Patel both looked forward to.

Alok had texted her early again, and she knew that the murder investigations would take more and more of his time. He had shared a few details of the case that he felt she could help with. He even asked if her family would know anything about Nadia's family. Usma seldom paid attention to her mum's tales of the young men and women she recounted when she went to the house. She vaguely remembered the name when her mum had chatted about young women in the community, but was not sure if that was the same, Nadia. Also, it was years ago when Nadia had married Salim, her mum had mentioned about a young, divorced woman. She had paid scant attention to it.

Mum and the 'aunties' often assembled either for a sewing session or to gossip after a visit to the mosques on Fridays. Pakoras and samosas were consumed in large quantities and with ample cups of tea, and the tongues wagged with juicy bits of gossip. Conversations also ranged from fashion, the price of things, to Bollywood films, serials, trips en-masse to a new film released with Shah Rukh Khan or one of the famous Bollywood stars. The main thing was the way they shared every little morsel of their family problems. Usma could never understand why such personal details should be aired. Was this because they had no extended families around or was it a hangover from meeting at the village wells or river, she wondered, getting the low down on all that happened in the community.

Just last week she had a run-in with her mum about this. She had walked into one of these sessions and one of the women, Bushara, immediately got up, hugged her and said loudly, 'Usma, such a pretty girl, still not married?'

Usma blushed, got away from her hug, and smiled sweetly and tried to escape to the kitchen.

Her mum said, 'What can I do? She is stubborn, refuses to see any of the boys we want to introduce to her.'

Bushara said 'Now you are in luck, my nephew is coming to Glasgow next week, from London. He's a big doctor there. Shall I bring him here next Sunday?'

Usma's mum said, 'Of course that will be nice.'

As soon as the women left Usma said quietly, 'Mum, I am working next Sunday. You know why I will not meet anyone. You know about Alok ...' before she could finish her mum put her hands over her ears and shook her head,

'*Inshallah*, such horrible words. What sin have I committed that she says such words?' she wailed touching a Koran that was on the mantelpiece.

'Mum, I can't even talk to you,' shouted Usma and stormed out of the house.

Usma resented such flagrant displays of disloyalty to one's own family. What did these women get from sharing such intimate details? From the behaviour of young girls in each family, how they dressed, disrespected parents, marriage plans or lack of them, to details of their own money problems, what each person earned and what they spent it on. Was this some kind of therapy session, vocalising issues that were so close to their heart, she wondered. Usma had often asked her mum to abstain from such conversations, and her mum had chided her, saying children never understood how much being close to one's own community meant to their mothers and aunts.

Usma took a deep breath. Alok would be busy settling into his work routine, she told herself. She paused for a while on the run, stretching as she took in the view, ran on the spot, and resumed the run, setting a good pace. After stretches she felt that the early morning sun was blessing her with its kind rays. She ran ahead, skirting around an old brown and white bulldog, its tongue hanging out of its ridiculous face (Usma never liked the pug ugly face of bulldogs) that was sniffing the path. An old man stood beside it, waiting patiently for the dog to follow him. He greeted her with a 'Smashing morning, eh?'

She nodded a 'yes' and moved on. She was glad that she was in the same police division as Alok. Maybe she could help him with the case. How would she cope if someone close to her was suddenly taken away? Then she shook off such morbid thoughts. It was an advantage that not many people knew of their relationship. A DI with a rookie would get the tongues wagging. It was fraught enough with the pressure put by the two families not accepting their relationship at all.

After the run she stopped by her car, towelling herself dry. A swig of sports drink and she was good to go and relax on her day off. She would meet her friend later on, early in the evening after Ruby had finished work at around five. They had been friends since primary school. They were close, had a good laugh when they went out and sometimes a heart to heart was on the cards. Ruby was going through some rough times with her partner, Roy, who had been made redundant recently.

Usma drove back to her flat. She had her housework to catch up on, which she had been putting off for a while.

Adele's new song, Hello, was belting out on the radio. Usma sang along with the track. Radio Clyde's George Bowie played a whole lot of her favourites. She enjoyed listening to the radio out loud and sang along with music that she was familiar with. The ironing table was already set up. She ironed her work uniform first and hung it up in the wardrobe. Then she ironed her T-shirts and dresses. She had just finished them and had put them in neat piles to take to the wardrobe when the phone rang.

'Hi honey,' Patel whispered. 'Love you' then he

changed his voice to a normal tone and resumed. 'I'm sorry but I need a favour from you. Could you run over to my flat and get something for me please? There's a piece of paper by the bedside table? I must have left it last night'

'Sure, I'll call you back soon,' she said.

She was in his flat in ten minutes. She ran up the stairs and took the paper and glanced at it and called him. 'Got it,' she said.

'Could you please read out the mobile number that I'd made a note of?

She read out the number, then hesitated and said,

'I recognise the number. It is my friend Shabnam's.

'Who? Have I met her before if she is one of your friends?' asked Patel. He was not sure if he heard her right.

'No, she is a family friend.'

'Why didn't you tell me you knew her?'

'You never asked. She's not involved in Nadia's case is she?'

'Well, she is the interpreter at Nadia's mum's old folk's home, and as always we follow all the leads. How well do you know her?'

'Not been in touch with her for ages, but I could text and ask to meet her. Would that be okay though, especially if you lot are going to interview her?'

'Kara has met with her at the old folk's home. Mrs. Hussain mentioned the first husband Roger, I wondered if Shabnam could find anything more from her when her mind is a bit clearer. So, maybe you'll be able to get some more information from her. Let me call you back, something has come up.'

'Yes, Joe?' said Patel and rang off.

The conversation with Patel had unsettled her. She called the number straight away.

She was so relieved that they could chat like old times. The phone call rekindled their old friendship.

Usma wasted no time. 'Hey, how about we grab lunch and a catch up? It's my day off.'

'That would be nice, meet you at Beanscene at Shawlands at one.' Shabnam replied.

Lunchtime arrived soon enough. Usma drove over to the Southside and waited for Shabnam.

After exchanging a few niceties and eating their salads, Usma broached the subject.

'That was awful, that murder of Nadia Ahmad.'

'Yes, the talk of all our Asian community,' said Shabnam. 'Her poor mum is at the place where I work. I feel for her, her only child.'

'How is she coping?' asked Usma.

'Well, she has her moments of clarity then forgets all about her. A poor gentle soul.'

'Can you do me a favour, Shabnam? If she mentions Roger, Nadia's first husband, and anything about his whereabouts, could you tell me immediately?'

'Why? What is it to you? Are you part of the investigating team? I thought you were still a uniform policewoman.'

'Yes, I am still a constable, Shabnam, but as an Asian woman, I'd like to help my colleagues solve this case. Surely you understand, we can't have the man who murdered her still walking around freely. What if he kills another Asian woman?'

'I know it is a bit scary. Mrs. Hussain chats about Nadia. All I remember her saying was that Roger drank a lot. Does that help?'

'Most men here drink, don't they? The pubs keep the economy going. We don't touch the stuff, of course. You do remember that fun time in my bedroom when we were thirteen,' Usma joked and winked at her.

'Wasn't that a scream! How silly were we?' said Shabnam. They both laughed as they thought of the bottle of cider that they had sneaked and sipped as their parents had chatted downstairs. Alcohol was a taboo subject as they were growing up.

'Right, if you get anything at all from Mrs. Hussain on Nadia and her family that may be relevant, will you text me please?' Usma asked her.

'I will. I know that there are photograph albums in Mrs. Hussain's cupboard. I'll take them out and see if she can remember anything. I do hope you lot find the murderer and soon,' said Shabnam.

As Usma drove home she wondered about the photo albums. Would they have photos of any other person in Nadia's life who could be the murderer? More importantly, would it help Alok?

Chapter 38

Amina, the Muslim Resource Centre, was in Eastwood Avenue in the Southside of Glasgow, near Pollokshaws Road. It was a hive of activity. Both Kara and Brian were surprised at the range of help offered to Muslim women. The leaflets spread on the table in the front room were engaging, colourful and well produced. The receptionist gave a copy of each to Brian. The list ranged from employability, befriending, refugee support and help for women suffering from domestic violence and even friendship groups. He glanced at them as they waited.

Rabia, a pleasant young woman dressed in a pretty light orange *salwar*, came into the reception area, introduced herself, and welcomed them into her office. She wore a dark blue scarf on her head. The colourful scarf framed her pretty features, her high cheekbones, dark brown eyes expertly tinged with kohl and her flawless skin made up to look very natural, Kara noticed.

'We need some information on one of your volunteers, Nadia Ahma ...' Kara began.

'Yes, I saw the news; I can't believe it, Nadia murdered!' Rabia the young lady exclaimed. 'Nadia helped one of our clients, she was extremely good.'

'Could you tell us a bit more about Nadia?' asked Kara.

'Nadia came often to help ... well, I'm not sure I can tell you my client's name. We try and find places at refuges for the clients, often far away from their homes. This woman from the east coast has a young child and had to flee from her husband who abused her for years. He was a violent man. Oh my god, don't tell me he might have killed Nadia?' Rabia looked aghast as she slowly realised that possibility.

'We need details of all the people involved, this is a murder inquiry, you need to tell us what you know,' Brian added.

Rabia began cautiously. 'Nadia had been working for a while with us then took time off when she had her wee boy, Mansur. She came back to help us and wanted to work with this client as she had a young boy like Mansur...' She noted Kara's raised eyebrows, then continued, 'well, her name is Nafisa and her husband, Kasim, is a real thug. We keep all the clients' information really secure so he had little access to her but because of the child, the court did give him supervised access to his son, once a month in a place chosen by social workers. Nafisa wanted to be near her child and though she need not have gone, the social worker would have taken the child, she insisted. Nadia volunteered to accompany her when he visited. Kasim would have seen only the child and the social worker.'

'Well, you know how ruthless these men are. He may have seen both Nafisa and Nadia. I'd like to have his address, phone number and work details. You'll have them I'm sure. I also need some information on the dates and how many times Nadia was with them when he met his son. You must have a log, right?'

'I have his mobile number.' Rabia pulled out a file and checked on the information on Kasim and Nafisa. 'The last date she was with them was fairly recent, June sixteenth.'

'Oh, I remember now Nadia saying that she had

been accosted by Kasim at the car park on the last day, June sixteenth when Nafisa, the social worker Alice, and Nadia had stopped at McDonald's for a meal. Alice was leaving for her summer break and wanted to leave early, she had just driven away quickly after the meeting. Nadia and Nafisa lingered on enjoying their food. He must have followed them to McDonald's. Nadia had given him a piece of her mind when he pleaded with Nafisa and asked her to come back and live with him.'

'Thanks, Rabia. Did Nadia say anything about Kasim? Or did she mention his behaviour towards Nafisa?' Kara asked as she noted down the details.

'Yes, we always had a chat after the meetings. Both women said that he was an unsavoury character, very rude and always made some derogatory remarks about women. The only good thing about him was that he adored his son. Nadia was always confident and gave him a piece of her mind when he said anything unpleasant to her or Nafisa. She was very protective of her. Kasim resented Nadia's presence, or at least that's what she said to me.' Rabia added.

'Did Kasim ever hassle Nadia in any way? Did she complain to you about his behaviour towards her?'

'She did tell me that he had followed her once from the Indian shop to her car and warned her 'to stop feeding his wife's mind with poison'. She thought it was a chance encounter, gave him a mouthful and told him to get lost. She was not bothered about him, felt that she could always give as good as she got. A second time was when she was at the mosque and they were collecting clothes for Syrian children. He came with a van to collect the parcels; she said he waited for her in the car park. She took out her mobile and said she'd call the police. He left then.'

'That is good to know, Rabia, we may talk to you again if we need more information,' said Kara.

They thanked her and left the office.

'I'm sure the boss would want to talk to this Kasim, perhaps even to Nafisa,' said Kara as she opened the car door.

On their drive back to the station, Brian read out the leaflets he had picked up: 'Our vision is to provide an inclusive and safe society where Muslim women of all backgrounds can fulfil their potential and participate fully. They seem to have a lot of useful activities too.' Brian was quite taken on with all the information.

'You know I've lived in Glasgow for so long I knew all about the Women's Aid but never knew that there was a separate one for Muslim women,' Kara said, 'I'm learning a lot more about our Asian people.'

At the office, Patel asked Kara and Brian to bring in Kasim for questioning as soon as possible.

Chapter 39

Later that day, Joe and Patel were in interview room three with Big Mo.

'Look,' he protested, 'I've told you all I know.'

DI Patel fixed his steely brown eyes on him. Big Mo squirmed in his chair.

'Mr. Morrison,' DI Patel said, his voice firm and low, 'where were you between ten and twelve p.m. on August fifteenth?'

'Don't know. Probably at home, asleep.'

'What were you doing with Mr. Graham at the toilets at midnight on August fifteenth? We checked the CCTV footage and you were seen together near the park on that night.'

'Naw, It wisnae me.'

'So, you were not in the park with Mr. Graham.'

'I told youse, naw.' Big Mo was sweating profusely.

'So maybe we have a double murderer in our hands, both victims killed in the same park and stabbed to death. Mr. Morrison was maybe even seen at both the scenes of crime,' said Patel to Joe as an aside.

There was a chilled silence in the room. Big Mo was not expecting to be blamed for Nadia's murder. He panicked.

'No, no,' he protested, 'I didnae touch that woman, just took that necklace, swear to God.'

'Well, now there is a confession, perhaps you stabbed her to get the necklace.'

'Naw, no way man, it fell aff her neck, I was standing

beside her and I just slipped it in my pocket.'

'Where is the necklace now?'

'That Romanian, he … he gave me good dosh for it. Nae idea what he done with it.' Big Mo was trembling. He sipped some water from the plastic cup and sweat collected on his forehead and ran down his right cheek.

'Then Paul Graham and you squabbled over the money and you killed him? We have enough evidence Mr. Morrison, your DNA, a strand of your hair was on Paul Graham's body. Time to tell the truth!' DI Patel's voice sounded like he meant business. It made Big Mo turn away.

His big shoulders heaved. Sobs arose in his throat, he tried to stifle them. His head hung down low.

'No, youse have got it all wrang,' he whimpered. 'Gazza is my pal.'

'No point denying it, Mr. Morrison,' Joe said.

There was a knock on the door. Kara stood outside as Joe answered the door and said to him, that they had found the murder weapon, a knife with Big Mo's fingerprints all over it. It was in one of the toilet bins at the park.

Joe came back in and whispered to Patel.

'Let's take a break,' he said to Big Mo.

They walked out of the room.

At his office Patel was informed that forensics had matched the DNA on the knife with Big Mo's, as his prints were already on their data base.

Patel and Joe came back to the interview room after a fifteen-minute break. Big Mo was holding a cup of coffee.

'Let's resume our interview,' said Patel making sure the video was switched on by Joe.

'So, tell us about the drugs that you and Mr. Graham used.'

Big Mo looked up at Patel. He started to shake; the colour drained from his face.

'Look I never murdered anyone, just the drugs get me all confused like.'

'Mr. Morrison, I'm losing my patience here. We have enough evidence to charge you with the murder of Paul Graham. How much money or drugs did Mr. Graham steal from you, eh?'

'He was my best friend,' Big Mo whispered.

'Sometimes best mates fall out, don't they?' said Joe.

'So, you and Mr. Graham were at the park and you confronted him about the money and drugs he stole from you, right? Unless of course, there is something more sinister?' Patel insisted.

'Whit, whit dae you mean?' Big Mo looked at Patel.

'You tell me, Mr. Morrison. This is not looking good for you anymore. We've found the murder weapon and guess whose fingerprints are all over it?' Patel's eyes bored into him.

'Naw, naw wisnae me,' Big Mo protested.

'Janette, Mr. Graham's ex-partner, and his two young children are without a father now,' Patel said this softly.

Big Mo's shoulders heaved.

'I'm sorry, I didnae mean to, he was pissin me aff, never paying me back, like. I lost it man...' a sob spurted out.

*

Big Mo might have had the gold necklace and given it to the Romanian guy, but Patel was convinced that he had nothing to do with Nadia's murder. It made sense now why he had seen him and Paul Graham at Nadia's funeral. Perhaps they were looking for more gold jewellery from the Asian crowd or free food at the funeral which was attraction enough for the two drug-crazed guys with little in their lives to look forward to except the next fix. Living on the edges of society and never able to distinguish right from wrong, they had their own code and lived by it with no idea of normal rules or responsibilities. Patel often wondered about this group of people that he came across almost every day in his career. Society looked to the police to keep them safe from these miscreants but forgot that they had created them in the first place. Not a single country in the world, 'civilised' or not, had been able to get this vulnerable group to lead a simple but safe life, contributing to society and keeping away from trouble. He had more sympathy with the likes of Big Mo who had drifted into a life of crime and petty pilfering than the gang leaders that profited from supplying the drugs or human trafficking. Now Big Mo had committed a murder! He had taken a life, that of his friend Graham. His own life was a mess from childhood. Trapped, unable to get the skills to escape a life of petty crime, he had committed this final heinous act.

Big Mo was charged with the murder of Paul Graham.

Nearly a month now and Nadia's murderer was still roaming the streets. That 'golden hour' when the murder scene yields clues had passed by ages ago, making the investigation harder.

Chapter 40

Hanif had walked confidently to the GUMSA group to give them leaflets on the behaviour of women in Muslim society that he had downloaded from the internet and had added his own words to. Some were wearing hijabs and scarfs, but a few were wearing Western clothes, tight-fitting leggings and tops. This made him angry. He strode up to them and a girl in a pretty green dress turned around.

Her grey-green eyes made him go all wobbly inside. Hanif had never felt like this before.

'Hey, Hanif, not that old rubbish again,' she said with a wide smile. The grey-green eyes and her smile made him feel weak at the knees.

How did she know his name? Her voice sounded sweet. He shook his head as if he wanted rid of that smile and words. He thrust the leaflets at one of the girls and turned to leave.

'Hanif, I want to talk a bit about this with you.' She picked out a leaflet from her friend's hands and waved it in front of his eyes. He was shocked. None of the Muslim girls had ever spoken so boldly to him. They either rolled their eyes or commented on him as he left their proximity. She was different. Cheeky and bold. It made him angry and yet he could feel a strange attraction. He could not ignore her.

'Shaz, don't waste your time on him,' said one of the girls standing beside her.

He looked down and took another step away.

'Hanif,' she called out again, her voice was mesmerising. Just that sound seemed to evoke some feelings he never knew he had.

'Look,' she continued, 'I would enjoy finding out why something not even laid down in the Koran seems to obsess you.'

A small lift of her lips and a wide-eyed look made his heart flutter again.

'I'm, I'm ... busy,' he stammered. He walked away, turned down Kelvin Way and heaved a sigh of relief. The cool shade of the beautiful tree-lined road made him feel better, as he hurried off. He wandered into the grounds of the Kelvingrove Museum and sat on one of the benches. He could not believe the lust and new feelings he felt for the young woman he had just met, Shaz. What was her full name, Shazia? Shameen? Shanaz? His heart was still beating fast. He was disgusted with himself. Such a weak man! How could he even look at such a person, that flowing hair that had copper highlights in it and fell in a tousled tempting way around her shoulders? He would love to run his hands through it, hold her face and rain passionate kisses on those lips. Was this love at first sight? He had read about it when he was younger, seen it in some Bollywood films. In his heart, he knew he was smitten. Again, those feelings of confusion took hold. These new surges of feeling meeting a girl for the first time had never been this strong before. He loathed himself for wanting to see her again. He chided himself. This was not him. He had to work off this temptation. He chanted a prayer as he walked home.

He locked himself in his room. He took out his textbooks and laid them out to work on them. Concentration on his books was the last thing that he could manage. He made himself some coffee and sipped it. He had respected and never felt anything more than a friendship with other girls that he had met. Some Muslim girls he loathed when he saw the way they dressed and behaved; they were blatantly going against the Koranic principles of modesty. The code was simple enough. He referred to the code in the Koran that he had on the desk and read it out aloud:

*And tell the believing women to subdue their eyes and maintain their chastity. They shall not reveal any parts of their bodies, except that which is necessary. They shall cover their chests, and shall not relax this code in the presence of other than their husbands, their fathers, the fathers of their husbands, their sons, the sons of their husbands, their brothers, the sons of their brothers, the sons of their sisters, other women, the male servants or employees whose sexual drive has been nullified, or the children who have not reached puberty. They shall not strike their feet when they walk in order to shake and reveal certain details of their bodies. All of you shall repent to God, O you believers, that you may succeed. * (24:30-31)*

Why was it so difficult for these women to follow the code laid down clearly in the Koran? he wondered. 'Shaz' was blatantly not following the code. Why was his mind straying back to her? How could beauty like that blind him to things he had started believing in. He was confused.

His lessons at the madrassa had taught him a lot. It had filled him with wonder at the simple and straight forward guide to clean living for all believers. It gave him a purpose in life, a higher purpose than just studying medicine and taking the Hippocratic Oath. The energy he got from such spiritual readings gave him an insight into his own identity and a world order that appealed to him. The extreme freedoms of the West started to grate on his soul. He had formed a good solid friendship at the madrassa with like-minded young men, something he had never had before in his life. No longer treated as a geek, not ostracised in ways only young men of colour who had gone through that experience could understand. The feeling of being one with God and with his fellow Muslim men gave him a focus that had evaded him before. He had never felt so confident. Hanif had visions of passing his medical degree and working for the common pursuit of the highest of ideals, help Muslims all over the world and perhaps one day Sharia Law, the will of God, will rule the universe. He had to start his contribution to this cause, so he worked at the university with young Muslim students who were from all over the country and abroad. Yet there were often conflicting thoughts in his mind when he was at university, mingling with other students and socialising with them at lunch times or studying long hours at the library then having a bite to eat with them. When he was at the madrassa his mood changed, he was convinced that following the path of faith was right.

Now, this young girl Shaz was challenging him. His beliefs were faltering.

Was God testing him? Would this Shaz change all the ideas and thoughts that he had rigorously followed all this time? For days, the confusion he felt raged in his mind. He could not concentrate on his studies. His strong beliefs that he thought he held were shaken. He started having some deep doubts and his beliefs were slowly fading away.

Chapter 41

Kasim was working as a labourer at the expansion of the new build of one of the largest cash and carry businesses owned by a Pakistani family. The huge premises on the Southside of the city employed a fair number of people. Kara and Brian walked into the office and asked for Kasim Abdullah.

The girl at the reception said she only knew that men were working at the building site but that the gaffer on-site would know their names.

Kara and Brian went over to the building site. The gaffer pointed Kasim out to them. He was a short man but well built, like a boxer, the muscles on his upper body visible under his thin T-shirt. He had a thick moustache and beard, and small eyes.

'Mr. Abdullah, we would like you to talk with you about your wife Nafisa. We would like you to accompany us to the station.'

'Why, what for? I haven't done anything.' Kasim was indignant.

'We need to talk to all the people involved, it's an important investigation' Kara explained.

'I don't want to take time off work.'

'Your boss knows, we've told him that we are taking you in,' Brian retorted. 'Just come along right now and we can sort it soon.'

Kasim accompanied them reluctantly to the car.

At the office, Patel and Joe did the interviewing.

Patel explained the reason he was interviewing

Kasim. 'Even if you knew Nadia only briefly, we need to talk to all who have had some contact with her. I hope you understand that Mr. Abdullah.'

Kasim nodded and said 'Yes, I do understand.'

'So, Mr. Abdullah, did you resent Nadia Ahmad helping your wife Nafisa?'

'Don't know what you mean?' Kasim gave him a defiant look.

'You were annoyed that Nadia was with her during your visit with your children.'

'It was with a social worker; they were not in the room with me and the children.'

'If that's the case why did you walk into Nadia's place of work and threaten her, telling her to keep well clear of your family?'

'What? I never did that.'

'We have a couple of Nadia's colleagues who saw you at the Bank, Mr. Abdullah and heard you accuse her of meddling with your life. Not once but a few times over the last few months.'

'They must be lying.'

'So, you never went near Nadia Ahmad at the bank?'

'No comment,' said Kasim. His demeanour changed. That confident and defiant man was starting to look nervous. Colour rose in his face. The muscles around his mouth pulled back, a definite sign of panicking inside, thought Patel.

Patel decided to go formal on him. A few choice words to make him realise his behaviour was not acceptable and the reason they were questioning him needed to be said.

'I do want to remind you, Mr. Abdullah, that under the terms of the Criminal Justice and Licensing (Scotland) Act 2010, the offence of stalking is defined as a course of conduct which causes fear or alarm.'

'No, I wasn't stalking Nadia. What do you mean?'

'To make it simple for you to understand, contacting or even attempting to contact a person if it raises fear or alarm is taken seriously by the Scottish courts.'

'I hardly saw her.'

'According to the law, not necessarily over a prolonged period of time, even if it has taken place on only two occasions,' said Patel.

Kasim fidgeted in his seat.

'Look,' he said, 'all I wanted was to see my son. Nadia had no business whatsoever, with how I behaved with my wife. Some of these modern women think they can do anything.'

'So, you threatened her? Were you at the Mela on July seventh, Mr. Abdullah?'

'Yes, I was, with a few of my mates.'

'Did you see or talk to Nadia Ahmad on that day?' Patel asked

Silence. Kasim said nothing.

'Well, a simple yes or no would do.'

'Maybe I did.'

'Did you talk to Nadia?' Patel insisted.

'I've nothing more to say.' Kasim clammed up after this remark.

Kara came into the interview room and said,

'Could I see you for a minute, sir?' to Patel.

Patel stopped the interview and walked out of the room with Kara. Joe stayed in with Kasim, who slumped in his chair. Patel's presence seemed to make him tense.

'What is it, Kara?' Patel's eyebrows were raised.

'Apart from the domestic abuse, this chap was in for a GBH a year ago. I just had a check on the database. I thought you should know.'

'Thanks, Kara.'

The interview was resumed after Patel came back to the room.

'So, Mr. Abdullah where were you on the night of July seventh?'

'In my bed I suppose. I can't remember.'

'That was the last evening of the Mela, the evening that Nadia was murdered.'

Patel changed tack.

'Mr. Abdullah, we see that you were in for GBH last year. There seems to be more to you than you're letting us know. You are an angry man who would harm someone like Nadia if she was interfering in your life, maybe?'

'No comment.'

'She was helping your wife and children Mr. Abdullah. Your anger management classes didn't help and maybe you took it out on Nadia.'

'No comment.'

Kasim looked down as if he were examining the carpet on the floor. He refused to engage with them. There was little from him after. He either kept quiet or said, 'No comment.'

Eventually, Patel stopped the interview.

Chapter 42

Nadia's murder investigation was still not yielding any clear leads. Patel was conscious of the budget restraints, so wondered if he should ask for more resources from Martin. He worked on the strategy and looked over more paperwork. The clock struck two, well, the Apple watch on his wrist pinged to remind him of the next interview scheduled for today. Patel got up and looked out of the window.

Patel watched them getting out of the car. He did not recognise Malcolm Watson for a moment. Nattily dressed, a broad smile on his face, with almost a spring in his step, Malcolm walked around the car to open the door for the other man, who looked older than Malcolm. Patel presumed this was his lawyer. He got ready for the interview, looked over Malcolm's file once more. Malcolm was the last person to see Nadia alive. He hoped that this time the interview would move the investigation forward.

As he expected, Joe arrived at the door and announced that Malcolm and his lawyer were here and happy to get the interview over with.

Interview Room Three was brighter today. The sun shone and the afternoon light made the pale walls reflect the light from outside. Patel started the interview with a statement.

'You can confirm that you were with Nadia at around ten-thirty on the night of the seventh of July, Mr. Watson.'

'Yes, I can.' Malcolm smiled broadly. 'She was my best friend; she came to help me.'

'So, what happened after she came in, Mr. Watson?'

'I told you I was well pissed, sorry, I had a lot to drink and she offered to make coffee.'

'You claimed that you could not remember anything after that.'

'Yes, that is true.'

'So, your fiancée dumped you three weeks before the wedding and she came over to comfort you? Was she more than just a friend, Mr. Watson?'

'What, no, no not at all.' He whispered to his lawyer and nodded in reply to his advice.

'I ... I am gay. I am marrying Andy, he's my fiancé. This is difficult for me. I am a very private person...' Malcolm lost his confident look. He was sweating.

Patel and Joe looked at each other.

'Andy?' said Patel

'Andrew Turner, we ... we had not told either of our families. His father had found out somehow and there was a huge row at his home. He was scared.' Malcolm twisted the fingers of his hands together and then rubbed them both on his thigh as if his palms were clammy.

Patel kept looking at him.

Malcolm continued, 'It may be legal since last year, gay marriages I mean, and it is 2015 but it is hard for gays still ...'

'So, you are saying that Nadia and you ...'

'We were friends, very good friends, like brother and sister. I miss her ...' Malcolm tried a weak smile. 'And please find the evil guy who killed her. I can't believe she's no longer with us.'

'We do need to check with this Andrew Turner,' Patel said as Joe took down the details.

'I am sorry I was too upset, and I did not want to involve Andy in this dreadful tragedy. It was bad enough he had to deal with his father.'

'I understand, Mr. Watson, but you could have saved a lot of police time if you had said so right away.'

'I couldn't then. I didn't know why Andy called off the wedding I didn't want you lot going to his place. Oh, I'm not sure. Everything was such a shock.' Malcolm shook his head.

The interview was over soon. As he left Malcolm turned to Joe and said,

'I am a law-abiding person you know.'

Chapter 43

The MIT room had a big whiteboard with all the relevant bits of post-it notes with Nadia's photo in the centre and various lines emanating from that central point. The purpose of Patel's meeting was to make the team reflect on all the information they had gathered so far.

He congratulated the team on solving Paul Graham's murder. At least one murder was solved.

'Now Nadia's murder. Kara, read over all the reports from the door-to-door and the report on Mrs. Hussain, Joe, you check out the Ahmad family reports again, Brian, the park employees reports ...' Patel reeled off the orders.

At his desk, Patel worked methodically. He wanted to find some clue, something to go forward with on the case. So many other things were distracting him from the main enquiry into Nadia's murder. The gangs' carry-on, Hanif the radicalised young man's behaviour, it had taken a lot of man-hours to deal with a sensitive issue, to find that the final Prevent Officers' report on him was that he was a harmless young man. On top of all that, the numerous reports to look over concerning the Black & Minority Ethnic support groups. Though, the last one was his own fault for volunteering to add extra BAME work to his busy schedule.

Patel looked out of the window, dark skies in the urban setting reflecting his own deep feelings of frustration. With an alibi from his neighbour, Salim was ruled out. The first husband was abroad, Nadia seemed to have no enemies. Malcolm Watson was no longer a suspect, his fiancé, Andy had turned up and they were patching up their relationship. He had stopped the wedding three weeks before feeling the pressure of such a big step and his dad's reaction when he had found out about his forthcoming marriage to Malcolm. Wedding nerves and fear of his father's reaction to his coming out as a gay man was the reason he had given Malcolm and the police when they had interviewed him. Malcolm's homosexuality seemed to confirm that his relationship with Nadia was platonic. He'd have no reason to have killed her.

Robbery as a motive was out since Big Mo had confessed to taking the gold necklace. There was no racist motive that he could find; the gangs seemed to be having their usual brawls, part of the youth culture in some sink estates that had spilled over to the Mela that evening. What else am I missing? he wondered.

Patel sat at his desk, late at night focussed on the CCTV footage of the park entrance near the Indian temple. He rewound the tape and looked at it again. The trawl had brought nothing of significance. Slowing down its speed, he noticed a shadowy figure but even zooming showed only a tree swaying. It looked like someone was there, but the figure was indistinct.

He looked again slowing and zooming in on one scene in particular. What was that on that telegraph pole? Was that a tangible mark, a dent in the telegraph pole? Was the murderer in a hurry to get away from the park and hit it as he raced away from the scene?

Patel's heartbeat quickened. He played it over and over again. Yes, it was almost indistinguishable, the marks on the pole. He read reports on Nadia's murder again and came across the fact that a taxi driver had noticed a blue Ford Mondeo, one that looked like his wife's car, parked near his taxi, at Kelvingrove Street when he dropped Nadia off. How on earth had they missed out checking the CCTV trawl more thoroughly? He needed to check that telegraph pole, but maybe that taxi driver would be able to give him some more information on that blue car.

The next morning, he and Joe called at the taxi office.

The tiny office was manned by a lady on the switchboard and a big gentleman, the manager, was seated behind a desk in a tiny room.

They showed the warrant cards.

'Aye, I'll need to get Bob over, he'll be parked near his last port of call,' explained the manager. 'Nice guy, our Bob, conscientious, he's not in any trouble, is he?'

'No, just want a word with him,' said Patel.

'I'd offer you a seat, but as you can see, there is not much space here, officer.'

'That's fine,' said Patel, looking around the tiny office. The wall had a rota sheet of the drivers and a calendar. The manager's desk was strewn with numerous papers, a plastic cup with dregs of either coffee or tea. He called Bob and asked him to come over right away.

'Aye, Bob Kerr, he's been with me for a few years now. They're all self-employed, you know,' chatted away the manager as they waited for Bob to arrive.

The switchboard was busy, and they heard the lady taking the orders.

Bob Kerr arrived in ten minutes. Patel and Joe took him outside the office to speak to him.

'Yes, I did drive Nadia Ahmad to that address on Kelvingrove Street. I've already spoken to the police, DC Johnson, I think was her name,' he said.

'You mentioned a car that was parked nearby. Did

you take down its number?' Patel asked him.

'No, I only noticed it because it looked like my wife's old car. And it had an Irish number plate. As a taxi driver I notice these things. It was a blue Ford Mondeo, a rather old model, 2004 or 2005 model,' he added. 'Not the new Candy Blue, the 2006 or 2007, that light blue, I argued with the missus, I liked the red, less mileage and in better nick, but no she didnae like the red. And she also crashed it quite soon. I'll remember that colour and model always.'

'Did you notice the driver of the car?' asked DI Patel.

'Sorry, it was dark, and I only glanced at the car for a moment. I was busy counting my fare and I had to listen to details of the next fare and pick up a guy from 'King Tut's Wah Wah Hut.'

'Thank you, Bob, you've been most helpful,' said Patel. He waved a quick thank you to the manager who poked his head out of the office, and they headed to their car.

'That was good to get the model and colour of the car, Blue Ford Mondeo, Joe,' commented Patel as they made their way to Kelvingrove Street to check on that telegraph pole.

They could spot it right away. Near the entrance of the Park, one of the poles was dented and had some tiny flecks of blue paint, consistent with possible transference on it.

'Let's get the forensics on it right away, Joe,' said Patel. 'I'll check the traffic CCTV again; it will have the time stamped on it.'

A slow sense of hope rose within Patel as they drove back to the station.

Back at his desk, Joe checked all Ford Mondeo cars, models that had a distinctive blue colour that were registered on DVLA. He let Kara and Brian check if any car repair workshops in the West End had worked on a blue Mondeo. The technology was marvellous but to find a car of such a popular model ...

'It's like looking for a bloody needle in a haystack,' commented Kara as she switched the computer on to the various workshops in the West End.

'Aye, in for several hours, the night,' said Brian.

An Irish number plate, that was his last thought as Patel went to bed that night.

Chapter 44

A month ago, Hanif got this message after that first meeting with 'Shaz'. He could not get rid of her from his mind and his confusion only got worse when he got this message from her: Hey, Hanif, meet me for a coffee? Shaz texted: *I got your number from that classmate of yours, Harry.*

Harry? That plonker, he was the gentle helpful soul, thought Hanif. Harry had given him a hand when he first settled into the flat, as he lived in the flat opposite him in the same building.

He refused to answer her text for a few hours, but that smiling face just lured him in. He texted back: *Why should I meet with you?*

She texted back immediately: *I'll tell you if you come for a coffee.*

He couldn't resist.

His heart raced. He muttered the prayer for forgiveness, *'Bismillah ir-Raham ir - Rahim'* and made his way to the coffee shop. He fought with his feelings, he tried to stop changing his habits and behaviour, or style of dressing for her.

Messages with photos had been shared for a while now. He looked forward to each one. Hanif sighed as he saw a photo of her with the text message. His heart missed a beat. Against his better judgement, he had met her for coffee a few times over the next few weeks and it had left him feeling very confused.

Coffee led to some more meetings, to discuss, make

her change her ways, he told himself, but he knew in his heart that he had fallen in love with her from that very first glance. Those first few weeks with her were agony, his not wanting to change, interspersed with new feelings of love and excitement that he had never felt before.

'Can you shave off your beard, for me? Hanif, you are so handsome, I'd love to kiss you,' she said stroking his cheek.

He wanted that kiss; how could he not succumb to such charm? He shaved his beard, feeling like a traitor to his beliefs, but felt a shiver of excitement as he thought of that first kiss with Shaz.

In just a few weeks Shaz and Hanif had become an item. She had taken him on as a challenge, to drag him into the 21st Century he heard her joking to her friends. He was annoyed, to begin with. It was more than he bargained for. She was kind, loving and totally smitten with him. What did she see in him? he wondered. He was willing to change for her, slowly. Gone was the beard, the *salwar-kameez* and most of the old ways, they were only outward symbols, he convinced himself.

Hanif began to revert to what he had been during his teen years. He still attended the mosque and prayed five times a day, if he had time, but the rigidity was gone. He looked at the world through Shaz's eyes. He was in love, he was happy. Hanif justified it all to himself. Shaz was a Muslim. She was not immodest, not really, she did not object to his praying five times a day. 'I'm sure I can get her to change soon, once she is all mine,' he told himself. Sometimes he enjoyed how those feelings of relaxation and happiness overwhelmed him, he wanted to be what Shaz wanted him to be. Carefree and in love was a new feeling that filled his being.

His family and Ali Hassan noticed the change in the

young man but did not comment. Better that he was slowly getting away from the radical elements in the madrassa, they thought.

Not only did Hanif change his ways, but he also seemed happier to his parents. The glum young man, with a simmering resentment, was no longer evident. They saw him take an interest in shopping, talking to them about ordinary things, a change that they were happy with. Now, seeing Hanif happy made their hearts feel a little lighter.

Chapter 45

The no-nonsense, 'Up here you two,' call from Jim Arnott, the Superintendent, made Patel and Martin get up to his room in double-quick time. The meeting was to inform them both of the call from the anti-terrorist squad of a bomb plot to take place within the next couple of weeks in Glasgow.

'Everyone on the list needs to be under surveillance. I called you Patel as one of your suspects, Hanif, seems to have some connection with Iqbal and Eiman who have travelled to Syria and are back now in Glasgow. They attended the same madrassa as Hanif. I need you to question Hanif to see if he can shed any light on his friends. It needs to be conducted in such a way that he doesn't know we are onto them. He is not on the Prevent list but looks like the other two may be worth a watch. Martin, I'd like you to be with Patel for that interview. Can you arrange an informal chat with that young man, Patel?'

'Sir, I am sure I can do that', said Patel not surprised that the geeky looking young man could have friendship with people who may pose a threat to Glasgow.

Dismissed, Jim had too much to contend with, his brusque goodbye was enhanced by his ruddy face and red-rimmed eyes as he picked up the phone that rang as they left his office.

'So, we have our work cut out,' said Martin. 'It is important to keep all the people safe in Glasgow. Let's discuss how to get this Hanif to give us more on these traitors.'

'Surely Nadia's murder will have nothing to do with this.' Patel replied.

'Well, one never knows,' Martin shook his head in disbelief.

Scotland had been one of the first to take in Syrian refugees. The perception was that Muslims in Glasgow were well-integrated and they were powerfully represented, with a cabinet member in the Scottish Parliament, though it could not be denied, there were some incidents to disprove the good relations between the host culture and the new immigrants. The iconic Red Road flats had seen the murder of a Muslim immigrant. The bombing of Glasgow airport was seared in the memory of all the residents, the Dungavel removal centre had become infamous for keeping families in prison conditions. There were sporadic bursts of racist incidents that made newspaper headlines. On the positive side, there were no major riots like cities in England. Patel and Martin discussed whether the cancer of radicalism was seeping into a fairly harmonious society in Glasgow, shattering its complacency.

Martin commented 'Patel, it will be a pity if these kinds of jihadist incidents change attitudes towards our Muslim citizens.' He chortled 'I even know of tartans designed especially for Pakistani, Indian and the Chinese communities. Proper integration. I see *bhangra* bands wearing tartan; the Cabinet minister was wearing a kilt on taking his oath for his Ministerial post. Curry is almost a national dish. I would hate the acts of a few misguided individuals wrecking what has been achieved.'

Patel nodded and sighed. The tenuous link of one the suspects, Hanif, to a couple of jihadists who had made their way to Syria and returned to Scotland would now take some more time off his murder investigation, but it was too important, it had to be investigated too.

*

Martin and Patel went to visit Hanif that same day.

'Joe you hold the fort here and if there are any important clues about Nadia's suspects contact me immediately,' Patel said as he left the office.

Looking bemused, Joe glanced at Patel's diary. Nothing in it to show he was away to one of those various meetings about Ethnic Minorities. He sat back at his desk and started on checking his 'to-do list' for the day.

As Martin drove the car, Patel was still thinking that the list of suspects had dwindled again. Hanif's demeanour had changed, Ali had told him. He was not even attending the madrassa as often as he used to.

Hanif's appearance when he opened the door surprised Patel. He had not seen him for a few weeks. Gone was that beard, that serious look. He was in a T-shirt, a smart pair of jeans and had a bright smile. He had none of that brooding stare or that reluctance to lock eyes when talking to him.

'Hanif, you are looking good, may we come in.' Patel smiled and started the conversation.

'Come in,' invited Hanif. 'Have you found Nadia's killer?' he asked.

'Well no. This is DCI Martin and we would like a chat with you.'

'Oh, what about?' Hanif sat opposite them looking relaxed.

'Do you still go to the madrassa?' asked Patel.

'Yes, but not so often. Why are you asking me about that?'

'Do you know an Iqbal Quershi and Eiman Razaq?' asked Martin.

'They used to come to the madrassa, I know them, yes. Why?'

'Did they go to the same the University as you?' asked Patel.

'No, I've known them for years. We went to the Koran classes since primary school. Then I stopped going to the madrassa for a few years, but they were good students. Regular attenders, not like me.'

'Can you tell us anything about them, what you chatted about with them?' Martin asked.

'I didn't see them recently. Think both had travelled home to see their relatives.'

'Home?'

'Pakistan, they went for a wedding I think.'

'Pakistan? Not Turkey, then from there to Syria to fight for the jihadists cause?'

'What, what do you mean? I don't know any of this.' Hanif looked shocked.

'Are you sure? Looks like these two guys have been busy since they came back to Glasgow.' Patel said, looking keenly at Hanif for his reaction.

'You've not seen them since they've come back?' Martin and Patel took turns to ply him with questions.

'Look what's this about? I've not seen them for a few months at least.' Hanif squirmed in his seat.

'Hanif, these two men are in serious trouble, so it will help us a great deal if you tell us anything you know.'

Hanif kept quiet for a minute. His mobile pinged, he glanced at it and then switched it off. He began slowly to open up.

'These guys used to come up with videos and literature about what is really happening in Syria. You know the Western media shows only what they want to. It is so biased. I was taken in with what I saw. I even wanted to give up my studies and go help the Syrians, humanitarian aid I mean. Those poor children.' He stopped again. Tears glistened at the tips of his eyelids.

'And what about Iqbal and Eiman?' Patel prompted.

'They became more and more involved. I do know that they went down to London for a few weekends then said to me that they were going to Pakistan. I was not happy with their attitude when they returned from their visits to London. I kept my distance from them. I am unhappy with what is happening in Syria. I'm also very unhappy about the Islamophobia here in Glasgow, but you know my parents taught me right from wrong. Glasgow gave my parents a better life than they had in Pakistan. I am passionate about Glasgow. I am Muslim and Scottish. I will never harm our country. I truly have nothing do with those two losers. I do have their mobile numbers and addresses, but they've probably changed the mobile numbers. I'll help all I can but to be honest I can give you little more than what I've said now.' Hanif finished his spiel and looked directly at Patel.

Patel jotted down the numbers and addresses of the two men. He knew that this was not any new information at all. The anti-terrorist team would know much more about them. In a way, he was relieved that Hanif had never been attracted to their fundamentalist ideology.

As soon as they reached the station, Joe told them that Superintendent Jim Arnott had called them up to see him immediately. They were relieved to hear that the counter-terrorism team had got the two men and a plot to bomb St. Enoch Centre, a busy shopping mall, had been thwarted.

The Breaking News headlines broke the incident

first. It was the top trending news item on Twitter. 'Police Scotland had successfully stopped a terrorist attack in Glasgow.' The comments on Facebook and Twitter updates were a fascinating insight into the world of twenty-four-hour news. Some hiding behind their false names and identities were coming out with conspiracy theories.

'This was a plot by the Islamophobic media' said some.

Others said, 'Get all the immigrants out.'

'No more room for bombing aliens, throw them all out,' said another.

'Our wonderful boys in blue,' praised some.

'We owe our lives to these brave men and women,' was another comment.

Patel read a few of them but was too busy with his work to pay full attention to it. There was the whole department on cybercrime to deal with it. He worked on, glad that a devastating bombing plot in his home town had been thwarted and people were safe.

Later at home, Patel watched on TV how Jim Arnott handled the media. He wanted to learn everything from his seniors. He aspired to be in Jim's position one day.

Chapter 46

Ali sat on the settee watching the Asian channels TV. It had started again, the Kashmir flashpoint between India and Pakistan which dated from 1947, when the British had partitioned the sub-continent on religious lines. Kashmir was a state that had a Muslim majority but was acceded to India in 1947 by the Hindu king and Pakistan has laid claim to it ever since. The two wars fought by the two countries had been bloody but India had won both.

The new conflicts, with the terrorism spilling over from Pakistan to India, including the 2008 bombing of the iconic Taj Hotel in Mumbai on 26/11 (as it was referred to in India), had made the relationship strained. The latest conflict on the Line of Control was highlighted on both the Indian and Pakistani news channel. Ali watched it with growing despair. His family were from Kashmir and he had heard all the stories on his grandfather's knee. The beauty of the state, on the foothills of the Himalayas, always part of India, often took his breath away. He remembered his boat trips on the Dal Lake, the cold crisp mornings as they paddled along the banks, selling flowers and vegetables to the people living in the big fancy houseboats.

These memories were almost part of his DNA now. The aroma of the coal-fired heaters, cooking pots, the smell of the flowers and vegetables that his grandfather sold was still palpable when he closed his eyes and thought of those days. It was an idyllic childhood, just enjoying nature at its best. The blue of the lake, the sky and the snow-covered mountains and the green of the grass, all spectacular in his child's mind and imprinted like a postcard to be brought out whenever Kashmir was mentioned in the news.

After partition, his family had moved to Pakistan, but like many of the Muslim families he still felt his roots were in Kashmir, that beautiful state, now permanently used as a pawn between India and Pakistan and a political settlement had never been found. India, the militarily more powerful, had kept hold of the state and like most Pakistanis, he felt a resentment that went deep. This morning the news that more people had died in further incursions made him angry. Just a few days ago he had heard that his young nephew, who was in the Pakistan army, had died in that latest war.

As he got older, he found the effort of being friendly with the Indians in Glasgow a strain. Being lumped together as Asians was an attitude he resented. Muslims in Glasgow were more politically powerful than the Indians who were largely Sikhs or Hindus and he wanted to use this to get the Kashmir problem highlighted and resolved. There were Muslim MSP's in the Scottish Parliament who could contact Muslim councillors in Glasgow. He resolved to get something constructive done. It was the wrong moment to be nostalgic. He needed to be more pro-active. Perhaps he needed to look after his own folk more.

The last time he was at the mosque he noticed that Hanif had become very different. That young man looked happy and cheerful. There was no furtiveness, a change even in his dress. Ali spoke to him after the prayers at the mosque.

'Hanif, what's up, looking very dapper, new suit?'

'Yes, Uncle,' Hanif, blushed.

'Is this a new you? What happened to the *salwar-kameez*?'

'Just wanted a change,' he smiled.

'Looking good, young man,' Ali complimented him. 'Any reason for this new you, not going to the madrassa, I heard.' he added.

'Well, been busy with my studies.' Hanif said.

Hanif's dad arrived and greeted Ali. Hanif moved away to talk to some friends of his. They were obviously commenting on his suit, Ali watched one patting him on the shoulder and making some remark 'Moss bros, bro?'

'Hello, Ali. How are you?' Hanif's dad adjusted his skull cap and continued, 'I see that you are talking with my son, good to see him smile. Even his mum says he has changed.'

'Very good, wonder if you know why he has changed so much?' Ali asked.

'Some rumour that he has met a young girl, but he's not telling us anything. I was getting concerned about his behaviour, what with all that you see going on in the world. Even the imam had a talk about ISIS fundamentalism and gave some examples of kids going from Britain and how wrong it is.'

'Yes, we all need to be alert to some groups on the internet brainwashing our youth. This must be stopped right away. If you find out about the girl, do let me know,' Ali winked, 'I need to go. I'll see you next Friday.' Ali hurried away to his car.

*

The phone ringing distracted Ali from his music he was enjoying. He was relaxing after a long session with his councillor who seemed to have little time for something that was not of local interest. He had ten minutes to

233

relax then take Salma to the doctor as her arthritis had flared up again. He was of the old conservative stock. His wife looked after all his needs. Ali did not fancy coping with all the jobs Salma did quietly to make his life hassle-free. That last month when the roles were reversed, he had to look after her. She could hardly move. This was an added stress.

'Yes, Patel what is it? Ali's brusque voice demanded.

'That boy, Hanif ...' Patel started.

'DI, Patel,' Ali growled on the phone, 'you don't seem to be able to catch the murderer and instead just focusing on this poor young innocent boy. Just because he's Muslim, you are hounding him. Look, forget I said I'll help you.' Ali banged the phone down. Hanif had changed. Was Patel not aware of this?

Ali bristled with anger. He cared little if the bemused Patel had wondered about his sudden outburst and his rudeness of hanging up on him. He turned up the volume of the music and relaxed.

Chapter 47

'So back, here again, Kasim?' Alan Brown was in charge of the interview today. Kasim had arrived with a lawyer.

'Let's get it started,' said Alan, switching on the tape as John sat beside him taking notes.

'Were you at the Mela on July seventh, Kasim?'

'Yes, I've already said I was.'

'Where were you after ten-thirty that night, Kasim?'

'I was at the local pub, and then went home later.'

'Can you be more specific? Which pub was it and when exactly did you leave the pub?' Alan asked.

'It was the Arlington in Woodlands Road. Not sure of the time, lateish I suppose.'

'Not far from the Mela then? Anyone with you?'

Kasim consulted his lawyer.

'Aye, a couple of mates. I left after ten and walked home.'

'Short cut through Kelvingrove Park?' Alan leaned across the table.

'Look I had nothing to do with the murder. I don't want people to know I drink. I'm a Muslim. You can ask my flatmate; he'll tell you what time I crashed in.'

'We'll check that all right, but it would be easier if you tell us now. Did you kill Nadia Ahmad?'

'No, no, no. How many times do I have to say it? I didn't touch her.'

The interview was over.

'John, do you think his alibi is solid?' Alan asked.

'Can never say, but he was certainly more

comfortable after he said that he did not want people to know that he drinks. The lawyer being with him may have helped too.'

*

Later that day, John and Alan interviewed his flatmate and found out that Kasim was home by eleven. Kasim's alibi was solid.

Chapter 48

'Over a month now and no one arrested yet for Nadia Ahmad's murder?' A journalist friend had asked Superintendent James Arnott at the charity function.

'We'll get him or her and soon, don't you worry,' replied Arnott with confidence. His smile however never quite reached his eyes.

'Well, our newspaper have not forgotten the case, Jim. We may have done the last update on it a few weeks ago but the nibs are all sharpened and at the ready,' he quipped, sipping his glass of wine.

'As I said ...' Jim began, fortunately, the MC for the evening turned up the microphone to get the proceedings underway and they were swept along for speeches and awards for the Police Memorial Fund.

It was not just the journalists, the Superintendent felt the political heat on him from Muslim councillors and MSPs who wanted to know if the case was not solved quickly because it was a Muslim woman and the DI in charge of the investigation was a Hindu. It was not in the media yet, but the Superintendent had his ears bent. Political machinations affected him rather than the rest of the force.

The next morning Jim drove to work, anxious to get answers for the delay in solving this murder. He noticed that the autumn colours were visible. The berries of the rowan trees hung in scarlet bunches and the rhododendrons were in full bloom, the sturdy Himalayan origin bushes that flourish in their new home of Scotland. He loved flowers and colour. His office had paintings of flowers in bud and bloom done by his talented daughter. Her paintings adorned the wall along with a couple of Monet's prints. It soothed him to look at the beauty of nature when the work stress made his blood pressure shoot up.

Jim arrived at the office and sent for Martin and Patel immediately. There were no niceties. His opening gambit to the two who stood in front of him was brutal.

'So, the murderer of Nadia Ahmad is still elusive? Put me out of my misery, just what the fuck is happening?' Jim's face was already pink with fury.

'Sir, we are trying our best, the leads are not yet yielding results...' Martin started.

Jim cut in.

'Patel, what have you got to say? Let me have it.'

'We've managed to solve another murder case in the West End, sir.'

'I'm talking about this one, Patel!' growled Jim, his jowls shaking, the red spreading all over his face and neck.

'Sir, my team have followed up all the suspects and questioned them, either they have alibis, or we have no evidence to pin them down.' Patel felt his shame, it sounded like the whole investigation had dried up and he could do nothing.

'I want answers; enough people are breathing down my neck.' He banged a file on his desk.

'Sir, we could do with more men and extra budget,' Martin interjected.

'What? If it is a lack of manpower why didn't you come and see me right away? This murder is causing a lot of bother for the city fathers and you know it.' He shook his head in disgust.

'Sir, we're all working really hard. Patel and his team

have not let up.' Martin used a placatory tone.

Jim turned on him.

'If it is a lack of manpower, you should have come to see me. I can't believe it is taking so long.' He shook his head in disgust.

'Sir, we'll get him soon.' Patel said quietly.

Jim gave him a black look.

'Go find the killer, I want results and SOON,' he bellowed, dismissing them with a wave of his hand.

The pair walked out of the room. Patel sighed. As they walked down the stairs, Martin said, 'It's all part of the job, Patel. Not every case is solved in a few weeks. He must have had pressure on him.'

'Yes, I know Martin; I'm working damn hard at it. My team has worked tirelessly, done hundreds of door-to-door interviews.' Patel shrugged, despairing at the rollicking they had received.

Chapter 49

'These electronic cigarettes are fucking hopeless, a waste of my fucking time,' Rita almost spat the words out to no one in particular, as she stood outside the Sanctuary pub. She had had a difficult week at the Western Infirmary, across the road. The auxiliary nurse had to do an extra shift as the staff had been reduced to a minimum. Her whole body ached.

Cigarettes gave her that nicotine kick to settle her nerves and get on with the job. Foolishly she had been persuaded to give them up and she had resorted to this new-fangled Vape idea. What a waste of time and money. She had been conned by the wonderful adverts. It had cost her good money to get the right kit to get smoking the e-cigarettes. It was over a month now and she had tried to get used to it, at least to recover the thirty-pound worth that she had spent on it. More often than not she had slipped back to a packet of 'proper' cigarettes. This was one late night that she needed a good draw from her favourite Silk Cut, the super king-size that she treated herself to. Well, she had done a time and a half, so decided to get a pack from the corner shop that was luckily open at this ungodly hour.

That corner of Dumbarton Road and Church Street never seemed to sleep, always having custom with students from Glasgow University and night-shift workers from the Infirmary and Yorkhill Hospital just a few yards down the road. She had spent a good couple of hours at the pub; the crowd was getting younger as the pub became more like a nightclub with disco-music blaring. Rita wanted out. She felt relaxed and decided to head home to a nice bath and a cosy bed. A long lie-in next morning was on her mind.

She ordered a taxi and stood smoking a proper cigarette, drinking in the night air. The old 'Hovis' flour mill had been converted into student flats. How many more are they going to build? she wondered. The tiniest plots in the area had new flats built to accommodate the ever-increasing demand for student flats. She had laughed aloud on the bus that day when she had seen an advert for flats offering widescreen TVs, WiFi, and a hot breakfast for students. Rita watched the smoke rings she had blown out of her mouth when she almost dropped the cigarette.

It was the screeching of the tyres of the blue car, that had attracted her attention and she had looked up. It had slowed down to take the right turn at the corner of Church Street. Was that her taxi coming so fast? But the car turned into Dumbarton Road, clipping the man crossing the road and sped away.

'Oh my God, oh my God,' she muttered and ran over to the man lying in the middle of the road. A member of the public must have called 999 for within minutes she heard the sirens. A police car arrived and parked at the corner of Church Street. The constables, Kara and Brian, rushed over to the man as Rita was trying to help him up.

'No, don't move him, he may be hurt, the ambulance will be here, the Western is close enough,' said the constable pointing to the hospital that was just a few yards away as she took over.

'Oh my god, hope he's not dead,' she said to the policewoman who was shooing her away. 'I saw that car speeding away,' she said as she was asked to move.

Rita was worried in case the young man was seriously hurt. Fortunately, the ambulance arrived and the paramedics took over.

'Is he okay?' Rita asked as Kara took her aside.

'I'm sure he's in good hands. Now tell me what did you see?'

'Well, I was just standing smoking, waiting for a taxi when I saw this big blue car that turned that corner there and next thing I knew I heard a thud and saw this man on the road and the car just sped away.' Rita coughed.

'What model was the car?' asked Kara.

'No idea a big blue one, maybe a Ford, quite old, bashed up a bit. I only took notice as I was waiting for my taxi,' she said. After taking her name and address Rita was told she could go.

A few more people were questioned by Kara and Brian, as the paramedics checked the man for injuries and helped him into the ambulance. He had jumped and fallen, leaving him with only a few bruises on the shoulder from the hard tarmac. He was more in shock that he had been so close to being hit by the speeding car. It had scraped him but had not had any violent impact.

*

Patel requested an ANPR, the automatic number plate recognition, from Traffic Scotland for the CCTV on the hit and run after Kara had typed up the report and told him the eye witness had said it was a battered old blue Ford. It was lucky that the car had had its MOT recently and the details had been passed on to the DVLA. The database also showed that Daniel Kelly had been picked up a few times and warned of breach of peace and once brought in in an inebriated state and spent a night in the cell to sober up.

Brian and Kara set off first thing next morning to the address given by DVLA. The rented flat in Drumchapel was easy to spot as the battered old car was parked on the road in front of it.

'Not far from Big Mo's place,' said Brian to Kara. 'Aye, the big man is in Bar L now, out of harm's way,' he added.

Kara nodded as she knocked hard on the door.

How can an area with three-quarters of its residents unemployed over a few generations retain any sense of hope? Kara thought as she waited on the doorstep. It may be just a couple of miles from the leafy suburb of Bearsden, but it had an air of despair. No buzz of people rushing out of the doors to get to work, revving up their car engines providing a noise of energy. A couple of dogs that looked like cross pit bull terriers were chasing each other in the small strip of grass further away. That was the only signs of life in such a grey place. The dull stillness felt poignant.

Daniel Kelly shuffled over to the door, annoyed at being woken up so early. He opened the door in his pyjamas, red-eyed, dishevelled and the scars looking more pronounced on his unwashed face.

Brian and Kara showed their warrant cards.

'What now?' growled Danny. His scowling face was animated with indignation.

'Mr. Daniel Kelly? Brian inquired.

'Yeah.'

'Need to come in and talk to you about last night. The hit and run that you were involved in.' Kara said firmly.

His eyes widened.

'Me? What are you on about?' He tried to sound very surprised, but Kara saw his hands started to shake.

243

'You must be mistaken,' he added.

'Let's come in and explain, Mr. Kelly,' said Brian.

Daniel led them inside. For a bachelor flat, it was in reasonable condition. A black leather sofa and an armchair faced a large TV mounted on the wall and a games console lay on the armchair. Only a light summer jacket lay on the sofa and a used coffee cup was on a side table beside it. Brian moved the jacket and sat on the sofa along with Kara. Daniel sat in the armchair.

'Mr. Kelly, your car was caught on CCTV at the corner of Church Street and Dumbarton Road on August the twentieth, around eleven twenty p.m. A young man was hit by your car the blue Ford Mondeo with an Irish number plate and yet you did not stop.'

'No can't be my car, I was home,' lied Daniel. His red-rimmed eyes swivelled around the room, and he avoided looking at either of them.

'That blue car parked outside, is that yours?' Kara pointed to the car that could be seen clearly from his window.

Daniel was quiet for a few minutes. Brian and Kara could see that he was searching for a suitable reply, anything that could get him out of answering the question. There was little point in arguing.

'That blue car ... well, I ... my uncle's, well, yes, it is mine ...' he said haltingly.

'You need to get dressed and come to the station right now,' said Kara.

As Daniel went to the bedroom to change both Kara and Brian had a quick look around the small flat. Kara noticed the kitchen was in a mess, lots of takeaway leftovers still in their original containers were lying, emanating stale odours. Not much of cooking done in this kitchen she thought. She looked inside the cupboards, a few tins and jars were stacked. But interestingly enough on the worktop, she noticed a knife block and one of its knives missing.

In a few minutes, dressed and ready but a cowed figure, Daniel accompanied them to the station in the police car. There was clear evidence of the car and, a few eyewitness statements apart from Rita's for the hit and run to charge him for dangerous driving. Kara rang Joe.

'Could you ask DI Patel to get the Fiscal to charge Daniel Kelly?' She gave him the details. 'I'll bring the file over,' she added.

At Patel's office Joe was describing the hit and run when he stopped him mid-sentence.

'Did you say a blue Ford Mondeo with an Irish number plate, Joe? There might be a possible connection. Could it be the same car that was at the park? Have you checked his driving licence, Joe?'

'Let's look at the file,' said Patel.

Kara came over with the file.

'He's a strange character, sir,' said Joe. 'Kara noticed something at his house when she went to arrest him.'

Patel's eyebrows shot up, as he looked at the various sheets of paper, diving down to look for the driving licence.

'Spit it out, McKay! I don't have all day.'

'Boss, when she waited for him to get dressed she glanced at his kitchen and there was a knife missing from the block of five that was on the worktop.'

'Well, he may have misplaced it, on the counter, in the sink for a wash. Or this could be the guy we are looking for.'

Patel got the driving licence out of the file.

'Well, well, well, so this Daniel Kelly has Roger Anderson's driving licence. Stolen? Or is there something more sinister? Could Daniel Kelly be Roger Anderson?' They looked at each other for a moment. Both felt a palpable excitement.

'This is brilliant, sir!'

'Let's go and get more information on his true identity.'

'I'll get him to the interview room, sir,' said Joe, his excitement mounting.

'No, this can't wait, I'll come with you now,' said Patel. He got up from his chair immediately.

Danny sat on a chair in the interview room. He glanced at the bare walls. Nothing to keep his mind from getting distracted, not even a poster. He was nervous and felt a tic on his cheek. He hoped no one else could see it. He kept his hand over it as if to stop the nerve from moving inside.

He watched as the door opened and a tall Asian detective walked in, his glance enough to send a spasm of cold fear through him. He was accompanied by that McKay whom he had already met before. He felt a shiver down his spine as he saw the officer sit on a chair across from him and start the interview.

'I'm DI Patel, and this is DS McKay,' the man said in a voice that was rich and firm. The video camera whirred on.

'So, Mr. Daniel Kelly, now that the formalities are over, let's start, shall we? You know why you are here, don't you?' Patel said to him.

'No.'

A tic increased on his cheek. Danny pressed his fingers on it.

'We have witnesses who saw your car hit a young man on the corner of Church Street and Dumbarton Road late last night.'

Danny looked down, said nothing for a while and

kept shaking his head. Finally, he said.

'Not my fault, it was dark and the guy shot out of nowhere.'

'Why didn't you stop?'

'I ... I thought I'd just scraped something on the road. Not a person'

'So, you didn't see the man? You didn't stop either. You seem to have dents in the car Mr. Kelly. I see that your car even has paint scrapped off on the passenger side.'

Joe placed some photographs of a Blue Ford Mondeo car in front of Danny.

'It was too ... dark.' Danny's hesitant reply came rather slowly. His fingers shook, and beads of sweat appeared on his forehead.

Danny sweated more as Patel seemed to pause and his eyes watched Danny's movements carefully, the nervous tic and the sweat forming on his face. Danny felt his legs starting to shake too. He wiped his hands on his jeans.

'How about telling us exactly what happened?' Patel asked. He moved nearer, his voice still firm and louder, his brown eyes razor sharp on Daniel.

'Eh? I've nothing to tell. I left the pub, got into my car and drove back home, and then I find this copper at my door.'

'The pub? That explains the breathalyser test results. I think it is time you come clean, Danny,' Patel paused, looked deep into his eyes.

Danny Kelly looked startled. His eyes were wild now, darting about all over the room.

'Perhaps there is something more you need to tell us, and we have taken your DNA as you know,' prompted Patel.

Danny tried hard to keep his cool. He asked for

247

a glass of water and gulped it down. He answered questions on the hit and run, agreed that he was a bit worse for the drink and did not see the guy who darted out suddenly. There was a pause, and then Patel continued.

'Well now maybe you can tell us a bit more about yourself, Mr. Kelly? Or is that really your name?' Patel probed.

'What? What do you mean? I ... I am Danny, Daniel Kelly.' His face drained of colour.

'So, this driving licence is not yours then?' Patel put the licence with a flourish in front of Daniel. 'Why was it in your possession?'

Daniel was startled. He said very quietly 'no comment.'

'Are you Roger Anderson?' Patel asked.

'No, no,' he said nothing for a while. 'I ... I need a lawyer. No comment till I have one with me.'

'It will be easier if you tell us the truth now, Mr. Kelly or is that Mr. Anderson?'

There was no answer. Danny looked down and refused to answer any more questions.

'We will have to detain you till we get a lawyer for you, you understand that?' said Patel.

Daniel nodded.

Patel stopped the interview.

Joe led Daniel to the cell to be kept for further questioning.

Death

He had come out for a walk, to clear his head. Overhead, the sky despite a few white clouds was a clear strong blue. It was like a mirage when he saw her there. He looked again. Was that her? She stood there laughing; looking so happy, with a little boy and a man he presumed was her husband. He had checked up on all her details. They were a beautiful family, enjoying the July sunshine. They seemed to be unaware of the significance of that fateful day ten years ago. The pain he felt seeing her happiness was like a knife plunged several times into his heart. He felt sick, he retched, vomited the alcohol that he had been consuming. Those months of physical pain that he had undergone seemed nothing compared to this heartache that seared him emotionally. An anguished mind made him want to plunge a knife into her. Get rid of her idyllic life that he could observe from a distance. Not because he still loved her, but because he remembered he had once loved her. And how deep was that love then? All that he had done for her, given up for her and he was left bereft.

Several times he had considered suicide, but what was the point of taking his life? Death had no fear for him. It would never bring anything back. That numbness, that lack of fear of his death had surprised him. Detachment, he thought that would give him peace of mind. But peace was elusive. The only answer he found was in blocking all those thoughts. His interest in life had drained to nothing, reaching out for a bottle of booze was all that remained.

Where was his happiness? 'Don't dwell on the past that is the way to happiness,'- -aye right - not when *your life is shattered totally. Why should he suffer more? He needed to live. He would restore that hope to live again. There was only one way to achieve it. Revenge was the only way. He was glad he had wiped that smile off her face.*

Chapter 50

The lawyer sat beside a sober Daniel Kelly. The interview started at ten o'clock. The tape was switched on and Patel began,

'So, let's start with who you are. Are you Daniel Kelly?

Danny nodded and said nothing.

'Let me help you,' said DI Patel getting angry at his silence. 'The car was registered to a Daniel Kelly. Shame that the poor man died after you used his hospitality and stayed in his house in Ireland. But obviously very helpful for you to steal his identity, eh?'

Danny looked down. There was silence again in the interview room. The lawyer looked at Danny, watching the red patches appearing on his face again.

'Yes or no?' Patel's voice rose very slightly.

The lawyer whispered something in his ear and Danny nodded.

'Aye.'

Patel raised his eyebrows.

'Aye, I did go to my uncle's in County Clare. I looked after him for the last few weeks of his life. He had no one there. We had a few jars together. After he died there was nothing. I loved that old man! I came back to Glasgow a few months ago. I wanted a new start to life.'

'So why did you steal his identity? Who are you? What is your real name? Not Roger Anderson by any chance?'

'What?' Danny's face drained of colour.

'So, you came back to kill Nadia.' Patel spat out the words.

Danny looked down. His body shook. He held the chair tightly.

'Looks like you are Roger Anderson, that's you, right?'

He nodded.

'Roger is suddenly lost for words. Where were you on the seventh of July, the last day of the Mela?'

Silence.

Patel got up and opened a file on the table. Photos of Nadia's body lay open on the table.

'I was at home,' Roger said weakly.

'No, no, no. Let's try truth for a change eh? You were at the Mela, followed Nadia and murdered her.'

Roger shook his head again.

'Your blue car was seen at Park Grove Terrace. The blue paint on your car matches with the paint on the telegraph pole near the murder scene. Your DNA matches with some fibres found on her body.'

Roger's shoulders heaved, and sobs broke out.

'She was living it up, happy with a son to love. I have nothing,' he sobbed.

Patel waited a few minutes. Roger continued.

'Those scenes of the tenth anniversary of 7/7 were all over the telly. I relived all that pain. I had followed her before. She looked so happy...' Roger's voice broke; he took a sip of water.

Patel's eyes bored into him.

'Nadia had everything. Her husband, her job, her son...' a sob came through, Roger shook his head as if mentioning her son was painful to him.

'Well,' DI Patel urged him to spill it all out.

'I had nothing, no job, no wife. I had given it all up to marry Nadia. I had even changed my religion for her. She dumped me. And my son Scott ... blown up by that bitch's religious fanatics ...' His voice trailed.

The three other men sat waiting patiently.

'I saw Nadia and her family at the Mela. I was livid. I went to the pub; the boozing didn't help. I went back home, got a knife, and drove to the park. I didn't know that the Mela finished so early. I sat in the car, just drinking, hating everything. I wanted to die. Then, out of the blue, she came out of this flat and walked into the park. I followed her with the knife in my hand. I was raging ... I just ... stabbed her.'

Patel could see that the revenge had done nothing to assuage that pain of losing his only son Scott in the London bombings. The Roger that sat in front of Patel was a pathetic figure, a scarred man crushed with self-pity and lost in his thoughts.

Joe took Roger down to the cells.

Roger Anderson was charged with the murder of Nadia Ahmad.

Later that day, Patel and Joe met Salim to explain what had happened. Nadia's young husband sat sobbing holding onto little Mansur Amreen took the young boy away as Patel and Joe described how they had found Roger.

Later, out of friendship, Patel also rang Ali Hassan and told him the news.

Chapter 51

'Mela murderer caught,' the headline shrieked. The doorbell rang as Marie picked up the paper. She opened the door. Cath her friend, stepped in and hugged her. Marie's red eyes and dishevelled state made it clear that the news was a shock to her.

'Cath, I can't believe it. It was Roger ...?' she cried, the disbelief clear in her voice.

Cath said nothing, just held her tight.

Later, they sat down with a cup of coffee and Marie wiped her tears and spoke softly.

'Was it my fault?'

'No, no, of course not! Stop blaming yourself.' Cathy held her hand.

'I couldn't bear to even see Roger after Scott's funeral.'

Cath gave her a hug. That hurt of a mum losing her child, that deep scar, brought more tears and loud sobs from Marie. After a while Marie dried her eyes and continued,

'He took him down to London ... I can never forgive him for that.' Marie sipped her coffee from her cup.

'Look,' said Cath, 'you took him back after he left that Nadia. You had just had Scott for God's sake. He was no good. He was a lousy father. Drunk often and couldn't even hold a job. Don't you go blaming yourself; you take care of yourself now.'

Cath and Marie sat in the lounge. The bare trees, with a few leaves in that cold autumn day were casting shadows on the dimly lit wall as they sat talking for hours and the darkness outside deepened.

Marie sat on the sofa, long after Cath had left. That fateful time in 2005 came flooding back to her. She thought of the letter that she had received from Roger after she refused to have anything to do with him. She had stashed it away in a box under her bed. Grief had overtaken everything else in life for a good few years. Burying her wee boy was heart-rending, the despair driving her to barely cope with keeping herself alive. The counselling sessions and sleeping tablets had helped her recover very slowly.

More memories of her time with Roger came cascading almost like a river in spate. She let them wash over her.

It had been another bright morning, and the sunshine lifted her spirits. It had been a trying few months. Roger coming back into her life, off and on, had not made it any easier. Making ends meet had been difficult. That dreaded thud of the postman's letters landing in the hallway. She had risen quickly and picked up the letters and The Daily Record. She left the letters unopened. The reminders of the mortgage payments made her shudder. Her part-time job at Asda had not helped much with paying all the bills.

He had asked her if he could take Scott to London to see the show Lion King as a special birthday treat. He had never been with him for his birthday before. After months of refusing and then only when he sobered up, she had relented and said yes. It was his genuine love for Scott that made her agree. Roger and Scott had left that weekend for London.

Neither of them came back. The police told her the news that Scott had died in the bombing on the bus. For months, the newspapers and the media talked of nothing else. Each and every aspect of it analysed, discussed, debated. She felt numb. No mother should lose her child. No mother should lose her child on his birthday. No mother should ever have to live those moments. It was too horrific to remember. She couldn't believe she was alive after losing him. 7/7 was chiselled in the psyche of the whole of United Kingdom. In her, it was a seeping wound that had never healed.

Roger had tried to contact her several times once he had recovered. She had ignored all his calls and refused to have anything to do with him. Roger's letter was the only thing that she had kept. All during the mourning period and years of grief, the letter was the last thing on her mind. She opened it up again and read it now. That was such a long time ago! Even the way he had started the letter was stark. She had never noticed it before.

London,
September 2006.

Dear Marie,

Fifty-two dead, seven hundred injured. Just a number. Yes, just a number for some. The newspaper headlines were soon forgotten, the newspaper itself used to wrap fish and chips in the next few days. Raw, raw anger, I see red. My bile rises. I feel the anger still, like a knife in my heart. The explosion on the bus that maimed and killed so many, was a faint memory for most people now. No, not for me. Number 30 was travelling its route from Marble Arch to Wick. At 9.45 am when the bomb went off destroying the rear end of the bus at Tavistock Square. It was near the British Medical Association building, and several doctors ran out to help.

Yes, I know all those trivial facts. They are

important to me because I was on it with our young son. I had left him at the rear end of the bus and was retrieving a bottle of water that had slipped out of his hand and I had moved to the front of the bus, chasing it. I fell at the impact of the explosion, knew nothing till I came round in hospital.

'Where is he?' I'm sure that must have been the first question I asked. I don't remember much in those first few months.

The endless silence, the indescribable void, feelings of guilt, all enveloped me like the bandages I wore for many weeks. Why did I run after the bottle of water? Why was my precious only son taken away from me? Questions raged often with no answers to be found. That deep depression and grief was something I could not get over. Months in the hospital took care of my physical recovery, but it was not only the physical scars that had changed me. All of me was scarred beyond recognition.

He smiles at me; the dimples hardly show in the photograph. I crumble. Photos, videos, memories of his few years on earth are all that I can cling to. I scream inside every day and night, and a ball of hatred screws tight inside of me. I travel to get away from it all but it stays with me. Never leaves me. Alcohol helps me forget it all for a while. The anger dissolves to numbness in the few hours that I pass in that state, but the pain is sharper when I sober up. Time heals say some fools. Not for me. Why does the pain get worse?

'Four suicide bombers,' said the papers. Cowards who had wreaked this horror had died as martyrs to their cause.

For a couple of years, I kept away from any news relating to the event. My mind could not absorb any of *the details. My son, my baby, was all I thought about. In those moments of pain, the innumerable operations that I underwent, I thought of him, his smiling face. What irked me most was the fact that I had not been there when he was young, missed him growing up and then at his sudden death I was not beside him either. I had failed, failed horribly.*

Revenge is the only way out of this pain. I must destroy everything that causes such pain. I must, I must, and I must, however long or whatever it takes. I must! You watch Marie, I will.

I will!

R

Marie wished she had shown that letter to the police when they came knocking on her door about Roger after Nadia was murdered. She had received that letter a long time ago when she had been mourning the death of her child, barely able to carry on with normal life. Marie had almost forgotten it was even there.

Now Roger had committed the ultimate crime. She shuddered as she made her way to bed. Marie tossed and turned in bed that night. Scenes of her life with Roger, little Scott and his smile came flooding back. The horrors of death seemed to supersede those few years of love and happiness she had experienced, despairing at the fragility of life.

Chapter 52

The Parikh's lived in another big house in leafy Bearsden, not too far from Patel's parents' house. Old-fashioned and filled with ornaments from all over the world, which was Aunty PP's obsession. She collected them with a fervour, asking all who travelled abroad to bring her some memento of their trip. She displayed them all over the house. Patel remembered the huge gatherings she had at the house every *Diwali* and the *Dandyia* dancing that they used to enjoy. The memories of those childhood days resurfaced as he parked the car and went in.

Awkward. That was the word that came to Patel's mind as soon as he saw the small gathering inside Aunty PP's house. Apart from his parents, Anita and her husband Dinesh, there were two other ladies.

'*Beta*, come in, come in,' PP was gushing all over him.

'Happy Birthday, Aunty,' Patel said handing her a bouquet, a card and a small gift box.

'Oh, you really shouldn't have, *beta*.' She smiled, quickly putting the flowers down and giving him a big hug.

'Now come and meet my cousin Renuka and Tina, her daughter. They've come all the way from Mumbai.'

'*Namaste*,' he said to the older woman and a quick 'Hello' to Tina.

'Hi,' said Tina, with a smile that he found quickened his pulse.

Tina was a bubbly young woman, with a Master's in Forensic Medicine and had enrolled at Edinburgh University for a PhD in Pathology. He found it easy to chat with her and he did not miss the fact that she was extremely pretty.

After dinner, they sat for a while drinking a cup of tea.

'Now why don't you show young Tina around Glasgow one of these days? Renuka and I are happy to visit the temple and meet with older people in our age group. Laxmi will join us.' Aunty PP had planned it all. 'I'm sure Anita and Dinesh would be happy to make a foursome.'

'Well, I am rather busy as you know, Aunty.' Patel protested.

'I'm taking Tina around the city on Saturday. Perhaps we can meet up for a quick lunch,' Anita intervened.

She winked at Patel, indicating that it is always better to say yes to Aunty PP.

'Yes, that would be possible, er ... nice,' said Patel.

The evening thankfully did not last too long. Aunty PP was convinced that Patel would be enchanted by Tina and she was happy her whole idea of pairing them up had worked.

Patel drove home, thinking of Tina. This was the first time in a long time that he had forgotten about Usma for the whole evening. A wave of guilt flowed over him, a new feeling, as he imagined a life with Tina with the approval of the families, no surreptitious meetings worrying about others feelings especially the tears of sorrow that his mother could turn on every time he mentioned anything about Usma.

Nearing his flat, he switched off the engine and sat in the dark for a while listening to his playlist. Relaxing and unwinding he told himself, but truly to make sure that he could face Usma. It was ridiculous to worry. He loved Usma and had argued so many times with his parents to be with her. She would be giving up even more as her parents were even stricter about her choosing her life partner.

Why was he complicating his life now? Could a single meeting with a woman make him feel this way? Was his love for Usma as strong as he thought it was?

*

Patel smiled happily at Usma. This was the first evening that he could spend with her in a long time. The kitten, Coco, mewed as if it felt ignored for the last hour or so. The couple seemed to have eyes and words only for each other.

Usma handed Patel a glass of wine, as they cuddled up on the settee, and he put her glass down carefully on the side table. She put her arms around him and said,

'Tell me all about it, Inspector Patel. How did you nail Nadia's murderer?' Arms tightened around him. She looked up at him with glowing eyes and he kissed her.

'All in a day's work,' he shrugged. 'How about we plan a getaway, a break that we both need? That's after the Edinburgh Book Festival, of course. I do want to see my favourite new poets and read their works. Then somewhere sunny, you choose,' he added.

'How about Tenerife?' she replied. Her smile made him want her even more.

'Wait, let me get you the present I bought for you, you'll love it,' said Usma getting up from the settee, to get the Hafiz poetry collection that she had bought for him.

Patel's mobile rang.

'Hi, Patel, Tina here.'

'Hi,' he said softly. He indicated to Usma who came in with a gift-wrapped book in her hand that he needed to take the call. He walked out to the hall.

'So glad we exchanged mobile numbers. I'd love to see you on Friday? I heard from Anita that a glass of bubbly is in order,' Tina's laughter was like tiny sparkle of stars.

Usma stood at the doorway. She had seen that smile and the look before.

The End

About the Author

Leela Soma was born in Madras, India and now lives in Glasgow. After working as a Principal Teacher of Modern Studies she has turned to writing, one of her passions from childhood. Her poems and short stories have been published in several anthologies and publications, including in the *National* and *The Scotsman* newspapers, and in the *The Grind, New Voices* and *Gutter* magazines.

She won the Margaret Thomson Davis Trophy for her first novel *Twice Born* in 2008. Her second novel *Bombay Baby* was published by Dahlia Publishing Limited in 2011. *Boxed In,* a short story collection was published by The Pot Hole Press as an ebook in 2013. She was commissioned along with 21 other writers and artists to write for the Glasgow Women's Library's *Anthology 21 Revolutions* for its 21st birthday in 2013. Her story *Pavilion* was published in the anthology as well as *Joe Stepped off the Train*, which raised over £1000 for the charity War Child.

Her two poetry collections *From Madras to Milngavie* and *Tartan and Turmeric* were well received and her poems have been published in several magazines as well as being shortlisted for the Erbacce Prize 2020 and The Pushcart Prize 2020.

She has served on the committee for the Milngavie Books and Arts Festivals and on the Scottish Writer's Centre Committee and is now on East Dunbartonshire Arts and Culture Committee. She is a founder member of The Bearsden Writers Group.

Her work reflects her dual heritage of India and Scotland.

Acknowledgements

In writing of this book, my debut crime fiction, many people helped to shape it to its final form. My special thanks are to my first readers, Frances MacArthur and Carol McKay for their sound advice and support. Michael J. Malone for aiding me through the intricacies of writing a crime novel. Norman Bissell for enormous help from reading some of the early drafts to supporting and encouraging me to keep the faith in the book.

I am forever indebted to retired Detective Inspector Douglas Weir who gave of his time tirelessly to explain police procedures in carrying out a murder investigation. John McBride, Chief Superintendent of British Transport Police and Divisional Commander, who helped me enormously with my research. I am immensely grateful to both for answering all my questions. Any mistakes in the book are, however, entirely mine.

Thanks to the support from Bearsden Writers and Strathkelvin Writers Group, who have given me unwavering support as have The Federation of Writers Scotland and The Scottish Writers Centre, especially David Manderson. The number of friends who have been there for me are too numerous to mention; but special thanks to Palo Stickland for decades of friendship and for always being there.

This book would not be what it is without the wonderful editorial team at Ringwood Publishing. Anna Jones, Liz Nolan, Rebecca Pollock, Chloe Murphy and Ruth

McQueeney. I thank each one of them for their honesty and making this book so much better. Many thanks also to Hannah Lee of Ringwood for her considerable support and social media help. Special thanks to Isobel Freeman and Dave Webster who contributed greatly to the final copyediting. Finally, to Sandy Jamieson at Ringwood for bringing this book out into the world, a very special thanks.

Last but not least, I could not have done it without Som and Nita, the two precious people in my life, who put up with my ups and downs and held me up with their love.

Other Titles from Ringwood

All titles are available from the Ringwood website in both print and ebook format, as well as from usual outlets.

www.ringwoodpublishing.com

mail@ringwoodpublishing.com

Cuddies Strip

Rob McInroy

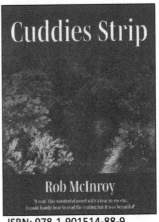

Cuddies Strip is based on a true crime and faithfully follows the investigation and subsequent trial but it also examines the mores of the times and the insensitive treatment of women in a male-dominated society.

It is a highly absorbing period piece from 1930s Scotland, with strong contemporary resonances: both about the nature and responsiveness of police services and the ingrained misogyny of the whole criminal justice system.

ISBN: 978-1-901514-88-9
£9.99

The Ten Percent

Simon McLean

An often hilarious, sometimes scary, always fascinating journey through the ranks of the Scottish police from his spell as a rookie constable in the hills and lochs of Argyll, through his career in Rothesay and to his ultimate goal: The Serious Crime Squad in Glasgow.

We get a unique glimpse of the turmoil caused when the rules are stretched to the limit, when the gloves come off and when some of their number decide that enough is enough. A very rare insight into the world of our plain clothes officers who infiltrate and suppress the very worst among us.

ISBN: 978-1-901514-43-8
£9.99

Ruxton - The First Modern Murder

Tom Wood

It is 1935 and the deaths of Isabella Ruxton and Mary Rogerson would result in one of the most complex investigations the world had ever seen. The gruesome murders captured worldwide attention with newspapers keeping the public enthralled with all the gory details.

But behind the headlines was a different, more important story: the ground-breaking work of Scottish forensic scientists who developed new techniques to solve the case and shape the future of scientific criminal investigation.

ISBN: 978-1-901514-84-1
£9.99

ISBN: 978-1-901514-80-3
£9.99

Not the Deaths Imagined

Anne Pettigrew

It's here, the medical noir novel you've been waiting for! The sequel to Anne Pettigrew's acclaimed debut, *Not the Life Imagined*.

In *Not the Deaths Imagined* we again follow Beth Semple, now a dedicated GP and mother in Milngavie, as she aims to navigate Glasgow's busy medical scene.

But when she starts asking questions about a series of local deaths, Beth finds her life – and that of her family – is about to be turned upside down.

Satan's Cut

Charles P. Sharkey

Satan's Cut is a tale of crime and the criminal justice system set in the gritty, winter streets of Glasgow.

Inspector Frank Dorsey and his partner DC George Mitchell come across a dead body they believe to be linked to the Moffats, one of the biggest crime families in the city.

However, as they begin to delve further into the case, not all is as it seems, as the victim was sent a cryptic text message days before their death.

What does the message have to do with the case? How are the Moffats involved? And will Inspector Dorsey be able to crack it before another body shows up?

ISBN: 978-1-901514-72-8   £9.99

Who Jinxed Jesse James?

Alex Gordon

Jesse James – real name, Frank – shoots straight from the lip: the controversial gossip columnist makes a living sullying the reputations of the elite and, like his Wild West counterpart, is no stranger to infamy. He finds himself with no choice but to swallow his considerable ego and seek the help of his former colleague, freelance sports journalist and amateur sleuth, Charlie Brock. They soon becomes entangled in the mystery surrounding the identity of an enigmatic scribe - known locally as 'The Red Phantom'...

ISBN: 978-1-901514-71-1   £9.99